Amethyst

The Email Draft Diaries of Bexley Martin

Second Edition

Brooklynn Dean

Brooklynn Dean Books

AMETHYST

Second Edition
Brooklynn Dean

ALSO BY BROOKLYNN DEAN

The Woman in Red Heels

The Word of the Rock God

Fiberglass Galaxy

2288

In another universe, this book would've been a love letter…

```
Prologue
To:
From
Subject: Autobiography
```

A lot of people wonder what their story is. What their life would be like if it were a movie, or a work of art, or a book.

Me? I know what my life is. I've known for a very long time what life is to me and what is important in it, and now... Now I know who it is. Now I know who my life is.

I realize now, typing this out, that my life is a story. Just a story? Maybe that's what you're asking yourself. Just. But a story is everything. A story is life itself because it can take on a life of its own and we can believe and buy into it, even if it's about us and we know it's not true, we still believe it.

But this isn't a rumor or a piece of propaganda.

Like everyone else in our society, I've heard rumors about myself. What I've supposedly done and with whom. How I've wasted my life. How I need to grow up. It's fine. It doesn't bother me because I've never bought into the idea that what other people think matters. Well, at least not what most people think. Specific people— a very specific person— whatever thought manifests inside his mind about me, yeah, that one matters. But more on that later.

Like everyone else, I was raised in a world of television and of ad campaigns and of what I should look like, dress like, act like.

Never bought into that much, either, and maybe that's part of what makes that specific person who matters matter.

Either way, I know who I am. I know what I am. And this is my autobiography. My journey. My story. Because I realize now that my entire life was spent trying to be someone else. My entire story is just trying to be someone else. Chasing someone else.

```
Chapter 1
To:
From:
Subject: Basement Dweller
```

How did I get here? My tattoos cost more than the opening band's vehicle. Yet they're elevated on a stage and I'm down here. Lowly.

They say the stage is set higher so you can see the performers. That's a joke.

The stage is set higher so those of us on the floor have to look up to the performers. Physically enacting the concept of idolization.

Except that I don't idolize anyone.

I don't idolize the men on stage, and I won't idolize the ones who come after, and I won't even idolize the final set, the main act, the headliners.

They're just people. And because they "create" something and "gift" it to us, we're supposed to care about who they are. I don't.

Do they care about me? Sure, they say so, but would they reply to the messages I sent if I were to send them DMs or tweet at them? Wouldn't they follow me back?

They don't.

And they won't. And they won't follow you back,

either. They don't care about you. They care about the contents of your wallet, all while they stand four feet above you and tell you that money doesn't matter, and that love matters, and equality, and everything sunshine and rainbows to trick you into believing they're something better than the rest of us.

They aren't.

All your screams are doing, all your praise, is making them believe that they are right to think they are better. As if they've achieved something no one else ever has.

The amount of shows Bridget has dragged me to in our ten, or something, years of friendship has proven to me just how dime-a-dozen those types of guys are.

They all want to be taken seriously, to be seen as artists, and philanthropists, and Abercrombie models who appeal to cheerleaders for their faces and to weird kids for their edgy clothes and to manly men for their screaming vocals and to everyone under the sun as an ideal. But it's all so fake. It's something carefully crafted to appeal to everyone and never turn anyone off.

Not saying this works all the time, but usually, yeah, it does.

And here I am because Bridget is my only friend, and I'm Bridget's, spending eight dollars on a quarter's worth of cranberry juice and a nickel's worth of vodka swirled into half a glass of water and another half of ice because she thinks the guy from London who claims to be the reincarnation of the world's most cliched idea of punk is "super dreamy".

I take a mouthful of my watered down juice and taste nothing of the berry, or of the sugar added to it, or of the vodka.

Shaking my head, I immediately tell myself that this will never be enough to get me through the night's entertainment, and I lift the cup— plastic, by the way. Whatever happened to dish washers and environmental concern?— and chug what remains of the drink.

I look to the bartender.

"Level with me," I say, "How many of these will I need to reach that magic blood-alcohol level?"

"Got a handcuff kink?" He jokes. At least, I hope he's joking.

"Death wish, actually," I say. "Unfortunately, I didn't drive."

"Not a fan of this band or what?"

"Not a fan of anything really."

"So you're doing a favor for your friend, then?"

"I am," I say and I lean in, lowering my voice as if Bridget, already fighting her way toward the hunk of plywood they call a barrier, might hear. "I'm about two more favors away from not being a fan of her anymore, too."

He exhales what seems to be a chuckle and turns around, grabbing the top-shelf vodka and putting enough in my plastic cup to quantify as two shots. "On the house," he says, "But keep that between you and me."

I wink, taking the cup in my hand and turning to face the stage.

This band has been going on for what feels like an eternity, but I check my phone and see that it's only been twenty minutes.

I bring the plastic to my lips and allow its contents to breach them.

I let the vodka swirl around inside my mouth for a

moment or two, disinfecting it from whatever pathogens must surely be circulating through this cement-floored, chipped paint, trying-too-hard-to-be-edgy basement bar, and then I swallow.

"This next song," the sweat-soaked vocalists pants into the microphone, "Is called 'Dollar Signs and Cocaine' and I wrote it because—"

I roll my eyes, turning back to the bartender and saying, "Does anyone really need an explanation for that one?"

"Could be more complicated than it seems," he shrugs, looking over his left shoulder to the stage.

I look over my right.

"I get high and count my dollars," he says and then the shit Bridget calls music starts.

The bartender looks back to me. "Okay. Maybe not."

"So poetic," I say.

"You want another shot?"

I take my debit card from my back pocket and set it on a dry spot on the bar.

He takes it, looks at it, says, "Bexley, huh?"

"Do you want to check my ID?" I ask sardonically.

"Nah," he says, sliding it through his register, sitting it back down in spilled water, or vodka, or spit, or piss. "Charged you for the shit but it's top again."

"You're too kind," I say and throw the drink back.

```
Chapter 2
To:
From:
Subject: The Heavens Part
```

My phone vibrates and it's Bridget: *Are you sure you don't want to get in the pit? I'm so close!*

I respond: *Knock yourself out.*

And she texts: *It's a possibility!*

Maybe I should join her. Maybe in the pit someone will punch me hard enough to drop me, and maybe the crowd won't even notice, and they'll keep jumping and kicking at each other and falling over until they trample me to death.

It's not that I want to die. It's just that I don't see much that makes living any more appealing. One state of being or the other, it's whatever at this point.

I've studied. I've worked. I've traveled. I've dated. I came. I saw. I found nothing worth the effort it might take to conquer it.

I'm indifferent. And regardless of what these guys say on these stages— these guys with their own self-destructive habits that our fucked up society has glamorized so vigorously that it could easily be mistaken for a violent attack on our minds; they actually believe they're righteous, and good, and in some mental position to preach to anyone besides maybe the junkies who are so far gone they sleep in their own puddles of piss to keep warm— apathy is not the enemy. Apathy is what keeps us sane.

There is too much violence, too much corruption, too much stupidity in this world to care about each individual instance of any of it.

No wonder everyone is so depressed.

Sure, it's chemicals and imbalances, but don't tell me how fucked up the world is makes that shit any easier to deal with.

I'm grateful I don't care.

I don't care about this life and all of its shitty consumerism or its fake art. I don't care about the afterlife, or whether or not there even is one. So how in God's name do these douche bags with their limited intellect and unlimited lines of horseshit expect me to care about them? I certainly don't care about what they say or what they think matters.

But then, right on cue, as if the empty recipient to these email draft diaries were some cosmic entity that has a sick sense of humor or a desperate need to prove us all wrong, he walks on stage.

There he is. Frail and thin and shorter than his band mates and everything no one ever thought a rock star should be.

```
Chapter 3
To:
From:
Subject: A Shift in the Paradigm
```

That sneaky bastard. God. The Universe. Whoever it is. It is an undoubtable bastard.

As I stand here, criticizing everyone for loving whatever staggers its way onto a stage, the heavens part. The heavens part but instead of angels singing, it's one man. A man who fills this hollow room with substance. Maybe he is an angel.

What is he doing here? I keep asking myself over and over again. *Why is he here? Why did he and his band decide to travel with these overdone copies of copies of copies who are headlining tonight?*

He's not a copy. No one's ever done what he is.

Why would he put his name on the same roster as a wannabe rapper with a drummer and a band who values only themselves and their drugs?

Sure, he just mentioned drugs in one of their songs, but none specifically and only in passing. Smart enough to throw it in as a way to connect with the people of this generation because he can't be from this generation.

He doesn't look like it, or sound like it, or even feel

like it.

But he's small. Tiny in a way that makes what bursts from his lungs seem all-encompassing. That voice, his eyes, the makeup surrounding them. His hair. The single cross in his left ear. I can't believe something like this exists. Maybe I'm hallucinating. Maybe there wasn't vodka in that top-shelf liquor bottle. Maybe I've been drugged, and it's only a matter of time before someone drags my body into the street and murders me.

But maybe the only thing keeping my eyes open is him. Having seen him now, having heard him, having bore witness to his grunge-glory, death suddenly seems less than appealing.

I can't imagine missing a moment of him. Not now that I can see his delicate lips trying not smile through his song, trying to hide his perfectly straight teeth behind a facade of apathy and anarchy.

How delicious is his purity wrapped up in the violence of his musical forefathers.

Oh, those forefathers, those trailblazers. Sex and blood and drug and rock and roll.

Suddenly I'm brought back to my surroundings, and I pause my admiration only for a moment. A moment of self-awareness during an otherwise trance-like state of him. A thought, a realization, an understanding pops into my head, breaking through the detachment I've held for thirty-one years and crumbling, with a single song as powerful as a cannon blast, the barriers built up because of it: I feel something.

I feel something from him.

I feel his energy, his presence, pushing out of him through his lips, pressing into the air, absorbing the oxygen, and becoming everything I breathe.

How is this possible?

I glance away from him to the crowd at his feet, and none of them seem as taken aback. None of them seem to care. Some of them still look down to their phones, entirely unaware of his existence, rudely ignoring him as he so evidently sings the story of his soul, of who he is inside the perfect porcelain flesh that wraps around his prominent cheekbones and his sharp jawline the way I want to wrap around him, the way I want him to wrap around me, and I realize that if he doesn't matter to them, then even the second coming of Christ wouldn't.

These fucking people. All show and no substance.

His show is all substance.

Chapter 4
To:
From:
Subject: Sermon

God, I love his voice. Even from this distance.

The feet between us feel like miles, and suddenly I wish I had joined Bridget on her journey to the center of the barrier.

Every word pronounced on his lips becomes my favorite word, and I hate that glittery pink microphone in his hand for hiding his lips from me.

Another barricade between us. A noisy barricade of screaming conversations, the clicking of keyboard letters for those who refuse to put their phones on silent even in the most public of places, and people are whistling and calling. One drunk guy in the back left of the pit keeps yelling out our city's name, throwing up his hands and waving them as if the savior of my sanity would ever notice such idiocy.

He's so far removed from this behavior, from this time; and all this generation feels is fun that he'd never be able to discern it from the other rumblings of such clubs.

His voice is deep and powerful when he sings, when he delivers me from the evil of this hell, but when he talks, when he speaks into the microphone, when he tells us of a country he calls home, he lowers his head. He presses his lips against the microphone as if he's afraid we'll see them. As if he doesn't want to admit that the sound they produce is coming from him.

Beneath the fishnets and the zebra-striped 80's nightmare pants, that seem to me the most perfect garment ever selected by a player of these dingy stages, underneath his collars and his clearly for-show kinks, he's soft. He's softer than his voice. I bet his skin is like a comforter fresh from the dryer, all warm and clean and too pure to use for anything sexual, though sex within the blanket, with him, would undoubtedly feel as blissful as the heavenly heat of paradise shining onto souls during the rapture.

I can't imagine him like that, in the act of everything he says he stands for.

Sex, drugs, rock and roll. They hang on a makeshift banner behind his band. The spray paint, evidently dripping wet when he raised the banner for the first time, smeared and smudged. Across the banner's edges, pink swirls of his too-eager fingertips.

He couldn't wait for his work to dry. He couldn't wait. He had to touch it.

I don't want to wait to touch him. To kneel before his altar. Give him offerings, praise. But given the opportunity, I'm not sure I would.

He's too shy, at least from what I interrupt, and too soft spoken to acknowledge the attention, much less enjoy it.

He looks envious of his bass player as the man with long, hairband locks pulls his cut-off T-shirt over his head.

His eyes move to himself, his body, his torso.

I see his hands jerk as if they wanted to reach for his own shirt and he forbade them.

When his eyes blink, they open upward. They peer into the crowd.

His lips still pressed into the safety net of his microphone, he sings. His sermon, it's anything but pure, but it is divine.

I wonder if he's an angel again, and I can't believe such a bullshit thought could even be produced inside my mind.

Who am I? Who am I in this moment? In these moments with him?

I'll tell you who I'm not.

I'm not someone who gushes over anything. I'm not some stupid girl who gets lost in songs about love and other meaningless crap because she has to tell herself there's something worthwhile out there.

There isn't. I know that.

I know that, even if love is real, it's the last thing on earth that would stop me from chasing a bottle of Tylenol with a bottle of this bar's supposedly top shelf vodka.

How pathetic are these girls, these women like Bridget, who haven't ever grown up because all they want out of their lives is some false sense of security in the adult popularity clique we call celebrity?

These guys, even on their most popular day, would never be in the knowledge base of enough people to call them underground. And no one here gave a shit about them until they hit that stage.

The bartender must think he's my friend now because suddenly my empty cup is full again, and this time I don't drink to numb the numbness of this boring existence, no.

This time I drink to numb the tingling sensation rushing through my lungs like centipedes with electric currents on their feet.

Slowly, this invading forces crawls inside my center, my core. It swells with each kick of the bass drum, intensifies with every note passing through my 80's nightmare's secret lips, until I feel it dripping down my abdomen like slow falling sand in an hourglass.

He turns. His smudged black, smoky eyes looking down at the keyboard at his side.

I watch the way his fingers move across the keys, the way his knuckles bend, his pinkies lift when he isn't using them, and he's still hiding behind his microphone. He's still hiding behind his music. He's hiding from me and I want more of him.

His left hand grabs a tambourine from a hook on the keyboard stand, and he shakes it with a fury so controlled it looks too precise to be spontaneous, but the smirk slipping out from each side of the microphone proves it isn't all logical either.

As that hand flutters through the air, his other presses into the keys. His lips still sing, still whine and groan and huff in a way far too erotic for such tame lyrics, and the sand in my stomach is falling more freely now, more quickly, hurried by each slam of the tambourine into his thigh, each violent connection of fingers to keys, and suddenly I'm in my own world with him. Just him, and just me, and no one else is in this basement, and this basement isn't a basement. It's a hotel room with floor-to-ceiling ornate curtains covering only half of the sliding glass door, and moonlight is shining onto the bed through that separation of fabric, and there are windows facing us from all directions, and the audience at his feet are just guests here in our space, guests of the hotels across the street, and they can see us through the window, but we don't care. We don't care. Because all that matters is him, and me, and him in me, and his voice hits a high note so sharp Michael Jackson would be proud, and his knee bends when he belts the words *yes*, and *losing*, and *heat*, and when he gasps his exhale, his boot hits the floor with a thud. It send shockwaves through the room, rushing over the sea of people because it wasn't meant for them, over top of them, and through the air, and it hits me, and I am dripping in ways so opposite the sand in my stomach that I'm not sure I can even handle the rest of his set.

God… I love his voice.

```
Chapter 5
To:
From:
Subject: Heathen
```

I come down from my high, from my untouched reaction to his action on the stage, and when I open my eyes, everything feels more real than it ever had before.

The floor feels more solid. The people look more animated. Everything has been touched by him. Everything is renewed. Everything is physical, material, and, in that reality, reminds me that what I just experienced hadn't really happened.

I look up to him, full of dread that what I thought was so amazing was just my arousal, that I'll see him and see nothing special, nothing different from the plethora of other men trying to be Bowie or Vicious or Cash, and I suddenly don't want to go back to feeling nothing.

I think I like the foreign way feeling anything at all felt.

My lungs fill and I hold the air in, my chest so swollen by oxygen and worry that even I can see the curve of my chest and the black cotton material that lines the flesh there in a V shape. Like a peacock displaying his feathers for nothing, I stand here for no one. He can't see me. Maybe he doesn't want to.

But I have to see him.

When my eyes finally find him, find his secret lips, and that pink glittering microphone, and his spiked collars and his chains, I feel terrible.

He's so pure and so beautiful and I don't even know his name and I've derived such pleasure to his image, to the sound of his heart beating through rhythms he'd surely written.

And I have the nerve to pass judgement on the people who just want autographs and pictures.

But they have no right to be demanding. Me? I do. I know it in this moment because in this moment I see him, I hear him, and I know that what I'm feeling is pure destiny. It's fate.

He's the reason I'm here. He's the reason I know Bridget, and the reason Bridget loves these shows. It was all some giant universal scheme to bring us together, and I have to know more.

"Grape Gardens," I whisper, reading the flashy drum set, and I pull out my phone.

Ignoring all of Bridget's texts, her Instagram posts, her Facebook lives, I open the social media apps I avoid like the plague and I type in this ridiculous band name.

I assume it's a play on Gray Gardens, but as I scroll through their minimal posts, their page only live for about eight months, I have trouble finding much depth here. But maybe that's the point.

Whoever runs this page, they don't tag the band members in the photos of them. Fine. There are other ways to find him, but at my fingertips right now are images of him, pictures, up close and personal and his lips aren't hidden, and there aren't a bunch of mindless zombies at his feet, and I can see him.

Oh, and his drummer. I forgot about him, but I glance up to the stage and sure enough he's there. And there's the pretty kid again, dragging my 80's nightmare guy by their clasped and connecting set of fuzzy pink handcuffs. He either likes the color and is forward enough not to hide it, or he's so far behind he thinks dudes in pink fur and glitter are edgy and taboo and bombastic.

The captions aren't very revealing. *Live dangerously so beautiful faces become souls.* What the fuck? *Danger, danger, said the amethyst alien, the galaxy's long lost lost boy.* My lips curl. Is he trying to be this bad?

I scan the comments.

"Daddy"

"Queen"

"Savior"

What the fuck? I scroll and I wonder how old these girls are. I recognized crap masquerading as art in middle school. Don't these girls read? Don't they pay attention to every word in every sentence, and don't they understand how each word changes the sentence? How "beautiful faces" coming before "souls" signifies something, and how "faces" gets an adjective to accompany it, but "soul" doesn't and how that means something?

My 80's nightmare, this amethyst alien, he's either saying that those with beautiful faces are soulless— given their many check ins in LA, I'd say he's onto something— and that living dangerously creates tension enough to give depth to those same hollow beings, or he's just vomiting out striking words like "danger" and "soul" and hoping that their nonsensical order will trick people into believing that what he's saying is too deep for them to understand.

Then there's a picture of him. Just him. And he's

looking down and his eyes are adorned with sparkles and sadness, and the pink microphone is covering his secret lips, and a collar with metal spikes and a ring is crooked on his elegant neck, and the ring blurs under the light of the flash like it's moving, and I can feel how hard that metal hit collarbone, and I can tell that we're one again. One soul in two bodies. I know it. I feel it, and all my life I've felt nothing.

Then I look down to the comments and I read "Is that like a cockring or something.?" and I don't know what's more offensive— her shitty grammar or her profane intrusion on something so spiritual.

I'm most beautiful when I'm alone.

Okay, Amethyst.

Carve yourself into my soul so I can seep into your skin.

Sure. Naturally.

I start to wonder if my 80's alien amethyst nightmare even knows what he's talking about. But I consume each and every Instagram-offering the band provide anyway, and I feel even more connected to him now.

I look up to him on the stage and he's taken the microphone away from its stand, and he's bouncing across a beam that looks like it's about to break, and he's singing behind the microphone, and his hands seem so small, and his body is taut, and he doesn't have those uncomfortably tiny male nipples, and his stomach is flat and half-hidden behind his high-waisted, plastic, black-and-white pants, and they're tied so tightly with a strip of thin chain-link he probably bought from Lowe's that they bunch all around the metal.

I don't understand what he's going for but all I can see is the physical manifestation of a television show character— a thirty-five year old man during his first season on a series I loved as a teenager, who is often written about in fan-authored stories on two fanatical websites I've been a member of since 2006.

When they write these other-universe stories— these stories that don't take place in the show's world, these stories where the characters are the characters but re-imagined— they make these middle-aged men into eighteen- and nineteen-year-olds, and my 80's alien up there with his small frame and his indifference to gender norms, and his small hands, and cute, little shoes, he's exactly what I've always pictured the teenaged version of that character to be. Not just in looks. In embodiment.

But he isn't a teenager. He's got tattoos and he's old enough to drink according to a Grape Gardens post that proudly proclaimed: *It's the alien's birthday. Buy him a shot if you're in Boston tonight.* And there's a link for tickets. I click it. And it's dead. And I knew it would be. And I check the date because I want to know his birth date, and it's February 10th, which has to be fate because mine is the 11th— not of the same month, but that's irrelevant to the numerical order— and I cringe at how awkward I feel in considering the possibility that he wrote this post about himself in the third person as if it weren't his thumbs clicking the keys and posting the photo.And I cringe because I care enough to want to know his birthday. And I cringe because I care. I care about someone I've never spoken to. I care about someone who doesn't know I'm in this room with him; who doesn't even know I exist.

The photo of him, lying back into soft, satin sheets. Purples and oranges and his beloved pink surrounding him, the way I want to surround him.

And suddenly the attraction to Daniel Crenels, the thirty-five year old actor in those fan-stories, that I've had since college seems superfluous.

My teenaged draw with a different fictional character, even shyer and softer than Daniel's characters, from 2005 seems less-than.

My nightmare is all that matters. My God, he is everything. And now he's lying down across the breaking beam, and his hair is so thick and so full and so purple, and he's shiny and new, and I feel ambitious.

I *feel* ambitious.

I look back to my phone because I need to know his name, but there are too many photos of his face, up-close, and I can't leave this page for another until I've consumed them all. Until I read every comment. Click every handle. Check to see who they are— are they fans? Are they kids? Are they threats? And threats to what? To me? Who am I to him, and why do I wish I could answer that question with 'someone who matters'?

Anyway, I find no threats; of course not. Not when you're discussing fate, and this is fate. I feel it. I feel it.

The next photo is him, and his band mates that I keep forgetting exist, and the caption is actually fairly normal.

Seattle, we're in your city. We're in your minds. Get a ticket if you haven't yet. And there's another link. And I click it. And it's dead too, but I realize I can go to the main website, so I do.

It looks the way their drum-set looks. Neon colors, 80's pop theme.

I call up my music app and check this theme. It's there, of course, but their category is listed as 'rock', and again my eyebrow raises. We'll have to analyze this later because

I have a website to consume, and then I go back to it.

I look through their merch— all cartoon purple eyes and purple hour-glass shapes with no heads and no legs, and purple cat-faces, and purple high-heels— and what the fuck are they marketing? And what does any of this have to do with aliens?

I look up to him, my eyes on him in reality, but head still facing his photo and my hand wrapped around it, and I can't understand this Sex Pistol jewelry with this disco design with this anti-pop pop music, and I realize suddenly that I can see him more clearly now.

I straighten my back and I glance around the club. The lights have come up— not enough to signal the end of the show of course, but enough that drunk people can make their way back to the bar and drunker people can make their way to the bathroom and even drunker people can clash their teeth together in some shot-induced attraction. God, it's so disgusting to be human.

Ah. Then it hits me.

My eyes roll to the left, to the stage, and connect to him again. I thought he was a god or an angel, but he *is* an alien. I always enjoyed the idea that our concept of a creator was just an extraterrestrial with earth as an ant farm.

But now the light is on his face, and now, as he tears down his microphone stand, he can't hide his lips behind it, and I see how thin they are, but how perfect that thinness is, and how pale he is, but how perfect that paleness is, and I start to wonder if I'm just fucking drunk because his hair isn't just purple, it's sparkling amethyst, and he looks small, short like a teenager, but he's got tattoos, and largely proclaims '86 on his wrist, and he can drink, but I can't imagine him drinking just like I can't imagine him taking "every hit of those drugs" like he sang in that first fucking song.

What is he?

Why is he here?

Why, if not for me?

```
Chapter 6
To:
From:
Subject: A Shy Calm
```

The headliners are on now, and I've had three more shots.

Everyone faces forward. Everyone's eyes are on the stage. I don't think a single person is on a phone.

When you think about it, maybe this is a miracle. Maybe that stage does mean something considering it's the only thing I've ever witnessed cause separation from fingers and thumbs and eyes to phone screens.

Even in this culture's self obsession, the idea of rock gods and movie stars and legends and idols can break through. To think it used to be a god that did that.

Neither man or god could do it to me. Until now.

Now that I've seen him, it's even gotten to me.

Part of me detests this; This connection to everyone else on the fucking planet. I do not want to be like everyone else. I don't want to be like Bridget. I don't want to be like these girls, these women who giggle when they approach men who sing for a living and cry when they hug them.

I want to puke but maybe it's the vodka.

Better have another shot. Just in case it isn't.

"Bro," I say, and my new friend has already filled my

glass.

I throw it back, and he does that weird finger-gun thing at me, and I'm drunk enough not to hate him for it.

I wish I could see myself. I think my eyes are narrowing in on him, my alien, as he sits at his stupid fucking merch table. I thought the opening bands didn't do that during sets out of respect for their fellow musicians, but considering the fact that there were only four little girls chatting with him and his guitarist (who looks like he's twelve, by the way) while the roadies— or whatever the fuck those servant-like dudes who do microphone checks and beer runs for the band are— set up for the headliner, I guess it really doesn't matter if he's there or not.

No one seems interested in him and I couldn't be more surprised by it. Part of me is upset that everyone is so ignorant to the Christ-like figure standing here at arm's length in this dive-bar. The other part, a very selfish part, is pleased. Imagine what Mary Magdalene could have accomplished if she'd kept Jesus all to herself.

I think I owe it to his barely legal (if legal at all) guitarist… Or bassist… Whatever he is.

You see, he's got this thick, shoulder-length hair, and it curls around his face in the most beautiful framing manner. He's a pretty boy. Big lips, straight nose, dreamy eyes, blond. All this I can see even from this distance. And I wonder if my guy, all shy and slouched-shouldered, is happy about the attention being away from him. Isn't it usually the singer of these bands that women and girls and boys and men drool over?

I think my guy is too shy to want that, but I wonder why he'd front a band if that's the case, but, my God, I've always had the biggest weak spot for shy guys, so I think I can sense it, even when it's masked so well.

I remember this cartoon when I was younger about a group of kids that always ran a muck in their neighborhood, and the nervous, smart one— the one that was always depicted shaking and fearful— I think I wanted to marry him. But I was a kid. Who knows?

Later in my teens I got weirdly invested in a show geared toward bored, middle-aged housewives, and my love of a new character with basically all of those same traits overtook all of my free time.

It introduced me to a world on the internet— still fairly fresh in those early 2000's days— of written debauchery and work warnings. Stories written by the fanatic for the fanatic, and I was fanatic.

I had pillows of this guy, shirts, followed his blogs— this was before Instagram or Twitter, but when those came along he was the first I found— and even began DVRing his show when such technology first appeared.

I guess my obsessive ass was lucky my parents have always had enough money to buy the latest technology just because it was available.

I think they are the only people I've ever truly loved, now that I think about it. The only real people, I mean. But maybe, just maybe, he— as he watches the headliners from his lonely little table of t-shirts— is the one who can change all of that.

He is the embodiment of one of those cartoon character. That nineteen-year-old version of this thirty-five-year-old man playing a billion-year-old god.

It sounds crazy the way I'm explaining it, but I'll blame the vodka for that too.

Genuinely, though, sober or drunk, I think I want him, and if that isn't the vodka's fault, it's destiny's.

With his little tattoos like a basic white girl's, and his Sid Vicious wannabe clothing, and his stupid little body, and those ridiculously appealing secret lips.

But I've never wanted something real before. And he's definitely not fiction.

Watching him, seeing him, the real him, something so meek and tender and soft underneath the display he's trying so hard to convince everyone is real.

You can't convince me, I think. *I see you. I see the real you.*

And now I wish I could see him on stage again. There's a significant difference in seeing someone for the first time on the stage and seeing someone on the stage for the first time. I want to see him sing now that I know his voice. I want to see him move now that I know his body. I want to see him smile now that his thin lips aren't hidden behind that god-awful, obnoxious pink microphone.

"Maybe he's gay," my bartender friender says.

I look over my shoulder to him, jolted a bit by the intrusion of his voice during my moment alone with my alien.

"Excuse me?"

"That skinny kid you're staring at," he explains, "Seems the type to me."

I roll my eyes and suddenly I hate my new friend. "You can't tell 'the type' just by looking at a person," I say, turning away from him as I airquote him. "People are much more complex than that."

He huffs, and I make no effort to maintain contact. This is what I've been saying about people— the longer you know them, and sometimes that length is only about an hour, the closer you get to some impending disappointment. Good thing I wasn't expecting much more than discounted shots from this one.

But he did serve a purpose. Let me realize that my staring was more obvious than I thought. Not that I thought much about it. I can't think about anything but my guy over there at his table, about how I want to be at that table, talking to him, touching him, fucking him.

Maybe I should go over. Maybe I should tell him how great his performance was. I'm sure that's all anybody ever says to guys like him though and I think I need to stand out. See, I'm not interested in him for his musical talents or the success that is achieved simply by having a job performing it, even if it makes you little-to-no money.

No, I think this destiny is something far more intricate than that. I think this is more personal than that. I think he was made for me. He was made with me in mind. I need to have him. A prized possession. I'll take care of him, protect him, keep his tender little heart so safe he won't need to cover it with chains.

I stand away from the bar, and my left foot slips forward on the floor.

I'm more drunk than I thought.

Maybe this isn't the best look for soulmate introductions.

I lean back.

There will be another chance, I'm sure. And for now, I just watch.

Chapter 7
To:
From:
Subject: Love Letters to Juliet

We leave and I'm obsessing.

Bridget talks about the headliners, their accents, and I slur, "Three countries under one tiny roof," while I tug at one of the stupid fucking space buns in my hair.

"What?" She asks, chuckling a bit.

"I can't find the pins," I say, and I'm really questioning why I even did my hair like this because I don't like my hair up. It gives me a headache, and I'm betting it would feel a lot worse right now if I hadn't had such a great friend in booze.

"Pins?" She looks over. "Like, in your hair?"

"Yes," I groan. Obviously. And I exhale a bunch of frustration because I hate it when I listen to the universe, when it tells me stupid things like, 'wear your hair in a way that you never fucking do' instead of important things like, 'alien boy is your soulmate so stop obsessing'. But it's weird when you receive a message and you have no idea why or who sent it. Like a thought that wasn't yours. Makes you wonder if any of our thoughts are our own.

"Anyway," Bridget says, "they're all British so it's only two."

"Those edgy 80's guys," I say as if I don't know their

name, as if I haven't found their Instagram, as if I didn't click through every photo of Amethyst. "I think he said they're from Vancouver." I feel her eyes on me but I don't look up. My eyes are burning. They're tired. The car ride is so smooth, and it's so dark, and the seat of her 2006 Volkswagen feels so much softer than I recall it ever feeling. Burning and tired, my eyes want to close.

"You were actually watching the show?" Her lips are held together by sheer willpower. I think, in my drunken state, I'd rather just see her stupid, silly-girl beaming.

"They have microphones, Bridget. Can't really help hearing them."

"Hearing is not the same as listening, Bex. You're the one who says that."

"Okay, so I was listening. But only because nothing they were wearing," no matter how attractive, "made any sense with their music," no matter how tantalizing, "and their music didn't make sense with their 80's punk vibe," no matter how sexual.

"Well, who cares about them?" She says, "What'd you think of Michael?"

"Who?"

"The singer."

"That's his name?"

"Yeah." Her brows crease. "I showed you his Instagram, like, a million times."

"No, you didn't. I didn't even realize you knew of—" Oh. The headliners. Right. "He was fine," I say and look out the window. He was fine. But he'll never be my alien.

I unlock my phone, and the bright light is blurry in the darkness. My eyelids are being weighed down by the alcohol, and before I know it, I'm lost to the three-hour trip home.

When I open my eyes again, I'm home.

I'm home, and I can't think of anything else.

I'm home in my shitty little apartment that I haven't cleaned in a week, and I count eight flies on the floor before I shoo them away, and I wonder if Amethyst has a fly problem where he lives, and what his house looks like.

I imagine it small, too. I think of all the grunge surrounding him in Grape Gardens' photos and I imagine it always surrounding him.

I imagine him, so small and fragile, trapped in the poverty of his chosen lifestyle. A trailer with mold on the shutters. Cigarette butts in ashtrays on the kitchen counters, the bathroom sinks, the floors.

I can see his parents in dirty clothing, coughing and not caring if he went to school but really wanting him out of the house.

I imagine his art was the one solace he ever found. The one place he could be normal.

Or maybe that's just the home-life his character leads; this Sid Vicious nightmare boy, this amethyst alien who certainly isn't the real… Whatever-his-name-is.

His family is probably wealthy, and he's got a trustfund so he's able to play with different characters and be edgy and drunk as profession.

I have to figure him out.

I wonder what the inside of his mind must be like— this uncharted desert island in some far-off recess of space. This place where bright pink glitter and pop music meld perfectly with dog-collared pretty boys on chains.

I see roses surrounding him. I see filth. I see the stars

dancing in front of his too-blue eyes, blocking out the dark world in which he's trapped and shielding him from it.

His microphone, that fucking barrier between my hungry eyes and his secret lips, it's who he really is. The leather jackets and the lock-and-key necklaces, those are who he thinks he should be.

Who I know he isn't.

And suddenly, this human being becomes a god because suddenly he makes my own art make a bit more sense to me. Suddenly, he's not just a musician or a singer or an artist, he's a muse. A living, breathing, flesh-and-blood piece of divine inspiration.

My book.

I need it.

I go into my bedroom and there are spiderwebs between my closet doors, and between my closet doors and the wall, and the wall and a fluffy gray pillow that fell from my bed to the floor a month or two-- or six-- ago, and I wonder where all of these spiders came from and why they aren't doing their job with all of the flies.

I open the closet doors. Step inside.

To my right is a small dresser my great-uncle crafted from wood, and inside each of its five drawers lie fragments of my soul.

My spirit, formed by pen and paper, lies dormant within each drawer, and as I slide them open, it awakens.

I feel the pieces of myself tremble and shake, vibrating in proximity to me, to the rest of themselves, and they want my attention. They want me to remind them that they're alive. They want to remind me that I'm alive, but nothing in this world— not even the tangible inspiration which stood only feet away from me in 80's nightmare pleather pants— could ever make me want to test the theory.

"Shh," I whisper, closing the top drawer, then the second. "Not now." I say.

I will be back for you.

For me.

I slide the third drawer open. There's an old notebook with Paris on the cover that an ex-coworker had bought me for Christmas one year when I was in my early-twenties. It's covered in re-hardened melted wax because I only buy candles from a store where everything costs a dollar, and that means they have no glass enclosures or even tin cases, and instead of spending another dollar on a dish, I set these candles on notebooks, on the edge of my bathtub, on my X-box, anywhere I happen to be when I need to see a fragment of a fire. A flame. A spark.

Under this notebook is a tattered yellow one. Beneath that, the tiny purple one that I abandoned a story inside almost ten months ago.

Purple. Amethyst. It's got to be a sign. An indicator. A truth. It's got to be, because I started this story about a punk-rocker, about a gentle soul, a meek man, and I tossed him aside like yesterday's trash when I realized pure innocence couldn't manifest itself inside the world of sex and drugs and violence.

I mean, how could I corrupt someone who drank and smoked and fucked and partied wilder than most people even thought possible?

It seemed simple enough: Don't let him do those things. He's pure after all. He's innocent. He's shy and scared and humble.

But then how could he be what he was? How could

he be Sid Vicious 2.0? It made no sense.

He made no sense.

But I was wrong.

I've seen it now. I've seen him. I've seen my character realized in flesh-and-blood.

Amethyst, my Grape Gardens alien, he is an innocent. He is pure. I could see it. Like rays of sun pushing through gray clouds and rain, the genuine trickled through the copies of copies.

It shone onto those of us intelligent enough to witness it, most clearly when he forgot his insecurities to the music and smiled as he danced.

His shoulders were still tucked in and his arms were tightened against his sides, but his hands shook melodies from the metal disks of his tambourine, and he closed his eyes and let himself get lost in it.

Like I want to be lost in him.

And I pick up the notebook, and I don't read what I wrote all those months ago because I know my story. I know every story I've ever written, started to write, thought about writing, wrote only in my head at night before bed.

This was how I started with stories. I'd tell myself bedtime tales. I'd fantasize. How could I be? Who could I be with? What if, what if, and then what if?

I remember them all.

But this one, as I stare down to the slop of handwriting written in a burst of unconsciousness too passionate to read, this one was different. Special. I think I was waiting for him. I think I knew him before I could even imagine his existence.

I stare at the paper and there's already a pen pushed

inside it, and I want to hallucinate the story.

It comes inside my mind, I see it, I watch unfold. I write and draw and shape faces, without seeing the paper or the pen or this world at all, everything happening inside my mind like a projection. And it's absolutely blinding. Someone could be murdering their child three feet away from me and I'd be deaf to it. I can't see. I can't hear. I just sketch and write.

But I'm too aware of the process right now to get lost in it, and I'm too drunk to stand without swaying, and my eyes still burn and they're still tired, and so am I.

When I step out of the closet, a spiderweb wraps around my shin. My lips curl and I brush at it but whether or not I got it, I can't say.

I close the door, and I turn off the closet light. I shrug. I turn off the main light and get into bed.

From this angle, I can see the moon shining through my window blinds and I hate it. It reminds me of how thin the barrier between me and the rest of the world is. I want to be a shut-in but I can't be. Not if I want to have enough money to eat. Or heat. Or be alive.

Who asked for this?

I know I didn't.

It's not that I want to be dead, not now that I am alive, but if I were never born, well, that'd be okay.

Trade happiness for money. Everyone picks money because happiness doesn't provide rent or AC or gas or ramen.

Unless you're one of the lucky few— like my nightmare— who gets paid to do what makes them happy, then you can probably relate to this. Even if you've never considered it before.

Consumed, possessed. I lie back in the softness of the bed and the sheets and the pillow, and I open my email and I pour my emotions into the screen. I don't know what to do with them otherwise.

Then it occurs to me.

I should be saving this. Channeling this emotion into the only thing I've ever cared about— a failing career creating graphic novels and comic books. I'll take any world over the real one.

But I think I'm too drunk to hold a pen, and too drunk to see anything but Amethyst's face, and I feel my phone slipping from my hands before the darkness encompasses me.

```
Chapter 8
To:
From:
Subject: Sobriety
```

My eyes are open and they still burn.

Fuck, my head hurts. I lift my hand to my temple and feel the way my hair isn't falling, and I remember I have these godawful space buns in.

It hurts when I dig at them, pulling out pins, and tugging at the ponytail holders. God, the relief that washes over me when my hair finally lets loose and falls down.

I rub at my head, then at my eyes. I feel clumping mascara on my lashes— Guess I didn't shower last night— and I don't remember disrobing, and I look down to see the tight black shirt and jeans I wore last night still clinging to my body.

I feel disgusting. I smell like smoke and mildew, and I taste booze and smeared lipstick.

My hand falls to the bed as I move toward the edge, and I feel paper. A notebook. That's right. My story.

I pick it up and take it with me to the kitchen, where I make a single cup of instant coffee and feed my fish while it "cooks".

I know it sounds insane, but I feel more connected to these little guys than any human being I've ever come across. If I had a bigger place, I'd have a cat— or two or ten— and rescue senior dogs from shelters.

But I'm stuck here in this box with only two windows in the entirety of the place, and no closet to hang my coats in, and these shitty baseboard heaters that do nothing but leave streaks up the walls.

"Love you, guys," I tell them. Because I do. Then I go over to the counter and open my notebook.

Staring at the words there, the idea, the brainchild, I take a sheet of stencil paper and I start to sketch.

First thing's first: Those bluer than blue eyes.

I remember their shape from the band's photos. Their size. The way the lids crease and fold, and I think I can even see them moving, blinking, closing, blocking out the world while he performs his music. The lashes, the waterline.

The left brow next. Unkempt but still delicate. The right one almost identical save for a few extra hairs that grow wildly against the pattern of the left brow, edging their way toward the center.

It may seem like a flaw the way I'm describing it, but it's beautiful. I couldn't imagine him without it.

From there, I sketch lines that become his straight nose— almost too straight. Not that it isn't appealing, but it seems too perfect to be natural.

Alien. Supernatural. Inhuman.

Whatever he is, my mind is full of memory. There isn't alcohol strong enough to stop me from remembering him, his delicacy, his sensitivity. The way he looks down to smile and bites his lip to try to hold it in.

The water is still dripping into my Styrofoam cup from the coffee maker with an echoing thud, thud, before a gust of steam pushes out, and I wonder what Amethyst

39

would look like standing in the middle of a dark street just as the fog of a passing rain begins to settle around him.

I draw the lines of his defined jaw, roll my pencil downward to create his neck— which isn't as delicate as you'd imagine considering how short he looks in comparison to his band mates, and how fragile his falling eyes and secret lips seem— and before I can move away from his neck to pre-shape his shoulders, I feel compelled to add the chains he wears there.

Thick, construction-grade chain link. It's not a piece of jewelry inspired by the working force, no. As I sketch the loops, the bending metal, I see the images of Grape Gardens' Instagram, and I see Amethyst on the stage, and my hand recreates what I'm remembering, what I'm hallucinating here in my kitchen, seeing him as if he's standing before me, as if the world in which I exist doesn't exist, and I see his necklaces for what they really are— confinement.

He's trapped and tied down, and he wears his handcuffs willingly.

I wonder if he sees himself a prisoner, a slave to the lifestyle around him. He's within it, he lives it, but he's separated from it. He's detached from the materialism touching him. He caresses it. He embraces it. But he doesn't accept it.

As my pencil moves away from the entirely drawn and shaded chains on the half-sketched man, my mind takes on a life of its own.

My fingers trace the slope of his shoulders, the lines of his arms. I'm trying to remember what the tattoos on his left arm were, but all I can see in the hallucination is his face. His eyes. Those secret lips. I can see the chains around his neck, and I imagine myself holding the key. I imagine freeing him. I imagine binding him. I imagine *giving* him some purpose outside the shallow surface of potential fame, fortune, adoration.

I don't have to imagine giving him adoration because I adore him so much already. He has to be able to feel it through the miles separating us because I can feel him. I can see him. And I want to be closer. I need to be.

But I'm lost in my musings, and I've paid no attention to the paper in front of me, and when I look down, I see that the lines that will eventually be his right pectoral are too low to be his.

I erase, and I'm angry. I know him. I know him better than this. How could I have fucked up something so immaculate? And in my frustration, I take my hand and swipe it across the fresh illustration.

I crumble it up.

My teeth grit, and I hear the sound of the coffee finishing.

I breathe. I inhale the scent of the coffee and the paper and the air, and I open up my wrinkled drawing, and there are still eraser shavings inside.

I stare at the drawing, at the face I've crafted from lead and dead trees. Even with a pectoral muscle slightly askew, Amethyst is perfect. Even only half-crafted and incomplete, I've never seen a face more flawless.

I close my eyes in an effort to compose myself, and I step away from his image. I go into the living room, that's really just an extension of the kitchen, and I dig around in the desk drawer for my bulb brush.

It pushes away the pink shavings from Amethyst's face far better than my hand, with all of its oil production and last night's bar grime, and I smile down to him because none of the evidence of my episode has touched his face.

He's wrinkle free on my counter, just as he is in real life, and I take my pencil and correct my error, and I apologize to God or the universe or whatever for trespassing against what's surely its most magnificent creation.

I pause long enough to add sugar to my coffee, and I consider the article I read two weeks ago that suggested psychopaths drink coffee black.

I don't buy it, but I can't help wondering how Amethyst takes his coffee, and I consider briefly how fulfilling it might be to sit across from him at a breakfast table— his eyeliner run down his cheeks from the sweating and pushing and heaving of our night together, and his chains unlocked and on the ground at my feet, and my teeth marks replacing them because I've claimed him, not you or Bridget or the four-hundred-eighty-six people who liked Grape Gardens' photo of him singing into his pink microphone while his fingers press into the keyboard; he's mine— and how complete I might feel when we lock eyes and he smiles shyly as he stirs a spoon in his coffee because, despite the sex his band proclaims is the savior of society, he's never done what we did, but he gave it to me because I am the only person on the planet who can see who he really is.

But I don't know his name, not yet, and I don't know where he is, or who he's there with, and I can just feel the inspiration flowing into me directly from him, and he's buzzing around inside me, begging me to release him, and I have to finish this drawing, and start this story, and work on his name, and figure out his real one. But I have obligations. I can't be late.

I drink my coffee and it's cold. I was too lost in him. I don't mind. Nothing that frustrates me could frustrate me now. Nothing could anger me. It's fine because he exists and because I know it now.

I know him in ways the people who know his name never will.

He's mine, and I will release him.

Chapter 9
To:
From:
Subject: Aimless

I have a convention to go to today so I stop my sketching long enough to go over last night's eyeliner with fresh and touch up my mascara. I smear foundation over last night's, cakey and sweaty, but I don't have time. I apply fresh lipstick. Curl the very ends of my hair so the kinks from the space buns look purposeful.

I have an hour and a half before I need to check in, and it's a forty-two minute drive.

I know that because, no matter how many times I go to this every-two-to-three-months bullshit, I never remember the directions.

I space out too much. I lose sight of reality. The roads, the traffic, the scenery. I go blind in my surroundings, lost to songs of screams and heavy metal or the dulcet tones of an actor's voice reading my favorite authors to me.

These hallucinations aren't new. As I've explained, I've done this since I was very young. You see, I don't just hear words inside my mind; I see scenes. I always have. Projections. Hallucinations. I'm not sure if I'm creating them without knowing, or if I'm attached to other people in other realms of existence. They don't exist here, not in my world, but maybe I don't exist in theirs, and maybe every time I write a graphic novel, they're writing one about me and they think I'm the fictional one.

I wonder if any of my characters will be sitting at a flimsy table with their name draped over it, signing photos of me that they've drawn, thinking I'm a figment of their imagination, thinking they've created me.

Maybe they did. And maybe the only reason I haven't   crashed my fucking car during one of these hallucinogenic projections is that they haven't written a car crash into my story.

Maybe my fictional characters are actually God, and maybe everything I think is real is just lines and shading. Maybe my line of vision is so limited because I'm inside a box on a piece of paper, and someone in a world I'll never know is writing what I see.

Maybe.

An hour and ten minutes. I have time to eat something quickly, but I'm too excited to get into the car. I want to Google Grape Gardens. I want to turn the radio as loud as it will go and be surrounded by Amethyst's voice.

I need to know his name, but I'm hungry, and my stomach yearns for food the way my eyes yearn for his face.

There's nothing in the refrigerator but dead, frozen gnats and coffee creamer Bridget left here once. There's a tub of yogurt in the door, and I have no idea how long it's been there, so I look in the cabinet above the stove.

Most of my cabinets are full but not of food.

One is full of epoxy and resin and old molds and glitter. Another has jewelry I haven't worn since high school stuffed into a TV wall-mounting box.

The one where I keep my Styrofoam, it usually houses some crackers at the bare minimum. Today there's nothing but some lollipops that are melted and stuck to the shelf and an expired can of tomato paste.

I guess a few spoonfuls of yogurt will have to do. Until I take a spoonful of yogurt from the container and realize the taste is as foul as the smell, and the look of it should've given its state away, but I don't see this place. Not really.

I'm always somewhere else, wishing to be alive in a place that doesn't exist.

I lob the rotten yogurt into my kitchen sink and discard the spoon and the container into an old Christmas gift bag that's currently functioning as my garbage can.

I'd say I'd go hungry, but I know Amethyst's voice has been captured and recorded and is waiting somewhere in my phone for me; waiting to fill me up, to quell any hunger.

I yearn.

```
Chapter 10
To:
From:
Subject: Red Light
```

I've listened to no less than four of Grape Gardens' "masterpieces", and I'm fucking pissed.

Okay, I knew going in that I wasn't getting 80's hair band music or the screamo stuff I grew up on because Bridget's been force-feeding me her British R&B group obsession for weeks trying to get me excited for this show last night, but at least they've got substance and some of their lyrics are dark.

Drugs and money seem like idiotic content when artists used to bleed onto the page and into the microphone, when guitar strings calloused hands and pens made fingers bloody, but occasionally they'll say something deep about timing and addiction, and they'll tell stories about their pain and stupidity, and how they hide their insecurities inside the influences of such substances.

Grape Gardens, well, so far I've heard stories of Valley Girl beauty queens— so original— and holding hands for the last time— so insightful— and the sound of Amethyst's tambourine and keyboard are poppy and upbeat and light to the point of child-star level.

I think Justin Bieber may have been as poetic, and I am pissed. Or maybe I'm being too harsh. Positivity and upbeat music aren't exactly my strong suits. I think I can learn from him, my Amethyst.

Speaking of Amethyst and his music, his voice, it's the only saving grace of this entire production because it's the only thing that's pure. I can hear *him* when his throat grumbles and whines and sings about angels and streetlights, and I can see the melodies, and I watch the pretty boy guitarist and the drummer who looks like a fucking robot crowding around him, inching closer with this superficiality, cloaking him within its dankness like the last burning flame of decades of sweat and blood and tears flickering out beneath the blanket of trends and marketability.

His perfect jawline. His bright blue eyes. The star-power quality that everybody tries to mimic. That power that countless musicians try to fake and fail, but that Michael Jackson possessed without trying. That spark that is appealing to everyone, but that can't be replicated. Amethyst has it; he owns it.

The others, his labels and his managers and his band mates, I think they're feeding off of him, his purity. Soon they'll consume him and there will be nothing left of the soul that shines so brightly in the darkest, dirtiest bars.

If he could make his own music, away from the world of insta-fame and pseudo-celebrity, if he could just stand on the stage with his instruments and his voice and his tender flesh and exposed ribs, if he could just sing the way he almost cries words like "connect" and "last", I know I'd love every second of each song.

I need to save him. But I don't know his name yet.

And I'm not sure it matters.

When he gasps and his words come up his throat like

gravel, when he says, "find" and "you", I don't think he means someone he's already met, and maybe that's why we didn't meet last night. Maybe my barfriender was a vehicle of fate— keeping me far enough away that he can feel me coming. He can prepare.

Whatever shockwave burst against my body and awakened senses I've been accused of being born without, it wasn't one-sided.

I received it, but it was sent to me. I didn't stumble over it. It wasn't gum attached to my shoe or a gun against my head. It was him. And maybe when he says he's calling out to this "you" that he can't escape, this force he can't imagine withstanding, maybe he's been waiting for me to awaken something in him, just as he's awakened something in me.

I don't know if he felt me there last night, or if he knew I was coming before the wheels of his van turned down the streets of that city, but he's been searching for the force that will free him. He's been looking for a way to find it.

Maybe our panels have just been sketched on opposite pages, and maybe he doesn't even realize how closely we've been drawn. But our souls came together last night. And maybe he felt it. And maybe that's why his eyes fluttered like they wanted to wander, but maybe they didn't because maybe he knows he's wearing blinders.

I think he's waiting for someone brave enough to rip them from his eyes, and it'll be me because I fear no one in this world of toxic smiles and plastic bodies; I fear no one when nothing's real, and I'll find him again, and he'll feel me even harder than he felt before because he'll know that I'm coming for him, and when I approach him, when his eyes find mine, I'll rip the blindfold away, revealing heavenly blue, and I'll restore his vision. I won't need a key to unlock his chains. I'll fucking break them. And before the world can sink its talons into his tender flesh again, I'll bind him with my own constricting control— this emotion we all so eagerly relinquish individualism to— but only because I need to protect him.

He'll be safe in his surrender.

He'll be free.

He'll never be chained again.

Chapter 11
To:
From:
Subject: A Sea of People

I arrive at the convention center. I tuck my supplies under my arm, and I run.

Marty intercepts me. "Bexley," he calls, and I hear his stupid expensive shoes slapping off of the pavement. "Wait!"

I don't even try to stop my head from falling backward. I feel my shoulders drop and I hear the sound of pencils hitting the ground.

"Oh, here." He's all smiles, jubilant as he bends down to pick up my fallen utensils.

I roll my eyes. Let my head tilt to one side.

When he stands up with the pencils, he offers them to me.

My eyebrow raises and I let my jaw shift. I take them, but he needs to remember his place.

"Be right in," he calls in that annoyingly excited way, and as I head toward the building, I hear him fumbling around in my trunk.

I don't have time for this.

I push through the crowd already starting to form, and I hear a group of girls go silent. One of them whispers my name.

Normally I'd stop to make introductions— I have to eat after all— but why should I know her name when I don't know Amethyst's?

I thought I was above it. I thought we were above it.

We don't need names or knowledge of the flesh or facial recognition to be connected. But I want it.

I want to know his name— first, middle, and last— and I want to know why he called his band Grape Gardens, and if he's inspired by Little Edie and her fashion, and which songs he wrote only lyrics, or only music, and which songs he created wholly.

In a sea of people, I see no people.

I see him, and I see the sanctuary of my table.

I throw my sketch pad down before Marty even makes it through the back "artist entry" with my bullshit banner and my bullshit comic books and my bullshit bullshit, and I open it and retrieve the crumbled-uncrumbled sketch, and seeing him bleed through the paper from my own fingertips makes breathing feel like a natural occurrence again.

I think my lips are even turning upward a bit. What a hold you have on me, my Amethyst, and as I sit down before his altar, ready to offer my only talent as tribute to his divinity, I imagine lying on a plush couch in his presence, saying it to him, proclaiming him mine, my jewel, my precious gemstone, my heart and my god.

And I'll pull on the thin, just-for-show chain hooked to his thick, black collar. And he'll giggle something pure and sweet and innocent. And he'll have hot chocolate. And I'll fuck him.

I draw his chest and I can see the creamy flesh there. I sketch his tattoos— the most "basic white girl" type of tattoos— but somehow they seem better when his skin is their canvas, and I can imagine him twirling lollipops inside his lips until his tongue is bright red, and I can see him sitting cross-legged looking like a lotus instead of a pretzel, and there's so much radiance in his smile and his eyes. He can't be human.

His hips are next, and the zebra-striped pants he wore last night were low enough to expose the bone there. Just for me. I know this because he's in five of the seven photos on Grape Gardens' Instagram page and in all of them he's wearing plastic garbage bag pants that rest just below his belly button.

Even that body part is exceptional. As if god were real and he existed only to swirl his immaculate pinky finger in perfect flesh and make that belly button. He didn't want it covered by garbage bag pants, but he didn't want it envied and desired and lusted after by fifteen-year-old girls who worship rock stars instead of gods, or by twenty-five-year-old girls who still think the only way to express love and gain power is by sucking dick.

Amethyst's belly button, it looks like god's thumbprint. It's proof that the most powerful, the most holy, the exemplary, can be very, very small.

Small like his hips that were on display for me. Small like the size of the zebra pants which curled black through white like reverse lightening— illuminating the path to perfect hip bones, but in a way only I could see.

I sketch his legs and my pencil shows darker where it runs over crinkles, and I'm sorry that I disrespected his altar. I destroyed his likeness. Tried to trash it.

I can see now, even as I finish his adorably-sized saddle shoes, that I'm nowhere near prepared for salvation.

Maybe I wasn't soulmate-blocked by vodka so he could prepare for me; maybe it's me who needs to prepare for him. Maybe I can't save him until I'm ready to be saved by him, and maybe when he raises my soul from this earthly domain, it's my spirit that will strip him of his chains.

I need to free him. He's so gentle. I can see it. He's soft. He's warm. He isn't what his image says he is, and maybe I *should* be destroying this image after all.

Maybe I need to shut the fuck up and pay attention to whatever the universe— or God, or the alien overlords— is trying to tell me.

I've completed the sketch, and I lift it, and I stare at it, and it's exactly him, except that it isn't.

It's not the real him. It's who he wants us to think he is. It's a mask, and it's a costume. A full character here for our consumption, and I bet no one even realizes the genius he's put into creating it.

Besides, he doesn't have to hide to be a hero; he doesn't have to hide to be a rock star.

My eyes remember the old notebook with the structure of a story and an unrealized main character. I blink back to the image of Amethyst, and my mind is finally clear, and I am listening to the universe— not the world around me— and I know what I have to do.

I flip open my sketchbook. I draw the lines of his jaw, his nose, his eyes. I shape his perfect body, his chest, his nipples. But I don't drape him in the style of Sid Vicious. I sketch him with no chains around his neck, with no harnesses across his chest. I sketch him in his leather jacket, but free of all binds, save for one: a tiny crucifix. His cross to bear.

His duality. This gentle nature— this shy stance, small footsteps— attacked and under pressure by the flamboyant violence of expectation when one pursues music over any other art.

He's heaven. It's hell here.

In my long-forgotten story, my character creation is at a standstill in his life. Should he continue such a sinful pursuit when inside he's delicate and devout?

It made no sense to me when I started it— how can someone who drinks and fucks and bar hops and pukes as he passes out *become* corrupted? He can't. But the thought of someone who stands on that stage drunk and in leather with a cigarette between his dirty fingers being pure, being *able* to be corrupted, felt like a fucking joke.

Until my Amethyst.

Now I see the Saint draped in sin.

Like a blanket of false narrative. It'll fool the many, but I'm the one, and you can't fool me, Amethyst.

I'll write you how you are, not how you'd like us to think you are, and I'll draw you how you should look instead of how you do.

This next work, this comic, this graphic novel, this tale, it will be what sets him free.

Through my hero, Amethyst will see himself— the rock star, the king, the god— all pure and perfect, and he'll thank me for releasing him from society and stereotype.

He'll let me pray at his feet.

He'll worship mine.

And when I lock *my* leash to his collar, he'll smile and say, "Thank you, Mistress," and he won't feel bad about exploring the things he claims to enjoy because he'll be lost in love and prayer, and all our purity together will be enough to satisfy this urge to be edgy.

He'll wear jeans and Chuck Taylors because he'll be confident enough in his message and his music to blend in with everyone else by sight alone. I'll let him see that sight doesn't really matter.

His face, his gimmick, there might be followers of this story now, but when he drops the act and just is, that's when the flocks will really listen.

And when he's playing guitar or piano or fucking tambourine, when he's singing as gently as I know he always wants to, when he writes real lyrics instead of covering his depth with hooks and pop-melody-shit, he'll look over his shoulder to the side of the stage. He'll smile that chin-lowered, shy smile that makes me feel like I'm sitting in hot-tub-soaked bikini bottoms instead of underwear, and he'll thank me for stripping his body of sight and for giving it back to his eyes.

His visage will change. His vision will change. But he'll remain. And he'll be mine.

```
Chapter 12
To:
From:
Subject: Fucking Marty
```

He takes peppy steps with a big smile. He's got my banner rolled under his arm, bags of books on both shoulders. "Care to give me a hand? Oh——" he stops and lets the bags roll off of his shoulders. Their straps slip down his arms and his fingers catch them, and he's standing beside me, leaning over me, looking at my sketch pad, and he gently sets the bags on the ground. "You're working," he gasps, practically whispering, but the excitement that coats his throat like super glue or sugar or unswallowable cum still manages to get stuck on every fucking word he says. "I won't disturb you," he adds, but he doesn't move.

"Marty," I say, slow and deliberate.

He's all smiles when I look up to him, and his bright white teeth are exposed and his eyes are huge behind his glasses. "Yes, Bexley?"

"You're disturbing me now."

"Oh," he looks stunned but only for a moment. His spine straightens and he brings a hand to his lips. A smile starts to creep out around it. "You creatives," he says, and he turns and starts unrolling the banner with my name across it.

I lean back into my storyboard. My shoulders hunch around my neck and over the sacred book, but I can't help looking back over to him.

"Bexley Martin, huh?" He'd said when we first met, when my publishers gave him— this stupid over eager intern— an actual job on the payroll because a real manager couldn't waste their time on someone so "small".

They accuse me of having "focus problems" and asked me, before assigning Captain Chipper over here to be my fucking babysitter, if I've ever been diagnosed with ADD. Idiots.

"Must be fate! My name is Marty. You know, Martin. No one calls me that, though." And the minute he said it, I realized that this wasn't fate. There was no fate— at least that's what I believed then— and someone up top saw his name on some employee list, some unpaid servitude kid, and it reminded them that they had a lazy writer/artist on their payroll who promised four more books by the time she turned thirty-two.

Well, here's number five of my books. Contract fulfilled. But maybe I won't give this one to the publisher. Maybe this one means too much to be fucked with by people who see dollar signs instead of symmetry, conventions instead of symbolism.

They want me to write my name six-thousand fucking times today and they send Marty to spy on me and remind me to write words that aren't my name, as if I'd have any time to.

"Well, what were you doing last night?" Marty asks after he pins the banner to my table.

I look up with my eyes, but nothing else moves. "Research."

"Oh!" He squeals and starts pulling comics from one of the bags. "For this? This that you're drawing? What's it about?"

"Do you get paid to interrupt me when I'm writing?" I ask, and he looks like someone kicked a puppy in front of him.

"Sorry," he says, and I almost feel bad for him, but then he adds, "I'm just so excited to see you so inspired!" And I decide to write him into Amethyst's story somehow just so I can kill him.

The doors open and people are already here. People will stand outside and wait in any weather to be the first one in the door. They do this here for writers, artists, actors, and they do it outside bars for bands.

Most times, it doesn't matter what a person creates. The fact that create anything means they're one step closer to being god.

The creator of everything is being replaced over and over again by creators of anything.

It's like those girls who fuck old men because their dad abandoned their family. It's close enough to the real thing, but far away enough to still reject it.

You're not god but you're my god.

I wonder how many worship Amethyst, and I wonder what his name is, and if I find his name, I can find his internet life, and I can see how many people comment on his face and his torso and his tattoos, and then I can comment something deep. Something pure. Something about him and not about what he does. Let's face it, guys like Amethyst, even in their smallest form, are told how amazing their music is all the time. But how many people tell him how amazing he is? How many people tell him that they can see through the bullshit, see through the disguise, and that they like what's underneath the costume?

This isn't Halloween, Amethyst. You're not a real bad boy. You're just dressing up as one, and maybe you're winning the costume contest, but I'm still here in the back corner of the party, and I can see where you messed up. I can see that you pulled the necklaces from the Sex Pistols and the belts from Bad era MJ and the shoes you've probably seen in an old classic horror film, and you're trying— you're really trying— to live up to the image.

But you can't. Not behind closed doors. No matter what you do on stage.

That's why I'm here. I'm here for you. To help you.

"Oh, my God," a girl says, and the hallucination is broken. "I love you so much," she gushes, and Marty slips her copy of "Crimson Crimes" in front of me with the fingers of his left hand and offers me a sharpie with his right.

My lips curl when I try to smile. I take the marker from him, and I look down to the book that means nothing because nothing means anything now that I've seen him, and I sign my name to it.

"Thank you," I say to her as I hand it back, and Marty accuses me of being short.

As the day progresses, I downgrade to "curt" then to "distracted" then to "I'm sorry to say, borderline rude".

I can't help it. I don't want to be here with these people. I don't want to be here with Marty.

I want to be with Amethyst. Since I can't do that in this world, I want to be in the one I've created for him.

But I need to know his name, and I can't decide if

drawing him is more important than Googling him.

I type *Grape Gardens* into Google and almost nothing comes up. It asks me if I meant *Grey Gardens*, and I think 'no, I thought that too', and I find their Instagram and their website and their Twitter. It's relevant to the searched term, fine, but it's his band and not him, and I want him.

Everyone keeps talking to me though, and Marty is trying to make me be nice, and the publishers are making me sit here, and I've had enough.

"I'm going to the restroom," I say and stand up and walk away from the table before he can even say a word.

He knows not to backtalk but I don't give him the opportunity.

Nothing matters but Amethyst, and I need to know his name.

```
Chapter 13
To:
From:
Subject: A Rose by Any Other Name
```

No, it wouldn't smell as sweet. Thanks, Shakespeare, but you got it all wrong.

My dumb ass never actually followed Grape Gardens on Instagram, by the way. I've just visited the page so much that it's first in my suggestions.

In the bathroom, taking a break from the chaos of people and my job and fucking Marty, I realized this blunder and corrected it.

A happy accident, however, because when you follow someone on Instagram, the app graciously suggests similar accounts for you to follow. You probably could've told me that; Bridget surely could have. Maybe if I cared about any facet of life at all, I'd be on the internet enough to know it. But I know now. I know, and guess whose beautiful face was the second in the line of suggestions?

Edited and filtered, cast in black and neon pinks, my Amethyst's gemstone hair was clear and cut like a 90's boyband model/"musician" and parted directly in the center.

His eyes so near the camera, the left is almost out of focus, but they're the most radiant blue— even bluer than I originally thought.

His fingers are curled and reaching for the chains and collars around his throat, and with his head angled for better visibility of this, his jawline looks like it could slice right through my phone screen.

I've never tapped my phone so quickly. Follow. Following. I'm following him. Connected.

I click his account and I'm treated to his handle— reedbarry— and I can't decide if I'd rather exit the app and Google that name to see if it's his real one, or stay here and consume, consume, consume.

There are only nine photos so looking through them all takes no time, and it appears the band just formed ten months ago. That, or he's only started his Instagram account at that point.

His photos are all in similar fashion— chains on bare chest; tattoos and wine bottles. In one, his purple hair looks damp, like he just came in from the rain, falling into his blue eyes to create a blur of beautiful color, and his lips, wrapping around a bottle, are covered in smeared pink lipstick.

It has to be his. I'm sure he was wearing it. I can't imagine him willing to touch someone he doesn't know in a seedy bar miles away from his home. He would be too shy. Too insecure standing next to Crop Top Big Hair Hottie. That guy, he's the one who gets all the girls. Not Amethyst. Not… Reed.

What a perfect name. It sounds as beautiful as it looks. It's smart. It's symmetrical. It isn't flashy. It's the name of a gentleman, and you and I know that beneath this image, that's exactly what he is.

"Your soul will follow mine to the grave"

I'll follow you anywhere, my Amethyst.

And above this caption is a photo of him, his handsome face, half-smiling but sad; his torso, wrapped in chains and a glittery harness, is covered in what appears to be blood, but it's purple, not red. I bet the ink inside the skin across his chest makes it even sweeter to taste.

"Carve out a hole in my soul so yours can slip inside"

I want to be inside him.

"Bexley?" I hear a familiar voice outside the stall. "Bexley Martin, are you in here?"

I want to say no, and even if I did, it wouldn't be a lie.

I'm not here. Maybe my body is, but I'm not.

I look down to Reed, safely cupped between my palms, and I'm somewhere else entirely. Somewhere with him. Somewhere where we know each other. Where our souls know each other.

"Bexley, Marty said you disappeared, like, fifteen minutes ago."

I get him. I get his poetry.

"There are only three bathrooms in this building and one is for men."

No one else in these comments seems to understand that this is what those captions are, but they're pure poetry.

"Actually…" her heels stop clicking against the floor. She's muttering now. "Maybe that's where you are."

But a poet recognizes a poet. Art knows art.

"No, you're in here…" her clicks are echoing in this empty room.

I want to be alone with Reed, so I say nothing. I don't even breathe, and I wonder how long I can do it. I wonder if I can hold my breath long enough to pass out and escape being alive for a few seconds.

"I can see your boots, Bex." And under the stall door,

her pointy-toed shoes are pointing directly at me. "I know you like standing out, but it doesn't make sense for someone who likes to hide so much."

"I'm not hiding," I huff as I open the door.

She points with her finger now. "You're on your phone, huh? Well, you better be storyboarding or something. If you're not at your table, no one is going to buy photos and autographs, and if no one buys photos or autographs," she follows me as I walk to the sink, "These events aren't going to want you on the roster anymore, and if these events don't want you on the roster, how are you going to eat?"

"I'll murder my neighbors and raid their fridge," I say as I stare at myself in the mirror. Dark red hair, light blue eyes, pale skin, and I'm such a good artist that every line drawn with concealer or bronzer or eyeliner or shadow is flawlessly crafted— straight and precise. The left eye matches the right eye to the very last detail. The purple shade I use to trace my lips hits each point of my bow and each slope of my mouth precisely.

I lift a finger and brush it under my eye.

"You're so vain," she says.

"I can't help it," I reply. "Talent is talent." But I don't think she understands what I mean. She's visual but there's no curiosity to analyze. No interpretation. Things are what they are. It makes me wonder why she likes something as deep and complex as music so much. I picture her watching Legally Blonde in her free time. I don't picture her trying to decipher each separate instrument in a song, each melody each instrument plays, each hidden meaning inside the lyrics.

Oh, well.

"Anyway, you can't actually murder your neighbors—"

"I can—"

"Well, you can't legally, so march your bootylicious booty back out to that table."

"Bridget," I exhale as I turn to her. "What are you even doing here?"

"Like I'd miss one of your events," she giggles and shakes her head. "You really are crazy."

And I wonder how long I can hold my breath until I pass out.

Chapter 14
To:
From:
Subject: Autopilot

I sign my name. I say hi. I say thanks.

Marty tries to flirt with Bridget. I tell him her brother is a veterinarian and will put him down in an instant. He asks why I'm always so negative and they bond over it.

I swear to God, the only thing worse than Marty alone is Marty with Bridget, and I wonder how I can get my hands on some of Vinny's drugs— the kind that will make holding my breath irrelevant.

But I'm excited when no one's at my table because creating my story— my Amethyst story, my Reed story— it's more important than selling the other ones I've written. It's more important than money, than food, than air.

I look over to Marty and I almost ask him if he'll publish whatever of this comic I get finished if I happen to die suddenly, or unexpectedly, or unintentionally. All of the above, or none of it. Does it matter?

At least he's silent right now. No one is around. Bridget ran off to get gourmet coffee, and I have no doubt she'll come back with bags of clothing and jewelry and purses and wallets, all with the faces of heroes she can't differentiate from villains.

When she comes back, she's got gifts for us, for her

brother. She shows us everything. Marty is engaging with her. They talk.

Small talk has never made any sense to me. I'm not good at it. I don't see the point in it. I want to discuss concepts, ideas, books, music, and I can never understand why so many people have the most simplistic answers as to why their favorite song is their favorite song.

Bridget has claimed to love a band since middle school and had no idea that their title was a reference to a classic piece of fiction from the 70's. She thinks her ass and her eyes are her biggest assets. She sees the surface, and no matter how hard I try, I can't stop seeing past it.

I wonder sometimes if that's why I struggle to make connections, but if I'm honest, I've never really tried to.

When I dated people, I think I only cared for them as extensions of myself. Don't cheat and don't lie but not because you'll hurt my feelings; don't do these things because I don't enjoy being disrespected.

I watched a movie once where someone was institutionalized with a mental condition that decades ago served as a sentence to life the insanity ward. Now people are just scientifically documented as unable to empathize and sent out into the world after an hour of healing. I don't accept most self-diagnoses, but for the longest time I thought maybe my brain functioned in whatever way creates this disorder. This mental health issue that seems more a blessing to me.

I've seen Bridget have meltdowns over traffic tickets, watched her cry over her body, saw her cheat on boyfriends because they cheated on her then get drunk and bawl about it. I've seen her cry because her daddy stopped paying her car insurance when she turned twenty-five. I don't know about you, but I think not caring about everything is fine when you look at the alternative.

When I got my fish, though, I disproved my own belief that I was a sociopath or something similar. I care about my fish. I love them. I prioritize taking care of them over taking care of myself, and I swear to God, if I had to starve to feed them, I'd do it happily.

I get Vinny to babysit them in my absence if work takes me too far away. And I don't hate Vinny. He's smart and he's tall and attractive, and he doesn't tell me I'm too attached to animals you can't even pet. Like Bridget does. He's nothing like his sister, and when I ask him for information on tranquilizers and body functions for my stories, he doesn't ask me if I'm crazy. Like Bridget does.

Vinny is too eager to be informative, too easy to explain deadly dosages, too convinced that everyone in the world is too unlike the villains of my graphic novels when they ask him for medical data.

So I don't hate Vinny, and I love my fish. I'm not entirely crazy. Not yet.

Further evidence— I love my family, even though we have nothing in common except blood. They've always cared for me, supported me, provided. But there's always been some strange disconnection of personality.

I look up from my storyboard, rest my chin in my palm. I'm certain there are black smears rubbing off of my hand onto my face, but the sight of Marty being a human, and Bridget being a human, and the idea that they don't really know how to do it as much as it an instinct to them is too fascinating to avoid.

I read an article once that said how young women relate to other young women is a direct reflection of how their mother related to them. I imagine Bridget's mom talked to her a lot. I bet she was the type of mother to have an actual sex talk with her children.

I'm sure as a child I appreciated skipping that chat, but now I'm wondering if it was detrimental. I'm wondering if everything in my childhood was.

That's not to say it was unhappy— it was the polar opposite. I had everything I ever wanted right down to extra television channels because we had a satellite dish while everyone else just had cable. It wasn't the time of DVR and DVDs, so everything seemed more exciting. Nothing was instant so the time spent waiting for it was fun. We were so patient. The drive to Blockbuster to rent a VHS was a thrill. Now driving to a convention where people know my name and my work and pay to praise me feels like a hassle.

I guess my point is that people who have everything rarely appreciate it, and growing up without a sense of how everything has found its way to you can be detrimental to who you become as an adult.

Sometimes it feels unfair. Sometimes growing up with everything, with every new toy and multiples of it because your parents are divorced and both sides want to prove they love you more by spending more when really your dad doesn't care if you live or die and your mom is more like your sister because your grandparents feel like your parents when you all four live together, when you grow up being the only child, the only grandchild, the only niece or nephew, well, you grow up thinking everything is easy because you've always had everything and everyone's attention and you never had to work for any of it.

When you're a teenager or in your early twenties and

you're used to only discussing yourself, you learn very quickly that any real social abilities have been lost upon you. When you realize everyone you meet isn't in awe of everything you do, you start to question if any of your talents were ever actually talents. You wonder if you're as smart as your mom always said you were. And when she isn't there to force you into studying at eighteen and nineteen and twenty, you realize how lazy you really are.

You see people of the same age ballet dancing professionally, and you realize that how lucky you thought you were because your mom allowed you to quit dance when you said you didn't like it anymore was actually really unlucky. You start to see how adults around you have mastered abilities that no one forced you into continuing.

You get pissed because you wanted guitar lessons and no one took you seriously. You get more pissed because your aunt bought you a guitar but you couldn't teach yourself how to play by Googling the chords to your favorite songs.

You remember how you wanted to apply for a college two hours away to study film, but your family and friends told you to be serious. Told you that weren't going to do that. Get real. And when you look at people who had those experiences, you know their parents were excited when they had big ambitions, and you become jealous of them and their lives and their decisions because you hate yourself for not submitting your own application anyway.

It takes a long time, but even after all of this— after all of the presents they still give you, the money you still get on birthdays and Christmas, after they help you change your flat tire, or pay your electric bill because your checking account is overdrawn and your book isn't selling

as well as the publishers thought it would— you realize
they don't care about you the way you don't care about
other people.

They provide for you because you're an extension of
them. They love you because society tells us to love those
with whom we share DNA. But when you try to talk about
the things you're passionate about, they don't care, and
they don't make an effort to hide it, and the close family
friends who give you Starbucks gift cards when you turn
thirty don't care either, and the people you text everyday
say "lol" and send smiley faces because they don't care
enough to read what you've typed.

It could be painful for anyone alive enough to feel
pain. But you don't care. You love them, and you worry
for them, and you want them to be safe and happy and
healthy, but you know they don't understand you. You
know the things they enjoy discussing aren't the same as
what you enjoy discussing.

Your mother rolls her eyes and groans that she
doesn't need a lecture when you try to explain some
thought you had on a TV show, or what a comic book
character can mean to someone, and how fun conventions
are, and how exciting small venue shows are, and how
music and words and art can connect us. She doesn't care.
She's bored with it. And eventually you just grow out of
the things that used to matter because no one wants to
hear about it.

Everyone wants to talk about themselves. They don't
care about the plot line of your book, or how kind the
architect of your most beloved band had been to you.

They make jokes about how they don't want to see
photos or how they can't be bothered to read over your

opening, but they aren't jokes. They're kind rejections of everything that makes you who you are.

Friends or family.

Or they simply don't respond and start telling you about a cake they baked for a sex party.

Friends.

Eventually you start telling people when you don't care about what they're saying. You hope it's the big wake up call that makes them realize how they make you feel, but it isn't. It just makes you a cunt. It makes them say that this is why no one wants to be around you. It makes them try to hurt your feelings.

Again, I suppose I'm lucky I don't experience much grief or turmoil or anxiety. But imagine growing up around people like this if you do.

I empathize, so again I'm not a sociopath. But right now, rewatching a movie I've seen a thousand times instead of sitting here with actual people sounds like the better option.

Bridget looks over to me and asks what I think of the stickers she bought for her nephew, and I smile and tell her they're great, but really I'm jealous that she has a nephew and I don't, and I never will be able to because my parents decided one of me was enough, and none of my five aunts ever thought having a baby was a good idea. I don't want kids either, but if I don't have them then my entire family goes with me when I die, and quite frankly I'm not sure I'm going to outlive any of them.

```
Chapter 15
To:
From:
Subject: Home is Where the Heart is
```

I come home and there are maggots in my sink.

I suppose most people would turn on the faucet and wash them down the drain, but I don't. I don't want to kill them. I tell myself they'll probably die there anyway. Then I feel evil for making them starve instead of drowning them. I just can't bring myself to do it. I'm not a murderer, am I?

Perhaps of fictional characters, but we can't really know that they're fictional, and if they are alive in some other realm, I wonder if I'm writing what they've done or if they're doing what I've written.

Who's God, and who's the muse? Creator vs creation. Parent vs child. I suppose it's proof that whatever you create— whether through divinity or DNA— will eventually turn its back on you.

If my characters plot against me, I've got no one to blame but myself. Assuming my thoughts are my own. Maybe someone else is putting them inside my mind. I mean, can you pinpoint the start of a thought? Can you trace its origin? Maybe thoughts don't have beginnings. Maybe they don't have ends. Maybe they are alpha and omega, just like God, and maybe God put our souls inside our brains because it made more sense than sticking them up our asses.

I go to bed hungry.

I go to bed angry.

I go to bed lonely.

I go to bed tired.

HALT.

Control your impulses. Self help. It's maddening.

I only know of this concept because it was mentioned in a movie I once watched when I was in high school, but it's so idiotic it stuck with me. I don't know anyone who isn't hungry, or angry, or lonely, or tired.

Most people I know are tired of their jobs and their boring lives. Most people are hungry for more. Or maybe that's just how I imagine them.

I roll over in my bed and look at my ceiling. It's plain white and there is a spider making its way across it. A single spec of black in the wide open whiteness. I bet he's lonely up there. A trip to my sink would solve his hunger. I wonder if maggots get angry.

I guess what I really want— what's really keeping me awake this night— is my story. I want to draw and shade and color and I want to write plotlines and dialogue. But all I can see when I sit down is the blankness before me. An anxiety in its own right: The excitement that beauty might drip from your brain onto the page; the horror of what cliched shit might.

And this is Reed we're talking about. My Amethyst. Everything in his story has to be beautiful, has to be perfect, and instead of answering any of the messages on my screen, instead replying to the people who want to talk to me, instead of thinking of my story or my writing or my drawing, I unlock my phone.

The passcode is my old number— a number I had to change because you couldn't just block numbers in those days and sometimes exes won't leave you alone when you tell them they'd handle this better if they just pretended you don't exist.

Every time I type that number, I feel nothing. I think nothing. But now I'm pissed about it. I'm pissed because the next time I see Amethyst's set, I won't get drunk. I won't befriend the bigoted bartender, and I won't be so fucking unprepared. The next time I see Amethyst's set, we'll meet after. We'll talk. And I'll have this comic book finished, and I'll present it to him. I'll tell him how nothing made sense, not life, not art, not music, not even my own stories, not until I saw him, and I'll tell him that his presence alone was enough to inspire me into being alive.

I'll tell him I think he's Jesus. He's an all-powerful, less-tactless Zeus. And because he's so delicate, so humble, and so shy, because there's a touch of insecurity inside his beautiful blue eyes, he'll hold it in his hands, his rings glistening under the low lights of the magically lit bar, and he'll stare in awe of it.

It's the Bible, Reed is God, and I'm just an apostle bearing witness.

He'll look up to me, and he won't know what to say because no one has ever cared for him the way that I do. No one's ever given him such a compliment before, but calling him God isn't a compliment; it's fact.

He might want to discuss it with me. But he's omniscient so he'll already know the story. And after our time together, just the two of us talking of art and inspiration in the silence of the empty bar, the Christmas lights surrounding us flickering from dead batteries, giving us the sense of darkness— calming like the kind you fall asleep in— he'll want to continue our connection, and he'll want my phone number.

I've had this one since I was twenty-two, but I'm not as confident in my memorization of it. I knew my old number perfectly. And because fucking Carl couldn't just move on when I told him I didn't want to see him anymore, I had to change it. Fucking 2010. Fucking low level technology. Fucking fuck.

Amethyst will ask for my number and I'll stutter and I'll worry that I gave him the wrong one, and I'll lose my soulmate standing right in front of me over ten digits after thirty-one years of not believing in him.

Maybe he doesn't exist.

But I'm on my phone for him, searching his name, typing Reed into Instagram and seeing his handle— reedbarry— and seeing his photos and being able to associate the name to the face.

I stare at him, and all I want to do is write.

```
Chapter 16
To:
From:
Subject: I am God to Those I Create
```

I got three hours of sleep last night, but I've written nine full pages. Story, dialogue, blocked and drawn.

Seeping into my veins, Reed's inspiration transforms by miracle the blood there into sparkling champagne. I'm drunk off of it. High off of it. I am God and all I create are subservient to me.

I draw Reed in chains. But that's for later.

I draw him with blond hair, with his pure eyes of gorgeous blue. I draw him in a simple orange T-shirt with only a leather jacket and chipped nail polish as signifiers of his profession.

He's innocent in my story, untouched and unknowing. He goes onto the stage with a message, one that's sung in a different manner and style than Grape Gardens. One that's deep and dark. One that would "frighten" idiots like this girl, Emma, I used to know.

She used to miss her car payments to buy expensive watches because she cared more about her image than her insides, and because I never cared about what anyone thought of me, we couldn't understand one another.

She hated heavy bass drums and blaring guitars, and harsh vocals scared her. God forbid men wear makeup around her. God forbid she wasn't married. But she cheated on both husbands and blamed everyone, right down to Jesus, for it.

No one takes responsibility. She said she cheated on Dave with Kel because Dave wouldn't go to church with her even though he promised before they got married that he would. I told her she was only worried about church now because Kel was a very proud Christian. She said I was absurd and didn't talk to me for a while, but when she finally left Dave for Kel and Kel didn't want anything serious, she settled for Jack. Jack who wasn't Christian. Jack who didn't go to church. And when they married, it was in a barn.

Emma wouldn't approve of men who look like Reed, not even who he really is, but I'm not certain she's ever been in any position to give out advice.

After all, we have the same four year degree and she has her master's, but she's one of the most ignorant and shallow-minded people I've ever met. And for someone who claims to be so liberal, she's insanely judgemental of anyone or anything that goes against what's considered normal.

Nothing like Reed. Reed and his deep thoughts and his concepts and his presentation.

I draw him shyly ordering a bottle of water at the venue in which he's playing. I draw him meeting a woman there. I draw him timid. I write him whispering his words.

Slipping into his space, this serpent woman bumps into him. His water spills. She replaces it with alcohol.

This woman, surely she's the reason for Reed's downfall. Somewhere along the line, someone told Reed he was too fragile to be a rock god. Someone filled his head with the same lies society tells us all from the time we're old enough to understand the words: Men are tough and bold and strong, and women are meek and sensitive, and if you're a man who is sensitive, you aren't correct, and if you're a woman who isn't, you're wrong.

Well, my darling Amethyst, please know that society is misleading and illogical. Society is sorely mistaken. And here I am, you flesh-and-blood fallen angel, to show you how perfectly crafted your innocence was; how heroic you will be when you reclaim your modest serenity. I will stand before you as a woman who is all of the things men "should be" and you'll know that all I've ever wanted was you— a man who is everything I'm not.

You're a gorgeous demonstration of divinity— proof that fairytales are real— and all the dragons and demons of our dreams, they exist in a plane unattached from ours in any physical way, but is connected to us through our minds and our souls. That one piece of all living things that is the same through time and space and life and death. Spirits. Minds. What's the difference?

I draw him walking onto the stage and I draw the screens of phones lighting up the faces below him. He wonders if anyone cares about the message masked poetically inside his songs.

I care, Reed, and when you read the story I've written for you, you'll feel appreciated. You'll know what love is, and not this ridiculous Hollywood love. Not the kind of love that's written in the stars or in songs or in books. Not even the kind of love so built on trust you let your girlfriend fuck you with a strap-on. This is beyond anything documented, or desired, or imagined. This is not fantasy.

And like you, my Amethyst, your comic book doppelgänger is someone tangible and alive and real, someone I've connected to through mind and aura and some strange blinded sight.

I know him because I know you, and somewhere in his world, the other me is trying to save him. I draw her meeting him, talking to him, praising him. I draw her understanding the song lyrics no one takes the time to interpret. I draw him in awe of her, like she's the angel, but really it's him and it's you, and we two women are only here to remind you of your divinity.

We're connected, Reed, my Amethyst, in ways we can't see or touch or smell or even feel. Not unless we're open to it. And I'm opening up to you. I'm letting you invade me, and guide me, and direct my mind with your words, and my fingers with your image. But the question is, my dearest Amethyst, are you opened up enough to allow me inside of you?

I pause and call up Reed's instagram. I zoom in on his secret lips, on his torso and his tattoos. It isn't that I want to know every detail; it's that I have to. To draw him, to show him as he really is, I need to see everything everyone else sees, not just the things only visible to me.

There's a small scar on his left collarbone and his chain-and-lock necklace rests just above it. Almost like an accent to it. For whatever reason, I can't help zooming and staring and imagining how soft it would feel if I'd run my fingertips across it.

I draw it, and instead of the Sex Pistol chains, I draw a delicate strand of silver with a crucifix and saint Cecelia glistening from it.

My own little Amethyst angel, my lord and savior

from all that is apathy-worthy. I care for you, Reed, and because of you, I care at all.

But there are only a handful of photos and I want more. I need more. The story does, and because the story does, Reed does. And then it hits me: check the photos people have tagged him in.

A plethora of perfection at my fingertips now, I see him on stage, smiling, purity radiating through dark eyeliner and messy makeup. He couldn't mask it with any amount of darkness.

I see him in bright pink eyeshadow, the word *FREEDOM* scratched across his neck in what must be red sharpie, dripping down his chest like blood, and when I click to enlarge, I'm treated to a surprise. It's a video.

A bright light shines into a darkened room, and Reed's face is ignited by its heat. The skin cascading over high cheekbones and a straight nose is pale and neutral, smooth, creamy. Soft and delicate. Not a single flaw in his flesh, but sparkles shimmer under his eyes and across his cheeks. The brightness of his pink eyelids is still diminished by the brightness of his eyes, and when the light reflects inside them and they flicker gently under a slow, deliberately seductive blink, toward the lens, I gasp. How they're real, I'll never know— not unless he is a magical being or a god. My second coming.

His brow raises over his right eye, the nearest to my phone screen, and his chin begins to lift slowly. He's teasing us. Tempting us to read what's written beneath his sharp, bold jawbone. And when the first few letters are visible— the *F*, the *R*, the two *E*'s— he turns his head in the other direction. His eyes look down as his cheek all but rests on his shoulder, and we see the remaining letters.

We're given the message. We're allowed to read. We may witness his word.

FREEDOM

But he isn't free.

His eyes are down cast and he's bound by chains and dog collars.

People in the comments praise him. They tell him they admire his freedom. They love a boy in makeup. They love someone who can break free. But they don't see him, not really. They don't even realize he's tied up just beneath the word. He isn't bragging. He isn't saying, "hey, world, look what I've got." He's asking for it. Begging. He wants to be free.

I know what's captured him. It's this stigma placed on his profession, placed on men. He can't be worshipped as a rock god if he's delicate, or if he's dressed normally, or even if he's sober.

He's a slave to his own false image. He wants freedom from it, from himself.

From Amethyst.

All this time and I'm only now seeing it— this Amethyst alien, this guy in Grape Gardens, he isn't the same person as Reed. They're both trapped inside the same body, maybe, but they're not the same mind, or brain, or heart, or soul. An artist hidden inside his art. A person inside the shell of his own character.

Amethyst is who Reed became when the world was too dark for his divinity, but I'll restore my deity to his throne. I'll give him back his body and his life, and through my story— which flows from me as easily and quickly as the lifeblood would if you were to slit my throat— he'll find the confidence to fight.

But that's the toughest wall to break— the hardest fight to curl your fists in preparation for— this battle we wage against ourselves, against who we really are, against who we want to be.

It's hard when you don't know who you are. It's harder when you know who you are and hate it.

Chapter 17
To:
From:
Subject: Gratitude

I wake up to a paragraph from Chelsea. She's thankful we're friends and she loves me. I don't even know what her middle name is.

Bridget texts. Bridget loves me and our adventures. Bridget feels like I'm her sister.

Vinny texts that he's thankful for me and he hopes he has occasion to fish-sit soon because isn't it funny how we only see one another in times of great distance?

I reply: *yeah.*

I have a Bitmoji from a family friend. A Facebook message from Harley, who I've known since college. A text from Connor, who used to deliver money to the bank I once worked in. Another text from Natalie, who I met at a show four hours away only to find out we live thirty minutes away from each other.

I'm thankful. They're thankful. I feed my fish and have some coffee, the last bit in my plastic jar of instant, and the eight dollars in my bank account is already dedicated to correcting the dreaded gas light.

I wouldn't have to go anywhere, and I could just buy coffee with it, but today is the last Thursday of November and that means appreciating family by sharing a meal with them.

This is the best part of my life— the most loving, the most secure, and the most connected. But it's the part I hate most. I hate it because it reminds me of what I'm not. I'm not as successful a graphic novelist as I'd like to be. I'm not anyone more special than everyone else in the room. I'm not someone who marries Brad Pitt; and I'm not someone more than three people would miss if I died.

Still, every time I drive home, I imagine swerving into the lane opposite me. The idea pops in my head as soon as I see headlights driving toward me, and my fists tighten on the wheel, ready and willing to jerk it and obey the thought, accept the call to action, as soon as I realize those headlights are attached to a big rig.

I write while I drive. I stare at my phone. I don't just check Facebook or type text messages, I write the dialogue to my stories. I call up photos of my panels, the character portraits I've drawn, and I study them. I imagine them alive, moving. I imagine what they're saying and I type it all out, and I never look up from my phone while I'm doing it.

It's incredible how the body must function on memory and instinct. I've driven the same roads so many times that even the butt of my palms can shift the wheel enough to turn the car around curves and up hills while my fingers hold my phone and type and write and my mind has escaped into an alternate reality that might not be real at all. So sometimes I close my eyes while I'm driving. Just on these too-familiar roads. These empty streets.

I test myself and my unseen, instinctual talent for navigating curvy and hilly roads without looking. Without really being present. My impressive memory.

I never die when I do this, and I'm not worried about

it. I imagine the statistics will catch up with me soon enough. And, no, I don't want to kill anyone else, but if I'm dead too then I won't be around to feel anything about it.

The last time I was with my family, I left abruptly. I wanted to spend time with them, and I wanted to enjoy it. I tried to engage and listen and converse. But no one wants to hear anything I have to say when it's my turn to talk. So I stopped.

I left. I took out my phone and I wrote while I drove.

Today I tried to manage expectations. Today I thought I wouldn't be upset if no one wanted to hear about Amethyst or how wonderful he is or how he's God but I'm a god too, and I'll set him free. No one likes the tattoos on my body, and even when I wear long sleeves and pants, I can't cover the ones on my feet.

They tell me I'm going to ruin my hair with all of this dye. They tell me they're worried about me and my hobby that I've turned into a shitty little career. It's not like I'm Stan Lee. But they don't have access to the sales reports. They don't see the people who ask for my signature. They don't see messages from strangers in England asking me if they could ask just one question about something that happened to Michael in the first comic. They don't see me as I am. And I think I see myself in all the ways I don't want to be when I see their interpretation of me reflecting in their eyes, in their voices, in what they don't say as much as in what they do say.

I try to stay. I try to get lost in my world with Reed, staring at his face, sketching with a cheap little app and my finger, typing into the notes app. I try to be there with them without being present to them, to what they say, and

I feel guilty for it.

Every time I tell them how I hate being around them, how I've wasted gas I don't even have to get to them, how they make me feel bad when I'm near them, I feel guilty. But it never stops me from saying it again.

I guess it would be nice to be accepted, but really I'd just like to be able to make a statement about something important to me and be met with some acknowledgment that wasn't negative or judgmental.

Who says you have to stop doing certain things and start doing others because you were born at a certain point in time— time that is a purely human construct.

My fish don't know how old they are, and they don't know how old I am, and they have no concept of a day or a month or even an hour.

They don't judge one another, and they don't judge me, and they don't judge the maggots squirming around in rotten yogurt in my sink.

I don't think Reed would judge me. I don't think someone so willing to stand out would mind much about a person that makes them odd or weird or immature. I don't imagine he'd approve much of how miserable I so often am, but I also think being close to him would fix that. Being close to him wouldn't just be okay. Being close to him would be good. He's God, after all.

And I'm just now realizing I have no idea how old he is.

So after I throw on my boots and exit the kitchen, sobbing because I feel terrible for being unkind to the family who has done so much for me, I suck the running snot into my nose, and I call up Google. I type Reed Barry. I type *birth date*. And in the pain I've caused myself, in the worry of what might happen to my family and what it might feel like if this angry interaction were the last experience I had with them, I see that Reed was born three months and one day before me. In 1986. And something tells me that he is the destiny I'm driving toward when I press the ignition button and back out of the driveway.

I choose my fate. And if I don't, I'm at least going to fight for it.

I type and write and become puppet master for Reed. My Amethyst. And I don't even need to stare at my phone because tears blur my vision.

It's raining and it's thirty degrees, and water falls from my rear view mirror and blurs my backup camera, and I can't see anything between the sky's crying and my crying.

I love my family. They love me. But I'm not interested in the things they find amusing, and they hate everything about everything I've become.

I blame my mother and father, I blame my aunts, I blame my grandparents for not having a sixth child who wanted a litter of kids because I'd be willing to bet that if all of their effort and energy and money and time and hopes and dreams and idealized images for their posterity hadn't fallen on me, they wouldn't be so disapproving.

If I had a twin sister who had pretty, natural brown hair, and delicate makeup, designer clothing, and a big-girl job, they wouldn't mind so much about me being a fuck up.

If I had a cousin with bare, creamy arms and legs, they wouldn't mind how I've messed mine up with tattoos.

If someone had benefited from all of their effort, they wouldn't feel like everything they'd had was wasted as it trickled down the family tree to nurture me.

This writer, this artist, this woman with bright red hair and tattoos. No one has ever said anything that I'm saying to you now, but I've known these people since the day I was born. I know what they're thinking when I catch them looking at my sleeve. I know they're wondering why I never use my bachelor's degree, and why my aunt wasted so much money to pay off those student loans for me.

They know that I know how I've been given every opportunity to be successful, and I know no matter how happy my art makes me, they'll never consider that worthwhile unless my name becomes as big as Stan Lee's.

We just don't get each other. But it's harder to love the black sheep when there aren't any clean, normal, fluffy white ones to thank God for. And what is God anyway?

Isn't it the spark of creation that ignites inside my mind and urges my pen forward? That inspiration, that unseen and unheard hallucination that my body makes tangible through pen and paper, that's the only god I've ever known. And because Reed sets what was once that little spark ablaze, he can only be the almighty.

I don't need to waste time on anything but worship, and I write to praise him.

Chapter 18
To:
From:
Subject: Black Friday

I made plans to go shopping, but I dread it. I know I have to, though. If I don't entertain these stupid friendship activities— rituals that mean nothing— then how will I ever expect someone to go with me to see Grape Gardens when they inevitably perform nearby again?

According to Twitter, they're running their own "headlining" tour simultaneously with this one, but really that just means they book itty bitty bars when they're in the same city for more than a few hours.

Bridget, of course, is a sure thing, but I just don't need her energy spoiling it. I need something less irritating. I need Natalie.

I watch her try on clothes for forty percent off, and she doesn't notice when I slip into the other realm.

I draw Amethyst in the bathroom of a dingy bar, red spray painted words splayed across the grime-covered, green-from-mold walls, looking at himself in consideration as he tries on his new Sid Vicious accessories. I draw him with his lovely hands holding open his leather jacket, head tilted, brilliant blue eyes scanning his bare torso. His crucifix lying in the sink clogged with cigarette ashes.

I name him Reagan, like Reed, and like the poor

possessed girl from The Exorcist. Reagan, a tribute to all Reed was, is, and has become, and I explain why. I explain where it came from— this external mismatch of his internal self. And when he reads it, when he sees himself through my eyes, he won't have to fake it anymore. Or maybe he'll tell me to go fuck myself. Who can say?

My book, it's the Bible. I'm the exorcist. Okay, I'm God. My divine inspiration will free him from his demons.

Reagan, standing in the bathroom mirror as the speakers of the bar blast rap music, his hair is parted the way Reed's hair is parted. Down the middle. Curling into his eyes. The thin lips of his secret mouth are forever parted. Fragile and small, but the life that bursts from them when he sings is more powerful than simple breaths and muscle spasms.

I draw Reagan looking at himself in uncertainty. Is he really someone who takes his shirt off to perform? Who likes the idea of being bound and tied and owned? Is he free?

"Okay, TV next," Natalie says when she emerges from the dressing room in her leggings and her flannel-pattern knit sweater. "You're sure there's nothing here you wanna look at before we move on to the next stop?"

"No, thanks," I say, still sketching, "Give me one second to finish though," and I draw the tag-line *JUST FUCK* above Reagan's head. A similar sentiment to what I saw above Reed's, above the Amethyst Alien on stage.

Reed, with his innocent hands, actually spray painted the words FUCK GOD, FUCK EACH OTHER and was too impatient to let it dry, or maybe he made it up on the spot when the band's old sign blew out the window of their van. It was either extremely thought out, or it wasn't thought out at all.

Knowing Reed the way I do, I'm sure he put his entire soul into that seemingly insignificant, substance-lacking statement of nothing. But maybe that's deliberate.

"Actually," I say, looking up from my panels and closing my pad, "what I need is in the electronic section too."

"Cool," Natalie smiles. "Off to the techie paradise we go."

Chapter 19
To:
From:
Subject: An Image Different from
the Images

While Natalie fights a ten-year-old in a Skyrim shirt for the last television behind, I walk to the CDs. A very specific CD in mind.

FXCK GOD, FXCK EACH OTHER.

Parental advisory.

Explicit content.

But I haven't heard anything explicit besides the title.

Reed sings gently over retro-pop guitars and calming melodies about aliens flying down to the earth, helping him find the woman he lost to the his inhuman mannerisms. He says he could never let go of this woman, but if you pay attention to the rest of the lyrics, he doesn't seem to know much about her.

She was wearing a yellow shirt and their eyes met. Boom. He couldn't let her go. Can't give you up. Can't stop loving you. All that love-song crap I've never believed in. But maybe I've been too cynical. Maybe it's me.

I let my fingers brush across the plastic wrapped souls. Little circular souls inside square cases.

I want to hold Reed's soul in my hands. I want to feel the plastic pulling away from its case. I want to free him from this manufactured idolatry. Keep him safe inside my hands, inside my home, inside of me.

But I get to the G section, and I see nothing that says Grape or Gardens or Grape Gardens, and I know their album is available now. I've seen it on their Instagram. I've seen it on his.

Hear me, Reed typed below the saved story on his profile. *Hear me.* And when I tap the circle, a nun pegging a beefed-up, overly sun-kissed surfer-dude shows up with that explicit content warning and Grape Gardens scrawled across the top in bright pink. Pink and glitter. Like his microphone. His safety net to hide his secret lips from the audiences who don't deserve his soul.

I'm getting off topic.

The point is that I wanted his album. I wanted to hold it in my hands and I wanted to flip through the booklet. I wanted to read the lyrics and see his name credited to them. I wanted to breathe art and life and sex and drugs, and I wanted to exhale it out onto the page the way it should be.

But there is no Grape Gardens section.

"Hey, Natalie," I say, rounding the corner to see her now arguing with the boy's mother.

"Bex, hang on," she says, her hand on her tiny hip and her other arm pressing the large television box against her side.

"This is a child," I can hear the woman saying, but I'm only half here so I only half hear.

"Okay, but I beat him to this TV…"

I pull up Instagram while she's fighting. I want to see the cover. I want to hear his voice.

"It's the last one…"

And I follow Reed's command. *Hear me.*

"Lady, come on. There will be more before Christmas…"

And when the nun giving it to the ball-gagged surfer overtakes my screen, I hear his angelic cries.

"He got games for thanksgiving…"

And I turn up the volume.

"Who gives their kid presents on—"

Connect to something else about your eyes within your soul.

"Bex?" Natalie says, and only my eyes move up to her. Something no one has ever found.

"Whatcha listening to?"

The air is still and silent but the night is anything but calm, my Amethyst sings.

"Bex, seriously," Natalie says, and her brows crease.

I'm chasing the footprints of your sound.

"It's called 'Echoes'," I tell her when the clip finishes and the fucking nun and surfer disappear back into Reed's profile. I look over to the woman, then back to Natalie. "I was going to get the CD here but maybe they don't carry it because there's a nun fucking a guy in the ass on the cover."

The woman gasps, spits something about disrespect, and drags away her bratty little kid.

Who gets presents for Thanksgiving? Well, Natalie, I always did. For the Fourth of July and St Patrick's Day too. And look how I turned out.

It's better that the kid learns a lesson now. Maybe he'll grow up and actually work for something.

```
Chapter 20
To:
From:
Subject: Better Without
```

Maybe it's better that I don't have his album. It isn't him on the cover. Who knows what's inside and who chose it.

I'd like to think Reed chose everything himself, that because he wrote the songs and probably established the entire band, he'd have some say so. But I'm sure that isn't always the case in music. It definitely isn't in publishing.

I mean, I wrote this entire story. I drew it. It wouldn't exist without me, and I alone am the god of these people who exist somewhere visible to only me. Until I draw them anyway.

But I don't get to choose the cover and if someone who makes a lot more money from my work than I do doesn't like an entire spread of panels, they can cut them out. Who cares what they represent? Who cares why I took the time and effort to draw and shade and color and write them? I don't know my story, right?

Well, I know Reed's. The real Reed.

"So, Natalie," I say as she drinks her caramel-coffee-Christmas concoction, "that song I was playing earlier…" I look down at Amethyst, Reagan, the real Reed. "I think I'm connected to that guy."

"Connected?" She sips and everything smells like caramel and salt and Christmas cookies around us, and it's pitch black outside the window, and there are red and green holiday bags everywhere that remind me of childhood around the tree, and it all creates this sense of warmth inside my stomach that most likely is just the searing hot coffee sliding down my throat, but still it feels perfect. It feels like confirmation of everything I'm about to say. She clarifies, "You mean you, like, connect to his music?"

"No," I say, still drawing him, "Not his music." I lift my pencil and look at the panels, the story, the most important one to me, and I wonder if he'll think it's important too. "I mean to him."

"Did you, like, talk to him or something?"

"I didn't have to."

"What does that mean?" Her nose scrunches. I turn my book around. I show her. "Wow," she says as she flips the first page. I see her eyes scanning the speech bubbles, the narration. I see her looking at Reagan, at Reed without the Amethyst Alien, and her eyes move upward. "So you're writing a story about some guy in a band?"

"About who he really is."

"He seems…" she looks down to the paper, "Unrealistic."

"He is unrealistic," I tell her, growing a bit defensive. "I've never seen anyone like him." I call up his Instagram. I show her photos of his secret lips and the sparkles that sometime dance below his blues. I show her his purple hair, it's 90's boyband cut, his Grape Gardens page, his bare torso, and his '86 tattoo, and the writing on his chest. I show her his dog collars, and the videos of young Mr.

Sexy Hair walking like a cracked-out zombie who is about to devour the purity of Reed, of the alien lifeform itself.

Amethyst, in this new photo by The Sandman, the band's seeming photographer, he's got on little 60's circular sunglasses, and blue comic book tears stream down from beneath them. "Maybe it's a sign," I whisper. "I've never seen this one before…"

"A sign?" Natalie looks confused when I take the phone away.

I study Amethyst's hands— thick and masculine, but small and delicate— as he grips a bottle with one and turns it over his head. It's empty, and I'm certain it was emptied by the others around him. He saw an opportunity to appear edgy when all he is is sweet and untouched by any mortal sin that leads to bullshit like escapism and Alcoholics Anonymous.

I zoom into this hand though, fascinated by the way the tight grip of his fingers pushes the ring on his pointer away from his flesh. I can see through the space between the glistening silver and his appealing skin. I've never seen his hands without the rings he wears on them, and I wonder if I were to lick the inside of the silver how the salt of his sweat might taste after a long performance in those rings.

"I've never seen him in anything but smeared makeup," I say, zooming out to see the black-outlined blue globs of drawn on sorrow. "Now that I'm writing about him, The Sandman posts a picture of him with comic tears drawn across his cheeks."

"Who is The Sandman?"

"Their photographer, I guess." I click his name to scan his page. "He tags Reed in everything he does. It's where I find most of the photos that inspire me."

"So it's actually the photographer inspiring you?" She says, taking the phone. "He's so smiley to be in black pleather pants and weird makeup. And what's with the bondage thing? Is their music kinky?"

"No," I say, taking the phone away. I wrap a hand over it. I'm not even with him and he still needs my protection. I'm here, Reed. I'll keep you safe. "I think it's a gimmick. That's what I'm saying about connecting to him. This…" I tap on my book, my manuscript, the Biblical passages which set Reed free from the bindings of the demonic world he's trapped inside. "This is who he really is. You know it yourself. Think about what you just said. He's too smiley to be the way he looks. He isn't edgy or grimy or drunk. He's not out there fucking girls in his van after the show. He just wants us to think he is."

"Bex, that's weird. Why would someone try that hard—"

"Because maybe he knew he couldn't make it being himself. Church kids get made fun of when they buy everything God is selling."

"So he's religious?"

"His album is called 'Fuck God…' something, but he's innocent behind that mask. Can't you see it? It has to be some manufactured rebellion. And I Googled him. He's thirty-three. I'm not saying it's impossible to be a virgin at thirty-three without some weirdo religious beliefs but—"

"He's a virgin?"

"I mean, I don't know," I say, and I do know because we're connected, because maybe God is real, and maybe he wants me to save his most prized creation. But I have no proof. Nothing that Natalie could see, and without seeing, no one believes anything. "Are you saying you'd be shocked if you found out he was? I mean, look at him. He's so small and adorable and shy. Watch this video," I say, and I click on one a fan took of Reed as another fan approached him.

Reed's purple hair is a mess. Wet from sweat from the show or a wine shower for the image. He's blanched and tired-looking. There's no makeup on his blue eyes and he doesn't need it. They're immaculate and they shine even though they're underlined with the dark circles of sleep deprivation.

He smiles, though, when he sees his fan approaching. And as they get closer, the phone's video flash lights more of the dark room up, lights up the shimmering sweat on his chest, highlights the slope of each exposed rib, almost blinding the viewer by its reflection on his pink, glittering waist-chain.

He immediately opens his arms and welcomes his small fan. She has to be a child because she's shorter than he is, and in his photos, and Grape Gardens' photos, and The Sandman's photos, he's always shorter than everyone.

When the girl speaks, Amethyst is really listening. His back is slouched and his neck is lowered. His brows move when she says certain things. He wants to be near enough to actually hear her.

It's fucking beautiful. He's pure and appreciation and light even in the darkest room.

"See?" I ask Natalie. "He's gentle and he's sensitive and he's careful."

"Bex, you just see videos and pictures. You see what he wants you to see."

"No, you're wrong. This isn't what he wants us to see.

That's the point I'm making."

"You think he wants us to think he's shitty to his fans?"

I roll my eyes. Of course she doesn't get it. "He didn't post this, first of all, so it wasn't recorded or distributed by him." I shake my head as I back out of Reed's tagged photos and into his profile. "This…" I show her the sex and atheism and liquor, the smeared makeup, the drugged-up walking he does as someone slaps a handcuff around one of his wrists, and he drags his other hand down his face.

The blue of his eyes go upward and we only see white as his skin is being pulled, and his secret lips, so small and tender, part and expose his lower teeth. "This is what he wants us to see. Not smiles and not tenderness. He wants us to see drunken parties and him as a submissive sex object. Look at the way he poses." I click on a picture of his head fallen back, his bare chest exposed as a torn-up, black jacket slips off of his shoulder. "He's objectifying himself. He's making a statement about it, or maybe he feels it's all he is. Maybe after years of learning music and guitar and piano and writing poetry, he considered the thought that all anybody chases after is a pretty face or the promise of fucking. So he made himself into that."

I exhale through my nostrils and I feel like a miserable, pouting bull. I'm pissed. I hate the world for what it is, for what it values. I hate every person in Reed's life who didn't tell him it was okay to be fragile. I hate Natalie. I hate Bridget. I hate Vinny. I hate Bexley fucking Martin. I especially hate Marty. "I can see when he's not looking at the camera traces of who he really is," I say lowly, pushing my book into my bag and locking my phone.

"Bex, I'm not trying to say anything about him. I'm just thinking maybe you should calm down about him."

"Yeah," I say, standing up. "Calm down," I exhale mockingly. I sling my bag over my chest and when I feel it land against the exposed skin of my upper leg, I say, "Imagine what we'd be missing if God calmed down about humanity." I pull my shorts down where the bag raised one of its legs, and I say, "Never mind."

Because, let's face it, if God paused to calm down, if God stopped to think about what he was creating, the universe would be full of angels fighting the devil, but there'd be no souls as prizes. Or maybe it wasn't Lucifer's destiny to fall. Maybe without our scummy existence, he wouldn't have ever considered himself better. Can't blame him for not bowing down to us. We're pathetic and everything we do is pointless. Yet we do it. And we've been given the freedom to do it. But how many of us don't? How many of us choose the road labeled SAFETY when we really want to walk down the path of hope.

I wonder if God liked the idea of us so much more than the angels because all they can do is follow orders, and we have the ability to create.

Isn't that what the soul is? Isn't that divinity?

Reed knows divinity because he sings and plays and writes and his music; he is a performance. His Instagram is. His existence is a show to be consumed.

It's not a life fit for a god.

I sit in my car and I don't turn it on. I let the cold air stay inside with me, and I let it make my nose stuffy, and when my nose starts to run, I inhale deeply through it.

I want to feel.

I want the physical sensations of feeling while I draw and write and express the mental ones.

Thank you, Reed, for existing. But soon you'll thank me.

You'll thank me for freeing you.

I will not calm down about it.

I will write you as you *are*, and I will set you free.

```
Chapter 21
To:
From:
Subject: Nighttime Calm
```

I drive down curvy roads. The streetlamps like dots of vision in the sky. I wonder if the headlights from passing cars are blurred from how quickly they're moving by me, or if I should go get glasses.

It's strangely calming, driving at night. Nothing above you but blackness and these few dots of light hanging from man-made material. The industrial and the natural.

It's all wrong for someone like Reed. For Amethyst, it's exactly right, but not for Reed. I bet wherever he lives, every building is clean and shining. Most couches are white. Everything in everyone's house is stylish and fashionable. I bet when he drives down the road, he sees only beauty in his headlights.

It was a mistake for me to try to explain our connection to Natalie. I should've known even she wouldn't be able to understand it.

She and I, we're the ones that make resenting all of Bridget's favorites so easy.

She's a writer too. Just a novelist, so not exactly like I am, but still. And all of her talent and passion, all of her effort and desire, it goes unnoticed by most people who love to read. Same as me. But guys in bands just have to look a certain way when they walk out onto the stage and thousands of girls will buy all of their merchandise and draw fan art of them.

Maybe I'm just jealous because they're succeeding in a way I haven't yet. But this story will change everything.

This is the big one for me and for Reed. It will bring us together. It will show him how understood he is. He'll never have to feel alone again.

I'm here, Reed. Ready and waiting for you.

When I shut my car off, I realize I haven't been listening to anything. A wasted opportunity but I still have the drive home.

Only four of the ten letters of Dollar Tree's sign are actually working. Two don't work at all. The others either flicker or only half work.

I see the way people look at my knee socks and my boots, my shorts. No one dresses like this, but it's the simplest outfit. Everything is black. Nothing screams for attention, and yet it's always on me.

I suppose if I wore pull-over hoodies and ponytails with jeans and hunting boots I'd be more acceptable. I don't even know why I live in a place that breeds nothing but my opposition. My total opposite.

But I need toilet paper, so I have to venture inside.

I hum the melody to Reed's song while I grab something rough advertised as soft, and I try to imagine that he's here with me, or maybe I'm there with him.

Maybe somewhere in Vancouver, Reed is grocery shopping right now, and maybe he's in the bargain aisle because his band is still too small to be sold in Walmart.

I'd like to think we're always on the same wavelength, always working together, thinking together, soul to soul, mind to mind. Maybe it's how I know him so well, and maybe one day he'll be here with me, making all of the small town folks feel uncomfortable just by going out sans camo.

I pause in the chip aisle to type out some dialogue. Reagan reuniting with his drummer, his drummer explaining how evil his lady friend is, how Reagan's other special friend told him all about it.

Reed is too naive to think anyone would ever take advantage of him, so I write a drugged Reagan that way. Disbelieving, worried, and far too afraid to admit it.

But I'm here for you, Reed, and no one will ever hurt you as long as you've got me. And he's got me for good. I'll never leave him. He never has to worry again.

When I exit the store, there are more eyes on my legs. I don't mind that everyone here finds me so strange because the last thing I want to be is someone who can fit in with them.

I call up Spotify and I type in Grape Gardens. A song plays called I'm in Love with You. I scroll through their artist page while my car heats up. When I click "see discography" it only shows one album. FUCK GOD. So I go back. FUCK EACH OTHER. I see radio channels similar to them and I don't care. I see bands similar to them and I don't care. I see that they're a verified artist and I click it. The band's Instagram is linked and so is their Twitter, and I can't believe I haven't looked up Reed's Twitter yet. I bet it's filled with elegant prose, small one-liner lyrics, pure poetry.

I think I need to be home when I read through it. I need to be in bed, wrapped in my blankets and warm. It should be dark so I can't even attempt seeing anything but

him. I need to fall asleep to his thoughts.
I need to be home with him.
I need to go home to Reed.

Chapter 22
To:
From:
Subject: What We "Know"

I go home and I have no room to write. My couch has freshly washed, folded clothing stacked on it. There are old fish food containers and frozen French fry packages lying about on my counter, and I can still perceive some movement in my sink which means the maggots have begun a venture down the drain.

I wish my mom had given me chores. I wouldn't be so fucking lazy about them now. It's remarkable how when parents give you shit things to do and say they're doing it for your own good, they really mean that.

Oh, well.

I go into the bathroom. I play "Echoes" and I wish there were a music video to go with it, and I don't know why it hadn't occurred to me until now to Google Grape Gardens music videos.

I sit on the toilet and kick off my knee-high socks. I type the words into the search engine as I wait for the bathtub to fill.

Grape Gardens - Expensive Lifestyle

I click on it, but something's off... with Amethyst. His purple hair, instead of being parted in the center, is flipped to the left side. He's got on aviators. He's dressed in a pink T-shirt and blue pants, and Mr. Sexy Babyface Big Hair is half yellow and half green. Their drummer, oh, so forgetful in his silent inexpressiveness, is purple, which is Reed's color, and red.

The music is the same. It's from FUCK GOD, FUCK EACH OTHER. But nothing about this style screams Amethyst. I can't even believe this is Reed, but in truth, it's a sort of confirmation. I mean, haven't I been saying all along that the chains and the meth-look weren't really him?

He lies down on the floor. It's painted brown and tan and beige. He looks into the camera as he mouths the words of his song.

The Hollywood sign is bigger than the universe.

And then he's standing in a tiny room, smashed inside with the dullard's drum set and the dullard playing, and Mr. Sexy Manchild and his guitar, and someone I've never seen with another guitar, almost as if they've all four had to squeeze themselves inside my phone. Inside my hands.

We wear money on her lips, they carry caviar in their purses.

I don't know what you're talking about, Reed, but at least the bright colors of the set make some sense with your sound.

But that album cover makes sense to my Amethyst Sid Vicious Alien.

But almost nothing's purple here. Nothing's Amethyst. Nothing's Grape.

Maybe this was all some big storyline. Maybe that's why the band was called what it was in the first place. But this video was released only eight months ago, and there isn't a single snippet or photo from it anywhere on his or his band's Instagram. It's like it never happened. Video evidence. But why did he wipe it clean?

My phone screen starts to fog, and I forgot about the bath. I turn the water off but what's in the tub is steaming, and when I reach my arm into to release the drain plug, it burns my flesh.

Feeling.

I exhale as the water lowers and I stare at this blond, blue-eyed Reed. This weird, retro 70's guy who isn't who I know he is, nor who he wants us to think he is, and I wonder if his issue is that he simply doesn't know who he is yet. Another character. An actor.

Who could blame him with so many people in his industry surely telling him what is or isn't punk rock. But then again, his music is pop, isn't it? He doesn't list it as pop. He thinks pop died the year he was born. I wonder what died the year I was.

What has he been doing for the last thirty-something years? Why did he suddenly decide to become a musician? Why did he just get an Instagram? Is he truly an alien who came to earth and just started a life in medias res?

Either way, I plug the tub back up, and I run more water, and when I immerse myself in it, with all the lights out in this dark room, I'm able to immerse myself in him. God, it's my favorite place to be.

To be with him, inside him, inside my mind. Drawing and writing and creating him as I knew he was. I knew his hair was blond. I drew it days ago. Our higher selves bonding. His higher self sending mine messages. He's telling me his story. I'm not writing fiction; I'm writing the realities of people I've never met.

But we will meet. Bridget will surely want to see her British R&B shit again, and this time the tickets will have our city's name printed on them.

I used to think she was insane for wanting to follow a band around the country, and she giggled and said, "Bex, it's not around the country. It's Ohio and Pennsylvania and Maryland and sometimes New Jersey. That's hardly the entire country."

And I thought it was so idiotic to pay to see the same show twice. To pay to see people. The way people pay to see me.

Maybe because I'm a joke I have better insight to this pseudo-celebrity idolatry. Maybe because Bridget is a part-time waitress and a part-time mail clerk and a part-time retail associate, she doesn't see these guys on pedestals as clearly.

I mean, the fascination with celebrity is the same fascination with God. When one dies out, we find another. Prove God exists or else we find one we know is real. But the problem with real gods is that they are human, and human beings are flawed and fucked up, and people like Bridget don't realize the human side of their divinity.

They're divine because they're creators. But they aren't gods.

Neither am I. And because I fall asleep in this dirty apartment every night, I know my own divinity is limited. I certainly don't have the cleanliness and godliness bit down. Maybe the Brits do, but they don't treat their bodies as temples and they write about taking bars and fucking random people, and by the time they're my age, I bet at least one of them won't even be alive.

It's fine. Because they aren't Reed. I'm not. Bridget isn't.

But she doesn't see the humanity in the modern-day gods. Most people don't. Because I'm one of them, I know none of us are much more than a passing thought we remembered long enough to write down.

Until Reed.

And all the things I found so stupid in Bridget, her need to know her gods, her need to meet them, her constant road-tripping and money-spending just to breathe the same air they breathe, well, I guess that all makes sense now.

It's just that I have real motivation. I have a goal. An important one.

I have a message to give to Reed. This comic, these images, my drawings and sketches of this hero cast in sin but crafted in purity, it will release him from the world's wicked grip.

I am a god.

Bridget isn't. I don't get what she thinks there is to gain or accomplish or give when she goes to these shows. When she meets the bands, when she takes photos with them, I wonder what she's getting from it. How does this contribute to her happiness? She doesn't even listen to the lyrics, and she barely hums along with the beats.

Since Natalie was a bust, I suppose Bridget is a go.

I draw another scene of Reed. Reagan has fully embraced this rock god life. The beautiful woman who represents the world and all we want from our delicate deity chuckles to herself as she watches him passing out against the motel room wall.

Her lord, the devil, will be pleased with such corruption, and Reed may read this chapter and cry because he's been there. He's experienced the world. What artist hasn't? Who among us hasn't felt the fire in our guts, who hasn't had it snuffed out?

I text Bridget asking her if there are any more shows she's dragging me to, and while I wait for a response, I start the next chapter.

Reagan's bandmate, his keeper and protector, sits in a room with another woman. This one who has kept an eye on Reagan, who wanted to make sure he stayed true to his righteous path.

When Reagan met this woman, she understood the secrets of his innocence buried inside the edgy, screaming lyrics. Reagan's music isn't Reed's music, but if Reed can play characters then I can make him into one too.

Reagan screamed into the microphone and his fingers were calloused from the guitar, and no one cared enough to search the lyrics, but this woman knew them.

She told Reagan she appreciated his chastity— something the demon worldly woman stole— and she told him he didn't need to toss aside his cross or his heavenly message to be who he always was.

Once, she stood between his legs in a bathroom wiping the smudged makeup from his eyes.

"I know who you are behind it," she said to him, but he was almost too drunk to understand.

I understand you, Reed. I won't let the world keep you. If you want to be someone else, you can be my perfect Catholic-boy doll.

Yeah, omg! Bridget responds. *I thought you'd only do one show per tour! Not the same torture twice, right Bex?! Lol!*

I exhale all the exasperation my body has been holding, and I type back: *When's the local show?*

My deadline. The due date.

I hear a ping as I'm drawing Reagan's drummer and the angelic figure trying to save him.

Two weeks!
Two weeks, and he's mine.

Chapter 23
To:
From:
Subject: Playing the Part

I've added four pages of his purity, and I have so much more to say and write draw and ink. But I'm too excited to see his Twitter. I want to see what he tweets. What he thinks. What he feels.

I feed my fish and I tell them I love them and I go into my room. I close my door. I turn off the lights. I curl into my comforters and I lean back on my pillows. I wait until I get warm. Everything needs to be perfect when I read him. When I connect in yet another way.

I call up Twitter. I type Reed Barry into the search bar.

His face pops up in that little circle and I can see that it's a drawing. It's cute and kawaii. It's his purple, parted hair, and his big, beautiful, blue eyes. The artist kept his dog collar and his bare chest. It's the perfect portrait of him. Sad eyed and beautiful.

His Twitter feed is full of retweeted Grape Gardens promos. Videos of Big Hair dragging Reed along by the collar of his ripped-up, white shirt. There are photos of them, of Reed and his purple hair in a cheetah printed shirt holding the links of his handcuffs up to his neck.

There are videos spliced together in hard, jarring cuts. Cuts of Amethyst with his head tilted down and his hair in his eyes, eyes that seem to bleed black eyeliner, and his shoulders slouch forward, his arms hang. He's basically saying *this is what I'd look like if I were so high I didn't know how to stand up* but I know he's totally sober. I wonder if anyone else does; I wonder if they know this is just a role. I wonder why no one gets that he's a performance artist.

The video flashes again. Another hard cut and we see Amethyst spray painting his album FUCK GOD, FUCK EACH OTHER on the concrete floor of some alleyway or club. His head falls, the pink, glittering jacket around his shoulders exposes one, exposes the tattoo on his chest, exposes his perfect nipple and his perfect ribs, exposes his spiked dog collar. Another flash lights the screen up in red as he spray paints, then a flash shows Grape Gardens name in an ornate, antique frame, and then it lights on fire.

The last flash shows his band members behind him, their faces each half hidden by the darkness around them. Chain link fence is their backdrop and cuffs hang from it. A sex-swing is set up behind the links, and someone with long hair hangs loosely in it; I worry that they actually killed her for this shot. Graffiti is visible behind the corpse, I mean, the sex-swing enthusiast.

Amethyst's jacket is pink still— pink like his microphone, but not glittering— and with a fuzzy cuff on one of his wrists, he leans back into the chainlink while his drummer clasps the other to it.

They walk away, leaving him alone there. Alone in the alleyway at night, all half exposed by his fallen jacket-shoulder. He's small and he's drugged up, but he's been drugged, he hasn't taken it willingly, and he's left handcuffed in a seedy part of town, vulnerable to the desires of any man or woman who should happen by and feel the need to release through sex or violence. He's the next victim. He'll be hooked up to the swing, or forced to fuck the dead woman still hanging in it.

Everyone in the replies, they think he's a willing participant. They think he gets high and likes bondage. They think he wants to be shamed, touched by strangers and publicly fucked. They think he's edgy. They praise him, and they call him god. He is God, but they worship him through misinterpretation.

They don't realize what he's saying. They don't understand him. But Reed isn't Amethyst, and Amethyst isn't real.

Reed invented Amethyst, not to experience life as a bad boy, and not so everyone would think he was one.

Reed is showing us through Amethyst how gentle men can be used and abused, how fragile boys get taken advantage of, how sometimes men can be victims in the same ways women can be.

This is why my presence in his life will mean so much to him. I will allow him to be vulnerable and weak and still be the hero. He makes himself the victim because he doesn't think society will let him be anything else.

I applaud him for not changing. I admire the truth he's exposing— the metaphor of it all.

He isn't Sid Vicious. He's a kidnapped victim. A sex crime in creamy flesh and bright blue eyes.

But soon all of this will change. Soon I'll set him free, and soon he won't need to show himself falling over into walls while he's dragged down a hallway by his wrists, lights flickering on him like he's about to be sold off to the highest bidder. Soon he won't have to post photos of his legs splayed across the floor while his eyes are closed and his head is surrounded by empty bottles of alcohol. Soon he'll be able to be everything he is without fear of rejection or ridicule. Soon he'll belong to me, not to this world.

As much as I want to continue consuming, Reed makes it really difficult. I can't see his face, or his eyes, his secret lips, his pink nipple, or even his chest tattoo without a flood of information pouring into my mind.

I swear, we are connected through sight alone, and when I see him, he sends me his story.

I don't want to get out of bed. I want to stay here in the covers and consume him. I want to be wrapped in warmth and Reed and watch Amethyst show me how fragile he really is, but I have to write. I have to draw.

I can see Reed, so innocent, sitting on a beaten-up leather couch as the band playing before his starts setting up their instruments.

I see his head hanging between his shoulder blades, the creamy flesh clinging to them— once warm, it's now clammy and pale.

He's suffering inside his drunken, fucked-out body. All the pleasures of the flesh are unable to nourish him.

I'm inking now, and he's running his hands through his wet, sweat-soaked hair. His lungs ache. He doesn't know how he'll sing. He isn't even sure if he can remember the keys to press on the keyboard. His rusted tambourine is lost, and when he plays the instrument now, the vigor isn't there. Not the energy and the raw emotion with which I watched Reed play.

I've finished two more pages completely. Who needs an editor? No one knows this story the way I do. Its subject is signaling all to me. And I go back to his Twitter.

I'm in need of him.

I need an army of angels. Any takers ? He posted merely minutes ago.

I scan the replies. Lots of "you're an angel". Lots of "here I am". Lots of girls quoting his own lyrics back to him. Lyrics from "Echoes". Lyrics about the sky and the sun and the moon and angels falling into him.

He hasn't liked a single one of them. They're generic. They're everything everyone else is saying. They don't get him. Girls like Bridget and their obsession to compliment and flirt and treat people like Reed as if they aren't souls inside their perfect bodies.

I don't objectify Reed, and I won't coddle him.

I come with a mind full of words, but my arsenal of replies doesn't contain lyrics he's written and it doesn't hold flattery. My words are passages from books and quotes from great authors.

I reply in quotation marks:

"There is no guardian for the guardians. No soul for a spirit. If you require followers, make the earth-bound beings yours, but you need not an army nor an angel. Bear your sword and shield alone."

I exit the app because the simple prayer has inspired me further, but before I can pick up my pencil, a notification slips down onto my screen.

Reed Barry liked your reply.

A hollow sensation empties my chest of all its contents. No air remains in my lungs, and my heart has either stopped pumping or has begun pumping so excitedly that it merely vibrates when it should pulse.

Calling up Twitter, my thumb shakes over the notification. Reed's name. Reed liking what I said.

I click the notification and I stare at it. I re-read what I wrote time after time after time, trying to imagine him with his beautiful face and his purple hair, him in a T-shirt because he's home and his camera isn't on, him free of his chains and binds, his short little fingers turning an empty heart red with the touch of his thumb— trying to imagine what he thought exactly when he read this. When he saw what I typed, when he saw my face, my name.

I scan through the other replies and he still hasn't liked any of them. Only mine. Only me. And I can see us sitting across from one another in the corner of a coffee shop, darkened by a burned out lightbulb but we're too in our own universe to notice, and the staff doesn't want to bother us about it because they can see the energy pouring from our eyes and into one another.

I imagine his smile, and his secret lips taste like cinnamon when I kiss them, and we don't care that we're in public because no one mattered to either of us the way we matter to each other.

Before Reed, I cared for no one, and before me, no one cared for Reed the way they should have. But I see glimpses of my future, of our future together, and everything is changed. A God and his archangel. Rulers of an awakened universe. This is art, these are characters, this is music, and Reed is genius.

I go to his Twitter and click on the tab to display his likes and heat surges through my body seeing myself there. Seeing myself, knowing no one else from those replies is with me, I'm validated. I'm confirmed. I'm feeling ambitious yet again, and I think I could draw an entire comic tonight.

Oh, Reed. He's pure and sweet and vanilla in the bedroom but I love him anyway, and nothing will ever—

Wait, what the fuck?

I feel my brows furrow over my eyes. They burn. I can't blink. I can't take my eyes from the feed because there, in Reed's likes, in the tweets his thumb stopped scrolling by and took the effort and time to like— effort and time given to me and my angelic quote— is a photo of a woman.

No, no, no, no, Reed. No. This is all wrong. You're not supposed to be the kind of guy who objectifies women online, and you're not supposed to *like* women because liking women means desiring them, and you're too pure to desire. You're an artist; nothing more.

I click her profile, and I see more of her than I needed to. I see her bimbo-makeup and her jet-black hair, and her too-tanned skin, and I can tell that she bleaches her nipples.

I worked with a guy named David, when we were twenty-two, who always bleached his asshole for this guy he dated and one night we got drunk and I found it in his bathroom and we decided to try it on the dark circles under his eyes, and then my tattoos, and then his nipples.

Four months worth of shirtless snaps showed me just how much he enjoyed the results, even though I told him he kept overshooting and his bright pink nipples had this white ring around them like a halo. Holy tits.

Still, I feel enticed by this person; This dark-haired girl whose naked body is riddled with the outward manifestations of her internal insecurities... I feel for her. Nothing about her is how she was born. Not her hair or her skin tone or her injected lips. Not her too-pink nipples, or her obviously photoshopped calves.

Nothing about me is real either. I'm not a red-head, and my skin is covered in art and ink. We are kindred. Two of the same type of souls in very different manifestations.

I've had my share of professional photos taken. Headshots for these dumb-assed conventions. Shit like that. I know what it's like to see a photo of yourself, and share it because reminding people you exist once an hour is the best way to get money from them, but not recognizing yourself in it.

I'm sure Reed has experienced this too, and it's why he went off on a different, more artistic path. It's probably why people like this girl, people like me, are so drawn to him. Oh, his freedom. His bound-and-chained freedom.

More fake shit. More industry shit. And Reed's Twitter is supposed to be his soul.

I'm disappointed in the thought that he can't see through her… Because it might mean that he won't be able to see through me. He should be wiser than this, wiser than her, wiser than me, wiser than anything less holy than he is and none of us are what he is.

I take my aggression out on the drawings of Reagan. I let the woman with her devilish, dark eyes corrupt him beyond reproach. I draw her practically forcing alcohol down his throat. I draw her scooping white powder into her black nail and offering it to his insanely straight nose. I draw her locking him in a motel bathroom while he's too gone to fight her, and I draw her fucking him.

It's attractive when it's fully sketched, but it's disheartening too. Purity is appealing; corruption is attractive.

Fuck this story. I toss it onto the floor, and I throw my phone at it, and if it breaks and sets the manuscript on fire, I'll lay here until the smoke knocks me out.

I sink into the covers, and I close my eyes before I get

so angry I won't be able to sleep, and I blame Amethyst. He possessed Reed. He did this. I know who Reed is, and this can't be him. He isn't someone who likes tweets from people he doesn't even know, and he isn't someone who looks at nudity without blushing. He isn't her. He isn't me. He's above us all. Isn't he?

This can't be him, human like the rest of us. Can it?

```
Chapter 24
To:
From:
Subject: Visitation
```

I dreamt of Reed last night. I know what you're thinking and no, dear reader, I don't mean that in some rom-com idiot way.

I think he came to me last night. I think he sensed how angry I'd become with him.

He was sitting across from me with his hair pointing in all directions and his leather jacket caused him to squeak when he moved. He was shy when I told him how I draw him and how I write about him. He was giggly and cute.

Reed probably never sleeps, this much is true, but he's probably awake and writing poetry. Drawing up concepts for the stage. Writing music. He isn't just an artist. He is art. Beautiful, and pure emotion, and fragile in its uniqueness. He's chained up because he's roped off. No touching. No contact. Stay behind the red line. Human hands would only soil him and his crafted beauty.

I get a text from Bridget and it's a Facebook post about the tour. *Officially less than two weeks away! So excited you're down to go see them again!*

Periods exist, Bridget. If you're excited about everything then really you're excited about nothing.

But I'm thankful for the text because I hadn't

considered Facebook either. I'm so old inside this body, it's a good thing I seem to be one of those "aging like fine wine" people. If I looked even half as bad as I think and feel and act, people would cross the street just to avoid me.

When the app opens, I immediately type his name, but before I can hit enter, fucking Marty is calling me.

I ignore him. I don't need him babysitting me. I'm fucking writing. I've been writing. *Oh, yeah, writing.* And I get back to it.

I remember Reed sitting at the table in my dream, and even if it doesn't end up in the book, I have to draw him like that. His elbow rests on the table. He leans into his forearm. The way he tries to take up as little space as possible makes him seem so small. I love him this way.

Needing a visual, I go to Instagram.

When I click on his name, the same few photos stare up at me from my hands. Of course he's posted nothing new.

Yesterday I may have found this endearing, but today I don't know. Today I wonder about it. I wonder why he only just made his account a few months ago, why he rarely posts to it, why everything is so vicious and violent and why that violence is draped in bright pink and shiny purple and glitter?

Maybe it's really as dark as it all feels. Maybe everyone's right in the comments and maybe Reed is everything he appears to be. Maybe none of this is art. Maybe it's all as fake and confusing as it seems. But I have to finish this story regardless.

I need more information to continue. I need him to talk to me. Communicate. Just tell me who you are, Reed.

You don't own people. You don't consume them. Not

the way I do. Not the way the other women online do. They're not yours, Reed. You don't get to objectify them. Not the way the word objectifies you. Or maybe you like that. Maybe you enjoy being less than human. Maybe you want to be an object. Trust me, I can own you. But if you're just like everyone else, why would I even want you?

I click the tagged photos. I want to confirm my suspicions. Really, I'm praying for denial.

My pupils widen with the lack of light. I swear to God, I can feel them expanding. But when the photos start to load and the color fills up my sight, I don't think they go down. I'm scanning, searching, hunting. I want to see Reed for what he truly is— whether it's this idiotic Sid Vicious who hates pop music but plays it, this drunk and cracked-out sex fiend, or he's the angelic entity descended from the heavens, all pure and innocent and untouched, all deep lyrics over heavy music, all saintly and divine.

I need to know if he's art, or if he's manufactured his divinity. Maybe he's only human.

There are photos of him on stage, photos of his eyes narrowed and loosely closing as he throws his arm around a smiling girl and takes a photo.

He looks weakened. He looks cold and clammy, just like Reagan when I drew him last night. Maybe what I have is more than communicating. Maybe I just sense when people are in trouble, or when they're trash, and maybe when I write and draw and ink, I'm just prophesying.

I see a photo of him in a bathroom, standing before the mirror. Just like I drew. I see him in his sweaty hair and on the stage. I see photos of girls with purple hair, claiming how inspiring Reed was for them, as if no one else in the world's ever dyed their fucking hair.

I watch videos of his druggy performance, and maybe it's not an act. Maybe he's shot up and snorted and drank his way into walking with his hips leading him, his back arching back as if he may fall at any moment. Maybe this is real.

He's still attractive physically if this is the case, but who would want him for that? In fairness I suppose most people who follow him only want him for his looks. I can tell by their comments and their tweets he's retweeted and their Instagram posts he's put on his story that they aren't here for who he is because they don't know him.

I know him, even if this version of him— my Reagan visions— aren't true now, they were. They will be. Maybe I can see the future, and maybe I'll steer him back onto the right path. After all, Reagan is being led astray in my artwork. He needs a savior to lead him back. Maybe art doesn't imitate life. Maybe life imitates art.

As I scroll through photos of Reed, fanarts, thank-you letters typed in the note app, videos by The Sandman, I stumble across one from three weeks ago. A video, that is. But I can see even from the blurry still that it isn't Reed.

This man, or boy, he's in a white T-shirt and he's got plain-Jane brown hair and a guitar slung across him. Is this someone Reed knows? Is it someone trying to get his attention? I suppose even talented musicians can be fans of bubble-gum pop calling itself rock art, but who would think such a thing?

And I know what you're thinking— what am I here if not a fan of Grape Gardens' bullshit? Well, I'm clearly not a fan. If it hasn't been made obvious from visions, my mental connection, our higher selves, I'm not here because I worship Amethyst, nor do I like what he does.

If I listen to music, I expect substance; not this watered down trying-to-be-famous bullshit. I don't appreciate song lyrics about being rich at the beach, and nothing about staying trapped in one facet of life forever resonates with me.

Forever, that concept alone is terrifying.

If you're like me, then you're counting down the days. Each second closer to the final curtain call feels like what I imagine a shot of Amethyst's heroin might be like.

A high to end all highs. A high to end so much pointlessness.

It doesn't matter though. The point of this piece of nothing is that Grape Gardens aren't substantial. Unlike their name, they aren't great vineyards over acres full of color and nourishment. They don't even realize it. Or at least Reed doesn't.

I think with all his cryptic captions about souls, he's eaten up whatever creativity is still pulsing through his deluded brain.

I think he dresses like Sid Vicious because the Sex Pistols were shocking, but it's 2019 and no one thinks you're scary or punk rock for chucking a flaming chaise lounge out of your hotel room window. What if you hit someone on the street, Reed? And more concerning, who is going to pay for that?

I didn't mention that video when she sent it to me with a text that read, *what are my babies doing touring with these guys?*, because I ignored her. I wondered what Reed was doing with them. But now I wonder if he's just a copy of a bunch of copies.

It's fine. Be Sid Vicious and dress like Johnny Rotten and sing like Michael Jackson and glitter like David Bowie.

It's art and character and metaphor; I knew that, but I bought it too. I feel stupid for having believed the fantasy behind the fantasy; for thinking inside those beautiful blues was depth and spirit and divinity. It's rare to find attractive organs inside attractive skin. Nothing breeds laziness and shallowness like a pretty face. Take me for example. Some of it's my parents' doing and some of it's society's.

You can't spend thirty years being told you're beautiful and not believe it.

Maybe Reed just didn't figure there was more to life like I did. But then, why would he decide to create anything at all?

Finally I click the video. The boy in the shirt begins to play his guitar— heavier riffs than anything that could be Grape Gardens— and I scroll down to read his caption:

Accentuate the Assent "Heart Failure" cover by me! Love these dudes.

What the fuck is this? Who is Accentuate the Assent and what the fuck kind of name is that? Fine, so it's got a ring, but why are we tagging Reed in it, and why do all of these band names have to be alliterations? Jesus, it feels like my eyes are being pressurized they're rolling so hard. But I'm curious because it's Reed. Because I can't imagine something somehow even vaguely connected to him without me knowing every detail of it.

I Google the song and it's from 2010, and I remember being younger and being dragged to shows because it doesn't take thirty years to start hating everything you've ever loved, but I don't remember Accentuate the Assent. Something tells me Bridget probably knows them, has probably dragged me to one of their shows, but if it wasn't

Reed, I don't care.

I click the video anyway, and the music is low. As it rises, its initial sound feels like something they'd play at a roller rink in 1997, but a huge kick of a bass drum crashes over it and it's followed by heavy guitars. After a few seconds of this shock of sound, a vocalist begins to scream his soul. It reminds me of Reagan, of what I always thought he'd play when I drew him yelling into microphones, but when he finishes a line about his heart pulsing one last time, a heavenly voice accompanies his. It's soft and delicate and it sounds auto-tuned just enough to fit with the opening beats of electronicore.

The camera swings wildly from the drummer, full of life and vigor, and zooms into the man playing guitar on his right. A short man, thin and fragile-looking, with mousy brown hair emo-swooped over his forehead. It flows around his face, his defined jawline, and when the camera comes around to face him, I see piercing blue eyes. Eyes that I'd recognize anywhere.

I pause the video, and blink around the room. The pain in my jaw suggests my mouth has been hanging open for quite some time, and I quickly Google Accentuate the Assent's members.

There, below Aaron Ither, harsh vocals, and above Stanley Jordan, programming and electronics, is the most melodic name in existence: Reed Barry. Clean vocals, guitar.

I can't hit the back button fast enough. I can't wait to see him like this, to absorb him like this. To watch this beautiful, angelic creature *knowing* it's Reed.

It's one thing to be introduced to someone through a performance or a persona; it's an entirely different thing to know someone already, and so well, and then see them inside a world of their own creation.

I play the video again, staring at the man on the right, the man singing and playing music. I stare at him knowing, consciously accepting, that this is Reed. This is my Amethyst before the Amethyst. Before the Grape Gardens and the Sex Pistols meets Bowie. This is Reed… As Reagan.

His legs are in that classic rock star stance, wide apart and stern and dominant, and the instrument hangs loosely between them. His shoulders still hunch forward and his back still slouches, but not as some performance of uppers, downers, dopamine, and orgasm.

When his body tightens and falls, when it bends, it bends into the microphone, into the guitar, as if he's curling his body into the music, around it. As if he's trying to become one within himself, to blend together his physicality and his spirit.

He's dressed in jeans, a common selection that seems so foreign on his tiny hips, and a navy blue shirt that's practically painted onto his frame. The sleeves are pushed up to his forearms and three of its four buttons are open, and hanging there between the parted fabric is a crucifix.

With his natural hair and his plain clothing, all there is to see of Reed is astounding beauty. I can't believe I've never noticed just how incredibly perfect his features truly are.

In this video, with Accentuate the Assent, there is no messy eyeliner or blinding glitter to detract from his face. Nothing to cover his porcelain skin. Nothing plastic or metal or leather on his body to distract the viewer from everything that is him.

As the camera rounds him again, I pause my admiration. Something is off, but in an appealing way. I think for a split second maybe it's the drastic lack of persona— Reed simply being Reed, that is— but it's clear to see that the profile of his face is remarkably different here.

His jawline is still precise. His cheekbones are still high. His eyes are the same blue and his one eyebrow is still trying to break free from the straight line the other laid out as a pattern for it. I pause. Zoom into the fuzzy stilled video, but it's never clear to me what's different.

I look up from my phone and I can feel the tug of my brow. For a second, I wonder about the stats on men who get plastic surgery, but he's not different in that way. Maybe he's just younger. I can't focus on it now;   my mind and my eyes and my entire being are all so stuck to the representation of Reed before me that I'm not sure I'm even processing my sight correctly.

This is the most attractive I've ever seen him. The most true-to-self. The most pure.

This is Reed as Reed. No gimmick and no facade. This isn't Reed playing a role to describe his emotion or his objectification. This before he became an object. This was when he was still a person. This is Reed playing and writing music and allowing us to feel what he's saying through his song.

I glance over to my book. Placing one palm on the stacks of inked drawings and sketches, I push them open, spread them apart. Staring at them in awe, all I see in my artwork is everything on my phone screen.

Okay, so I'm not psychic. But if this isn't proof of our connection, nothing ever could be. How else can you explain it? Our connection is sitting right here in my hands— an eight year old premonition come true, springing forth from my hands as his strum and pluck and slip down the neck of his guitar.

Reagan is everything Reed was. Reagan, my ideal version of the world's most ideal man, is real.

The other realm in which he exists, it's not some far off galaxy, and it isn't somewhere unimaginable to us, no; it's simply in our past. In our immediate past. The eight-years-ago version of Reed I somehow knew without knowing. I'm in awe of myself almost as much as I'm in awe of him, but as I stare to him and his innocence, watching his hand rise up from the chords and his fingers ball into a fist of passion as he sings "runaway from the past, a runaway from my past. Free of the hell fire, I'm home at last." I feel a hollowness spread through my chest. Something light in weight but cold; something that takes each internal organ and replaces them with air; this thing, this sensation, rises up from my stomach, surging through my core like the bubbles of a dead man's float until I have to gasp for air.

I don't even think my heart is tangible at this point. Everything inside has disintegrated with one fell swoop of the most secret lips singing biblical hymns through head banging and heavy metal.

As I stare at this straight nose and pink lips and this mousy brown hair and hear this melody of his soul with depth of lyrics and belief in devotion, it all culminates in one gutwrenching realization: Reed isn't perfect.

But he was.

He was, and I feel my eyes burn with the stinging threat of tears— the heartbreaking desire to know Reed encompassing me wholly, filling all of this emptiness with want and need and urgency to feel and see and touch and, oh, such hunger— because I really wish I hadn't met him as I did. I wish we'd met sooner. I wish in 2012, I'd gone to a show with Bridget and I liked some stupid band enough to go see them when they opened for some guys we'd never heard of called Accentuate the Assent, and I wish I'd been paying attention when my tiny twenty-two-year-old alien walked onto the stage.

I wish I'd gone to his merch table after, and I wish his eyes would've widened in the pursuit to consume me as I adore consuming him, and I wish I could've saved him before he fell.

I cry because I know I would've loved him then, and I cry because he would've been so loved that he would've never felt the need to expose his tender flesh and hide his beautiful soul in the desire to matter.

I would've shown him how much he mattered. How much the world needed him. I will show him how much it does. And whoever bruised his psychology, whoever tainted the way he trusts, whoever made him feel like connection wasn't worth the risk— because I guarantee you someone did— I hope I find her, and I hope she knows for what exactly she's paying.

I've seen her. I've drawn her. I've written her. A crimson sapphire. Nonexistent. She is a ruby because sapphires come in all colors but red, and I with my "ruby red" hair dye am here to absolve her sins. The reflection. The inversion. Everything she was supposed to be to him, that's me. And when I draw her dying violently, I'll find a way to make that piece of the premonition come true too.

No, Reed isn't perfect. But he was. And she ruined

him with her guile and abused his nativity.

I'll remind him of his value, and he'll never let people push drinks on him or themselves into him because he'll look to me and remember who he is.

Mine, something says to me. *He's mine.*

And the heavens part as he sings to them, and the riffs of his guitar thump loudly like a building drum calling to action all the forces of light still left in this cold wasteland we call the world, and my mission, as he flips his guitar behind him and then pulls it back up to his chest, walking slowly and with determination to the microphone— black and ordinary and not a shield through which he hides his words— as his band members approach the camera in line with him, becomes clearer than it ever before had been:

I am to restore Reed. I am to revert the converted. Polish his cheeks with warm washcloths and pat away the smut of the world from his eyes and his lips and his body.

Restore him, I hear and maybe it's Reagan speaking to me, I don't know. *Restore him*, the angelic nightmare of a face lost to corruption and greed whispers as its blanched flesh emerges from the black background of my thoughts. That clean slate onto which we paint our pictures, that backdrop for the photo shoots we snap inside our minds, it fills itself full of bloodshot blue eyes, of thin lips afraid to speak, and when the eyes cry, blackness spills from them, and maybe Reed wears his makeup to represent the darkness for which he weeps, and maybe he is bound after all, and maybe once purity is corrupted there is no saving it. Maybe I'm the last hope as a creator of comics, as a writer of worlds. Maybe I, as the closest to God a human can ever hope to become, am the only one whose soul knows his well enough to rescue him from whatever prison the past has locked him away inside.

The key hasn't been thrown away. If it has, I'll forge a new one.

But right now, I need more. I'm in desperation for Reed, for Accentuate the Assent, and all I need to know right now, as the next song shuffles onto my screen and displays my darling Amethyst angel in a sleek black coat staring up into the sky from a glass case above a cityscape, is who wrote the lyric "When false idols charge you, I'll be the angel to guard you"?

Chapter 25
To:
From:
Subject: Who Cares Convention Round
Two

Marty meets me at the fucking airport, and he huffs
when he opens the door and an avalanche of boxes and
sealed air and packing peanuts fall out of my passenger
seat. It's not my fault comic books can't be sent media
mail, and it's cheaper to stuff the envelopes so full
shipping them out like packages at $4.50 makes more
sense than shipping them sleek and slender at $8. What,
does he think I'm made of money? No. I'll tell him like his
parents should have: you cost a lot of money, Marty. The
publishers aren't paying you out of their own wallets,
sweetheart. You're an investment they hope to get back
with my next installment, and if they don't, it's fine
because they don't give me a high enough earning
percentage on my own fucking creations specifically to
fund babysitters like yourself.

Maybe I should CC him on this. And my agent. And
my publishers. And Reed, and Bridget, and Natalie, and
everyone else in the world who makes my head hurt so
badly by simply existing in this world that my only solace is
to escape into others.

"Bexley Martin," he says, scooping the mailing mess

into his arms as if each box is an infant, "What am I gonna do with you?"

"Get my luggage out of the trunk," I say, slipping on my sunglasses and heading toward the airport doors.

I dig my sketchbook out of bag, and I write down all the ways I'd kill Marty if I were the god of his story, the one writing his life.

I could decapitate him, make the trunk slam shut on him, right down on his neck. I could have his pant leg get stuck in the moving sidewalk and draw the rushing businessmen and egotistical models trampling him in obliviousness and hurry. I could turn around and shoot him. Well, if I had a gun, anyway.

And, okay, fine, it's not really Marty's fault he's my ass-istant. It's not my fault he's my babysitter. It was either accept this job or graduate whatever fucking college he went to for publishing or editing or English with no hopes of a job. Until I started writing my own graphic novels, I never used my degree. Shit jobs at the mall paid better than work specialized for my 4 years of studying skills.

Truth be told, I never needed college to learn how to analyze and interpret. I've been doing it since I was a child listening to Bon Jovi and watching Tales from the Crypt. The point here isn't that college is a sham (although it sometimes feels like it). The point is that I'm really mad at what Marty represents, not at him.

He's basically a living, breathing baby monitor— not just the type to invade my privacy and spy on me, but the fancy, rich people kind that also has a button they can click from their phones to yell at their governesses or their dogs or whatever.

And, okay, fine. It's not like I want to be a bitch to

Marty. He's just so fucking happy all the time and it really gets under my miserable skin.

"There's just so much to be thankful for," he told me the first time we went out on a "get-to-know-you dinner".

I asked him, "Yeah, like what?"

"You, silly!" He said with the biggest smile I've seen to this day. "If you weren't such a procrastinator I wouldn't have been hired!"

Fuck off, Marty. I know what I am and I am not a procrastinator. I am an artist, and I am a god, and artists wait for their muses, and gods take at least seven days to create a world just to watch it burn.

"Bexley!" I hear his stupid feet slapping off of the pavement behind me. "Wait," he huffs and I turn around just in time to watch him stumble over the dufflebag he dropped. "Oh," he cries as he topples over, "God bless America!" His arm is tangled in its strap, and he's chuckling, telling the couple walking by him how he's such a klutz and a butterfingers.

I turn around and keep walking. I have business to attend to, and while I might be Marty's job, he's got nothing to do with mine.

So I write as I walk. I jot down notes about Reagan and make his present-version even more vicious, even more disgusting and dirty now that I know how far Reed really fell.

I mean, all this time I thought his music was hijacked by the labels, but it was completely torn apart. They took the meaningful lyrics and the powerful sound and watered it down to something easily digestible by the masses.

No one likes to think. People don't even like to feel. Not without instruction. They like being told what to do, and with soft shit like Grape Gardens, consuming and buying and devoting is easy.

At least I'm sure that was their plan when plucked Reed from his holy writings, mutilated his mind and body and face, drenched him booze and boujee clothing, and told him to sing meaningless lyrics over some poppy catchy tunes. They stripped him of his clothes and of his message. They cut off his nose despite his perfect face. But they won't win.

I draw a boardroom meeting. I draw angry fat-cat managers and producers because— this really was their plan, if they were thinking *marketability*, that screamo Christian music doesn't have as broad a reach as a Freddie Mercury/Johnny Rotten hybrid bastard child— they were wrong.

That's just based here in reality. You can search Grape Gardens and Reed Barry and you'll see how both pages are lacking in follower counts. The currency of the realm these days.

Most of these shows I go to with Bridget, they're at small venues with small crowds because the bands are underground and no one in the mainstream world has ever heard of them. Those guys generally have more than double the count Reed has, but in a weird way, I like it. It makes me happy.

I'm overjoyed when I call up his page and see his follower count drop from 27.6 to 27.5, and I stare at that number trying to will it to go further down.

I don't need these people surrounding his pale, fragile body like vultures. Not when he's so close to losing himself entirely. Not when he's so beaten down and mind controlled and weakened. He's not dead. Not yet.

He's mine, the voice says, and I look up because the sound was so vivid I swear it came from a real person in this room.

Just in time, too, because I'm nearing the end of the moving sidewalk, and I get so caught up in the lives of my characters— of these real people only I connect with— and so caught up in Reed, and so caught up in who he was and who he is now and why, that I'm sure I wouldn't have noticed it.

And then it would be me being trampled to death instead of fucking Marty.

The thing here about this certainty— this insistence from some voice in some realm I can't see— is that it could very well be Reed's. It could belong to the part of him that is like God, the part that exists outside the binds of earthly flesh, the part that recognizes the ethereal part of my being and has been consistently calling out to it ever since the first night I saw him.

This voice reiterating my ownership of him confirms that he'll experience an awakening not only to me, but also to himself.

When our eyes meet for the first time, he'll see flickers of light, small beams quickly surging by the background of sight to which he's looking, and before he knows it, they'll overtake his vision completely.

He'll be transported, just as I was, to a place that exists only between the two of us; a place where the bar in which we're standing and the people there inside it with us are merely a backdrop, one dimensional and inconsequential, frozen in time like a screengrab of memory printed onto a life-sized photo.

The sounds of the blaring bass music, the beating of

drums, the cries of whichever artist on stage is expelling his oxygen into a microphone will all be replaced by silence after a hollowing out of our eardrums with one sharp whistle.

Nothing will exist outside of my eyes in his sight, and his eyes in my sight, and he'll see the movements of my chest when I breathe because I exist here in this plain and no one else does, and I'll perceive the subtle furrow of his brow— both the perfectly shaped one and its rebellious other half— because he won't know at first what's happening.

I didn't know.

But after he glances around, once he realizes everything we've ever been told is real because it's materialized is actually just a sham— a scare tactic to keep us from achieving our full potential so those in power, like the bullshit puppet masters of record labels and publishing houses, can keep their power— he'll look back to me with loosened brows and features full of relief.

Here I am, my darling Amethyst. I've come to save you.

And surely when he sees salvation in me, he'll want to be near to me, nearer than he's ever been to anyone else, and we've already accomplished that with this transcendental bond built between us by soul and higher self, but he'll want even more than that. I want even more than that.

I'll want to take his hand and lead him into the bathroom. He'll follow willingly, shyly lifting his shoulders toward his blushing cheeks. His lower lip will be planted in his teeth. His free hand will rise to cover those secret lips, and he'll look around to see the living ecosystem of bands and bar-goers is still flat and lifeless now we've experienced each other.

When we get to the bathroom, I'll pull him by our linked hands so that he moves in front of me, and I'll lock the door behind me.

I'll move closer to him, his hand instinctively reaching for me, for my waist, my hips, my chest, and when he holds me, the desperation of his lifelong search for who he is will force his fingers into fists, and he'll lift his perfect little ass onto the dingy green sink and cling to me like he'd die if he released my body from his grip.

I'll move into him, between his legs. I'll run my hands along his tight pants, curling them around his thighs before slipping them upward.

I'll want to touch him— *him*, not his pants— and I'll want to tear away the layers between us. I'll want to tug at the loop attached to his silver chain and jerk him into me.

I'll want to touch those secret lips with mine, devour his taste, drag my tongue down his neck, and across his collarbone.

I'll want to trace his tattoos with my fingers, and fuck him until he's gained the sight necessary to see our mingling spirits.

But I won't.

It may be fitting for Amethyst, but this isn't right for Reed.

I know it, and I hear the voice repeating it, reminding me of what he isn't and what he isn't.

Reed isn't the chains and spikes and the smeared makeup and the empty wine bottles of Amethyst. Reed isn't anarchy and sex and violence. You don't take Reed into some smalltown bar bathroom, and you don't fuck him against a sink that is constantly dripping thick, rust-colored water.

No.

No, the voice says.

No, you take Reed and all of his delicacy, his modesty, and his hesitance by the hand and you don't jerk at his arm or walk ahead of him.

You hold his hand tenderly. You pet his fingers once they're woven into yours, and you smile something small and gentle to comfort him as he relinquishes his self control to you.

You have to take the first step, you have to lead him, but you walk alongside him, only stepping ahead when you have to turn the street corner or urge him toward the parking garage.

You're the woman, but it doesn't matter when you get to the car because you don't subscribe to social archetypes, and the things you adore most about him are the traits too often assigned as feminine, so you open his door on the passenger side, and you watch his feet slip closer to the car— they don't step or stomp down or even lift— and when he lowers himself into the seat, his legs close into themselves and his back slouches forward and his arms cross over his abdomen as if he's suddenly too shy to be this naked.

When you close the door, you keep your eyes on him. You watch him through the windshield as you round the car, and you love the way he brushes a hand through his hair because his arm is still tight against his side, and he leans forward to bring his head to his hand, and everything about him— not just his height or waistline— is small and delicate and, oh, so desirable.

When you get in the car, you have to ask him if he's all right. You have to check in with him. You want to make sure he isn't frightened by you or your car or the prospect of where you might be taking him.

When he says he's fine, when he smiles that shy, perfect smile that brings light to the lips he often hides, you smirk. You wink. You let an eyebrow jump.

You remind him that, even though you take his desires into consideration, it is ultimately your decision what happens between the two of you.

He is yours. He is mine, and the voice I keep hearing repeats to me mine.

When you get him home— my vision is interrupted because when you get him home there shouldn't be maggots in your sink, and you shouldn't have empty fish food containers lying open on your kitchen counter.

There shouldn't be mold in your toilet, and you shouldn't have the clothes you've put off washing for two weeks thrown about on your floor.

You should've cleaned the spilled coffee by the door to your garage three months ago, and you should've bought some bleach the last time you were at the dollar store so you could clean your bathtub for the first time since the summer.

Shit.

If I'm going to have Reed, I can't bring him to a dingy apartment. I'll have to consider my options.

```
Chapter 26
To:
From:
Subject: Stuck
```

Don't judge me, but I sent Marty off for coffee. I just can't get lost in my work if he's sitting right beside. Pestering me.

Every time I call up Reed's Instagram, he scoffs. He tells me how the publisher would tell me to get off of Twitter.

I tell him it's research. It's not like I'm lying. And it's not like he'd ever really challenge me.

I mean, that's why he unloads my car at conventions, and that's why he carries my bags and gets me coffee.

I've learned early on in life, mostly by watching the people who take everything without ever having to give something back, that reality is all inside your mind. You have to express what you imagine life to be in order to get it. Don't focus on what is. What is is that Marty is paid to micro-manage. Marty is literally on the publisher's payroll to boss me around and make me write. What's in my mind when I see Marty is a young kid who's so eager to make his degree matter that he'll do anything I say so long as he doesn't get fired.

In my mind, Marty is my assistant. Marty is paid for by the publisher to assist me at the airport and hand me books to sign when I'm sitting my lazy ass at a table with my name across a big, stupid banner.

I'm the writer. I'm the artist. Anyone else in my life in association with that is here for me.

Take my advice, if you teach people who you are before they can see the real you, they'll never know the difference. And to Marty, I'm a celebrity.

Marty doesn't know how empty my fridge is, and Marty doesn't know there are maggots in my sink.

Most importantly, Marty doesn't know about Reed. If he did, I'm sure he'd find some way to ruin it for me. This is why I sent him away. I need space to research and write and get lost in Reed without worry that Marty's perpetual happiness is going to intervene.

So I put my earphones in, and I call up my browser, and Accentuate the Assent is still there.

That glorious image of Reed with his dirty blond hair and his eyes and his mouth and his straight nose is so fresh in my mind I'm sure I wouldn't need to revisit it to draw it. But I've already created Reagan's image, multiple times over, in that of current Reed's. Maybe that's for the best. This story is meant to return him to his former glory after all; it isn't meant to be a tale of what has already passed. Though the more I watch and listen to who Reed was, the more I realize that's exactly what it is.

It's strange to me, but not in a disbelieving way, how accurate my changes to Reed have been thusly.

I imagined his music heavy, and here he is in my hands playing heavy music. He strums, and he headbangs, and he sings with so much force the veins in his neck are bulging as they twist around beneath his skin.

I made his lyrics mean something, and in this time

period, they did.

I made his clothing more humdrum before his mistress of corruption arrived, and here in the video, in my hands, they were.

I feel the sting of tears again because, God, I wish I knew him then. I wish I'd met him and shielded him from the evils of the world; all of the violence and objectification and self-satisfying self-destruction this life offers. But I'll rescue him from it still.

As I listen, I sketch. I create panel after panel of Reagan's face full of fear, full of wonder, full of the rush of his first orgasm, full of the guilt of his first betrayal.

His best friend in my story, he's disappointed in Reagan. He always knew Reagan was the purest among their group of five, and he was so certain that if life hadn't corrupted him at this point in life, it was never going to.

Reagan failed because Reed failed, and as he sings to me about watching and guiding and protecting, I realize he wasn't placing himself in such a role. He was asking for someone to take the role on, to watch him, which I do, and to guide him, which I will, and to protect him, and I swear to God, every time I click on a girl's profile after they sweet talk him on the internet, that's exactly what I'm doing.

They don't get him. They don't get his living art. They don't understand his message in a rectangular bottle. He's begging for help. He become lost; he hasn't lost himself. No one sees him, and most of the time I'm sure he wants to be found, but other times... I'm not so certain.

On my drive in, the service was terrible. Music wouldn't play, Instagram wouldn't load. Luckily the push notifications still came through at certain spots in the road, and of course, the only thing I'm notified of is Reed.

I've shut off all notifications for me. No, I don't care if I've inspired you to draw, and, no, I won't send you a free copy of my latest because your mom said it was too violent for you to have. I don't care if you like my stupid photos, and I don't give a shit if you call me "hot" in the comments.

But I care about what Reed is posting, and I care about who likes his selfies, and I really need to know everything about every single woman in his tweet replies telling him he's beautiful.

When I caught my screen lighting up from the corner of my eye, I knew it was Reed. I was hoping he posted a photo to Instagram because I really could use more material, but it was a tweet.

Honestly, even better. Or at least that's what I thought.

AMETHYSTALIEN @reedbarry
Honestly so thankful @simonegale

I didn't realize I slammed my foot onto the brake until the seat belt gagged me. I gasped for air. The oxygen literally ripped from my lungs, the perfect physical manifestation of all I felt inside.

Simone Gale. Another object to be owned. A musician, this time. Another soul for sale. I hate it because it's her and it's me and it's Reed. The objectified ourselves. Thankful. So thankful. And in honesty.

I gasped for air still as I read. The longer I stared at the words, at the name, the harder it was to catch my breath. The more I eyed his profile picture to ensure it was his face within the circle, to see that it was, in fact, his twitter, the more painful inhaling became.

I remember whining. Not like spoiled little girl can't have what she wants whining; I mean emotionally charged, life shattering, lung twisting, heart thudding in my throat type of whining.

This was a physical, visceral, animal response. This was what I will forever assign to the pain of drowning. I just could not breathe.

My mouth was open and I was trying to inhale, but everything was shaking— my lips, my lungs, my hands where I held the wretched tweet, the wretched thought, this disgusting sentiment.

A car horn from somewhere behind me was able to rip my eyes from my phone, and when I turned to face it, I saw someone flipping me off in a navy blue Volkswagen as they blew by me.

I'm sitting in the middle of the road, I told myself, and I tossed my phone into the passenger's seat and tried to begin driving again.

Everything was still shaking. Everything was painful. Every organ necessary for life felt small, shriveled up. The life had been sucked out by a woman who was barely old enough to drink alcohol then by a woman double my and Reed's ages; by a woman who is valuable to those who follow her because her skin is airbrushed and her nipples are bleached then a second woman who sings her soul is sellable because of it.

The second woman proves something to me, something about me, something about the first. The young woman, she won't be seen in such a positive manner if she continues this career path at forty-five or fifty, at the age of singer/songwriter Simone that Reed is so thankful for, and that's the biggest "fuck you" to this all— that girl matters now because she's twenty-two and pretty, and Simone seems to have lost a lot of popularity in the past decade, and Reed, even though he's pushing thirty-five, matters, and will continue to matter, because he's male and pretty.

George Clooney could do porn and moms would still love him. The minute an actress turns forty, though, her career is over unless she's comfortable playing a rom-com mother-in-law or an evil business queen bitch.

But no matter how much everyone adores Meryl Streep, no one wants to see her naked, and how many people would pay good money to see Brad Pitt's dick?

So, no, it isn't just the absurdity that someone so pure and naive and innocent would find their way into a friendship with someone so adult, and, no, it isn't just the absolute insanity that someone with so much depth would be so taken by someone whose public (and sadly probably personal) worth is tied up quite literally to her ass, but it's this unhinged notion of equality and of respect; this idea that you see displayed on the crop tops of college girls in big, black letters: a woman doesn't have to be modest to be respected.

It's lovely in theory, but here in reality, it's just not the case. "Wouldn't it be nice if…" is not the same as "it is", and if I walked into the airport without my top on, I'd be arrested after the majority of men who paused to ogle me objectified me.

See, this is the problem with "groundbreakers" like Simone and porn stars and cam girls. They see what they're doing as empowering because they see themselves rebelling against the value systems of their grandparents. Sure, displaying your naked body to the world may prove that you're confident in that skin, but doesn't it also seem to suggest that you aren't much confident in anything else you have to offer?

Simone likes animals and I admire her for that, but her following consists of men remembering the good old days when they wanted to fuck her after a show, and the younger woman's Twitter, well, it's a glimpse into what Simone's would've been had Twitter been a thing when she was twenty.

These men don't give this woman money every month because they think she's a good person. They like her ass, and they think her chest is nice, and when she spreads her legs for all of them, they can stroke themselves imagining it's just for them.

They're really the problem. Being a progressive woman doesn't mean shit if the men of your nation insist on wanting you, obtaining you, returning you, just like you're a pair of khakis they wore once and then decided jeans would make their dicks look bigger.

You're not going to stop being an object in someone else's eyes until their vision is changed, and trying to insist that someone won't look at your naked body sexually because you display it freely isn't logical when you've done nothing to teach them better sight.

And while I don't think it's Reed's intention to objectify this woman, just like I don't think he used to objectify Simone, and while I see him only interacting with these women and others of our sex through gentle words like "thankful", "kindest", and "sweetheart", I don't think that means he'd have fostered such strange internet relationships with women who weren't in the careers they'd repetitively chosen.

I tried not to obsess over it. I really tried to stop thinking about it. But there was hardly any service so I couldn't scream-sing my feelings away, and when it did pick up all that would blast through my speakers were teasingly short two-second snippets of fucking Reed's fucking voice, and what once had seemed so heavenly now sounded like the blood-curdling wails of a crying infant in the booth behind you at a restaurant.

It had ruined everything— the drive, the scenery, the idea of my story, the idea of Reed, of Reagan, and all I kept seeing was my innocent Amethyst before Amethyst, with his plain hair and blemishes, all purely him and perfect, and all I could see were tanned hands with wrinkles and a few age-spots and long red acrylic nails pushing his emo-boy bangs off of his face before their claws tore his Abercrombie shirt away from his delicate torso.

I wanted to cry but tears didn't come. Instead, just the very real phantom smell of oil and gasoline and rubber as I plummet my car into the next big rig I see driving down the highway.

I wanted to fuck up someone's day, someone's job, someone's life. I wanted to get my ass to the airport so I could tell Marty what a fucking joke I think he is.

But I didn't.

Strangely, it was a Christmas decoration that calmed me.

Though my vision still blurred, my eyes seemed to dart from one focal point to any other— bouncing from stop signs to pedestrians to cars to gas stations to the sky.

Everything was dark, glooming inside the haze of my destruction and the bleakness of early morning. Nothing glowed. Nothing shone. Nothing was light; just mere flashes, streaks of white or of yellow. Comprehension was zero, for I was far too lost inside my mind, inside of Reed, inside of what could potentially be the act I thought it was, but for a different purpose.

Worried that he was simply a phony like the rest of his rocker brethren, consumed by the idea that such innocence was only present on him and not inside him, terrified that all I've gained and received and allowed to seep into my soul enough that it grew into something tangible absorbing into my muscles and tissues and was now pumping freely through my veins by way of blood and spirit and everythingness, I couldn't connect to anything here on this planet.

All I could connect to was the darkness that became Reed's higher self; the energy that was once light and airy and full of naive hopefulness had soured.

Maybe it's true, that old adage about how one should never meet their idols, but I ignored its warning for I do not idolize Reed. I don't worship at the altars of Grape Gardens, nor do I see Reed as something elevated about the commoner solely for the title of his career. No.

What I see as divine in Reed is all the divinity I see in myself and in Natalie and in all those create. But Reed is connected to me in some mystical way that neither of us were ever aware of.

We each spent thirty years unaware of it, and he remains blinded to it because he has yet to see me. I've seen him. I've bore witness. I've been enlightened. But our exchange was one way, and had I not been so intoxicated, it would've been a true meeting. An introduction of people instead of one person's introduction to another.

So I had to remind myself of this, of the fact that I was the one meant to save him, but his fondness for someone who wasn't me seemed to negate this.

After all, I've never been that thankful for someone else, and it seemed to me that this was because my spirit was so attached to the spirit of Reed, fully aware of the intangible bond that we couldn't witness with our eyes or feel with our fingers. But now I'm not so sure, for if that were true, wouldn't Reed be sensing the same detachment from all others of this world?

That's when my autopilot came to my awareness. That's when the lines of blurring color grew sharp and came into focus.

I felt my foot pressing gently into the brake, easing my car to stop instead of slamming it into a sudden halt, but I wasn't in control of it. Not yet. I was merely aware of my physical surroundings. And as they grew clearer, a blur of circular blue dissipated until I could see vividly what was in the road before me, and on the streets around me.

A flickering Christmas light, a snowflake covered in tinsel. Shining with white and blue flashing lights, the colors chasing each other, and made three-dimensional by silver strips of glittering garland.

It wasn't visible at all once— Nothing is ever as sudden as it seems— and as I stared to it, I imagined it a Star of David. As my vision returned entirely, however, I realized it was a snowflake, and next to it was a glittery Christmas tree with red flashing lights.

A calm crept into me, slowly at first— halted by my suspicion of it. I hate feeling something without understanding it. Even emotions must be interpreted. Otherwise, why would you follow them? But when the light turned green and I began to drive again, the service to my cellphone returned, bringing with it Accentuate the Assent. A brief encounter with their harsh vocalist flooded the car and jolted my body into a stiffness I can feel in my muscles at this exact moment, and then, as if whisked away to some place more heavenly, Reed's voice washed over it until the screaming faded and I was left with only him.

"Burning streets that I follow along," he sang to me, "Clouded skies clear my way through with snow."

My vision narrowed as I absorbed the lyrics, and without the context of what the screamer might have said before, I still can't say what the message of this song originally was. Maybe when Reed wrote it, he didn't even know. Maybe all he ever put into his music was his spirit reaching out for mine, and maybe all of what we've done in the last ten years was just us trying to catch the other's attention.

Right there, in those few seconds in my car, Reed was singing what I was experiencing. The road on which he stood was on fire, and I smelled the aftermath of my car bursting into flame. Snow cleared the clouds from his sight, just as a snowflake pulled my vision from its blurring stupor.

Reed was mine, and like the snowflake that I mistook for a Star of David, things aren't always as they appear. That tweet, it couldn't have been as it appeared. And I knew I had to dig further, but I was so close to the airport now that I didn't want to take my attention away from the road because dying now would never allow me to have the answers I was seeking.

When I arrived, yeah, I wasn't thrilled to see Marty, but I had shit to do, and now he's off getting a coffee because I still have shit to do.

I have a story to write, and I have research to dig into, and I have Reed's past to look at.

How long has he known Simone? I'll find out. Where did their interactions begin? Let me see.

I press against the earbud because I want his voice to be louder than the tweets I'm reading. I don't want to confuse who he really is with who he's appearing to be on twitter.

I scroll and I scroll and I let words of Reed slip by my eyes, words that promote his music, words that tell me what food he enjoys, words that show me Reed as is deep as I knew he was and words that show me his innocent thoughts.

I stop when I see shit like, *so drunk last night I don't think I'll be sober for the show tnght.*, and it drives me insane how he only half abbreviates his tweets. I mean, commit or don't. Are you someone who types out full punctuated sentences, or do you still like the shorthand of T-9 and 2006? Make a choice. Decide who you are.

4th of July got me fucked up, and I feel a shiver of disgust roll over my shoulders and down my spine before I can even finish reading. But I have to. I have to see if all, read it all, consume all of him. *American holidays are crzy but ilysm.*

I dig around my bag with my free hand to find some chapstick. I didn't realize how dry they were until they cracked and flaked in a surprisingly painful pull of my frowning lips.

I hate the thought of him drinking. I don't like thinking about him drunk and vulnerable at parties. Not alone; not without me to protect him. And I really don't like the idea of him saying "fucked up" or "fuck" or "fuck me".

Quickly I realize that what I'm searching for isn't going to be found in what he's tweeting. He doesn't tweet anything to anyone much. His tweets are musings, poetry. The occasional commentary on drunkenness or swear-words, but he's just being bombastic. Those aren't him. I don't know why I allow myself to fall for the falsehoods of his gimmicks. He doesn't get drunk. He doesn't get high. And probably when Bridget was blasting the British music about how sad it is when people who don't do drugs pretend that they do, they probably wrote it about him. But it isn't sad. It's self preservation. No one would take a rocker seriously if he admitted his sober lifestyle and lack of experience in intimate matters. Sex and drugs, they're synonymous with rock 'n roll— so much so that I don't even have to tell you that.

But I'll tell you what I figured out. I have to look through Reed's tweet replies to find the start of this thankful bullshit.

His friends and the bands he tours with, they're all unfiltered, and they do not have a carefully crafted presence the way Reed does.

I can tell— and probably most people can't— when someone is faking it, even through a screen. I can see how calculated it all is— this persona and the tweets like the ramblings of Edgar Allan Poe on LSD.

Like I said when I first found his Instagram, you have to try to create captions like his. His thoughts aren't his thoughts. They're what he wants us to think of him.

I've also said this before; about telling people who you are. I guess Reed just figures if he shoves this mystical prince of darkness who's part poet and part ET down our throats enough we'll believe that's exactly what he is.

With his obsessive control, this orchestrating of himself, this need to never share anything real, it's smart. Genuinely.

Like I said, humans lost God and had to find replacements. We can't function being the center of our world— well, most of us can't.

If you believe in nothing, your thoughts can get pretty dark, and I'm certain people like Marty and Bridget could never be alone inside a head like mine without blowing it off.

It's fine, though. Reed isn't manipulating me. I don't care how badly he treats the girls who worship him; they aren't going through what I go through every time I see his face or hear his words or watch his idiotic Instagram stories in dark rooms where he slaps his hand on his face and drags down his skin, pulls down his lips and narrows his eyes as if the downers he just consumed are too heavy for him to keep his eyelids up.

He's not at a party. He's not even at a bar after a show. The comments and the tweet replies all say things like, *lol Reed be trippin every night and be safe, sis, we stan our alien king* and they quote his lyrics *all those drugs keep my head in the clouds* back to him.

They don't pay attention enough to notice that any time Reed is around anyone, he takes a million photos. He fills up his Instagram story with men sitting at tables with smoke billowing from their lips and women in tight dresses on countertops drinking from bottles of bourbon. He brags.

He wants us to believe him when he sings about getting high and when he smears the word fuck all over

Grape Gardens' banner. He's not capturing fun times for the memories. He documenting the hedonism of those around him as some sort of proof that he's involved in it.

He isn't. If he were at a bar in those photos, we'd see the bar. We'd seen the booze. We'd see people everywhere. But all we see is his face and nothingness, and I type out *getting ready for bed alone in your room* but I delete it and keep scrolling.

It would prove that I get him in a way no one does, but it would also make him hate me.

After all, disillusionment hurts, and imagine how badly it would pain Reed to know everything he's been so crafting so meticulously isn't fooling everyone.

I could never do that to him.

Simone rants in her tweets. She's so angry so often and I feel so connected to her. She rambles as much as I do. Kindreds for sure. So if I find out that she is fake, I swear to god, I am going to scream right here in the middle of this airport and probably at Marty.

The world fucks us all up, but we can't save you when we can't save ourselves.

You're too gentle for these women, anyway. You're too soft. One is looking for an entrance back into the scene, and the other, well, maybe she likes to fuck around with guys with fanbases because pretty girls like attention (and no, I'm not being judgmental; I'm speaking from experience), and insecure girls get off on having things lots of women want. Just ask Bridget about that one.

Besides, messing around with people, their emotions, using them for followers or fame, that should feel creepy, Amethyst, and yes, I'm addressing you because whatever part of Reed that would even entertain this is you.

You're the violence and you're the FUCK EACH OTHER and you're the only one who would make such a sweet, devout young man turn to such power play bullshit.

What I share with Reed is something far more spiritual, and maybe Amethyst is only worried about the physicality of art, but Reed isn't. I bet he isn't at all, and Marty is near— I can hear his fucking shoes— and if he so much as exhales audibly when he sees me on my phone, I will hit him.

"Bexley," he says as he sits. "Oh, little Miss Martin," he chuckles something cute and small, and I bet if he created an alter ego for himself it would be something disgustingly sweet like chocolate covered cherries, and I'm here to tell you, Marty, no one likes chocolate enough that it'd make fucking cherries seem appealing.

"Marty, please," I grit out and he gasps before I can say anything else.

I look up to him, and his hand is covering his mouth. His eyes stare down to my phone, and for a second I realize that I don't know what color they are, and how am I going to kill him in this novel if I can't even ink him properly?

"What are you…" he looks up to me from his downcast head and his eyes are blue. "Bex, are you a… Do you not like… Men?"

I raise a brow. "Marty, are you a fucking homophobe? Because I will hire someone who is big and muscley and gay to kick the shit out of you."

"What? No!" His head rears back and he clutches his chest as if he's a southern belle truly aghast by my accusation. "No, I just…" he takes his lip into his teeth and, God, he's like every shy, awkward heroine in those weird monster romance books. What are you, Marty? Are you a sixteen-year-old in love with a vampire? Come on.

"You just what?" I ask, and he looks too nervous to answer. "What? You're concerned about what I'm looking at?" I turn my phone screen so Simone's acrylic nails digging into her spreading asscheeks are right in his line of sight. He looks away. "Oh, so it's no concerning that a woman is looking at a naked woman. You're just concerned that a woman is naked in general."

"Oh, no, it's not—"

"It's not what? It doesn't align with your idea of femininity? Women should be modest, right?"

"No," he tries again, but he won't even look to the screen.

I turn it back so I can see it, and I back out of Simone's profile. I go back into Reed's replies. I scroll. I research.

"Bexley, I…" when he stops, I let my eyes roll over to him.

His eyes, they're careful not to meet mine, and while they're trailing down my arm, I see him biting his lip again, and the middle finger of his right hand is moving around the khaki on his thigh.

"You what?"

He smiles a bit. "No, I just… Guess I always kinda had a little… A little bit of a…"

He trails off and I can feel the dryness of my lips again, and I'm starting to wonder why I only remember chapstick exists when I'm frowning. "You what?" I scoff, and his eyes are on my arm again. His fingers are moving. "What are you doing?"

He looks up, brows lifted, and I nod toward his hand.

"Oh," he says, tucking it quickly under his leg. His stupid legs. They're touching, and his feet are turned in toward each other. "Whenever I get nervous I... I trace the tattoos on your arm— the chakra symbols, I mean."

I stare at him, feeling my face harden in the silence between us. "You what?"

"Well, I just remember you talking to a fan— I think her name was Jamie— in DC last year. You were telling her about meditation... And you told her how drawing helps to calm you if you're too anxious to sit down in silence."

I'm softening now. I can feel it in my features, and I don't like it. "You remembered a fan interaction?"

"No, I remembered you. I know you think it's my job to be your au pair or something, and I guess it is, but I really was so excited to get to work with you more closely because you always seemed so calm.

"I remember the first day I met you. Other people come in with manuscripts and they were always nervous and they were afraid, and some of them looked like they were going to cry. One, just in my first week, threw up; he came out of the restroom just as Hunter called him back to Ann's office. Not you, though. You sat there filing your nails. Slouching in the chair in your leather jacket. Legs thrown about everywhere. Everyone else comes in in slacks and nice blouses or button-ups, and they sit with their spines so rigid. I bet... You don't even remember what you said to me."

He smiles but it's scary how fake it is. I've never seen Marty look anything but optimistic, even when he's falling over luggage outside the airport in the freezing cold air.

I'm seeing him from the corner of my eye now, and I

shake my head just enough to communicate that, no, I don't remember.

He exhales what could be a laugh, but his expression gives away that isn't it one. "I asked you if you were related to Ann— maybe you were her niece coming to take her to lunch or something— and you said, 'Kid, if I were her niece, I'd only visit on Christmas, and just so she didn't cut me out of her will.'"

"Doesn't shock me," I say, "Ann's a bitch."

"She knows what she wants," he says lightly, shrugging. "And even though everyone else may agree with you, they'd never say anything so terrible."

"So you wanted to work with me because I'm awful."

"Not at all," he says, biting his stupid fucking lip again. "I wanted to work with you because you're strong enough to be yourself. You're confident enough in your work that you don't need to dress up or even act up. I admired you for your strength and your confidence. I do, I mean. That's why I really wanted this job when they offered it."

"Well, congrats," I say. "You got your dream job." And I take a sip of the coffee he brought. It burns my tongue far worse than my words do, and I hand it back to him. "But your coffee fetching skills could use something improving," I say, and I look back to my phone. "Hurry back with the next one. Coffee is supposed to be hot."

I try not to look at him, but from my peripheral I tell that he's hesitant to move at first. He shifts. He turns away from me. I think his head tilts back. After a short self-debate, he stands, throws the coffee in the trash at the end of the row, and heads back down the hall.

Chapter 27
To:
From:
Subject: Stuck, but in the Air this
Time

My sketches are subpar and it's definitely because of
these fucking tweets. Sure, art has to come from emotion,
but fresh, heightened, raw emotion is just manic.

It's furious, and it's teeth gritting. It's a rapid heart rate.
It's sore lungs. My ribs feel like they're on fire. My hand is
aching so badly but I need to get this shit out of me, so I
even try switching to my left hand for a minute.

It produces atrocious results, and I can't say I'm angry
about it.

It's what Reed deserves.

His shallowness, his willingness to be corrupted, his
turning away from something poignant and powerful for
something cheap and meaningless, here it is in black and
white.

Do I know him? Well, maybe not in most people's
understanding of the word. But do I sense things about
him, things directly from his subconscious, that she could
never know? Fucking yes, I do, and that makes my vision
of him here in these pages the truest reflection anyone
could ever create of his soul.

It's soured. It's rotting. It's sweetness dropped into a

bottle of pickle juice and becoming bitter by all of the acidic, petty, superficial, and uninspired vermin drowning in the dingy water around it.

I draw him passing out face first in his drummer's vomit. I draw him sharing cigarettes with plague-infested lips. Touching hands that haven't been washed after giving homeless men bjs in the back alley way for coke.

If this is the image he wants, if this is the life he wants, then I'll draw it into existence.

Are you my god, Amethyst? Or are you a saint coming to my altar and asking me to grant you the life experiences you'll never have enough guts to try for yourself? Are you talking to me? Are you?

If so, I can't imagine why. I can't see your point. If you don't want to be saved, why are you calling out to me? If you want frivolous friends and unsymmetrical conversations, why have you reached out to me? Don't you see my depth? Don't you see my capacity to create, and to understand, and to care? I never thought I'd care. Why did you do this to me?

I know it's real. I've seen too much to prove my connection to who he is— to who he… was.

It's irritating having to say that. I was holding out so much hope that all of this was artistic expression, but I've combed through his tweets and his replies, and I got all the way into last year before I gave up hope of finding anything to prove me wrong or right for certain.

Not that I'm normally a quitter.

Going through Reed's replies was easy enough with a goal in mind. That goal, figuring out exactly how close he is with Simone, well, all it did was show me that they haven't known each other very long.

Still, I didn't see a bunch of replies shared. I didn't find full conversations. Sure, they FaceTime. He helps her pick out lingerie to wear. Could be romantic, but what do I know? I've never loved anyone I said "I love you" to, and when they leave, I only mourn losing an extension of me. I can't say I know shit about love, or if I think it even exists.

Now, don't think I'm about to go into a tangent about chemical reactions. Unseen things, things we feel, they're very real. Trick or not, emotions govern a lot of our choices, and for some people like Marty they apparently govern all of their choices.

I glance over to him. He's reading while he listens to his earphones. I can't understand that, but maybe it's because I'm a writer. Maybe my natural pull toward words can't let me hear only the music of a song.

I think it's why I can't really enjoy Grape Gardens's shit either.

I mean, "Echoes", it has a mystic sound. When I close my eyes in the car and let it become all that is perceivable by my five senses, my mind paints for me a setting in which I'm walking through mystical forest, trees black and shimmering somehow in the subtle cast of light from the crescent moon. The grass appears purple in the darkness. My clothing is loose and silky and thin, and it flows in the breeze, but there is no breeze. Everything is enchanted. Nothing is real.

But the lyrics— this night where Reed sees a woman and can't let go of her— what do they have to do with such a mysterious tone?

Every other song discusses the nuance of beach-tanning girls vs every other girl, I type sarcastically, and why stuck up women wouldn't like guys in bands that haven't been popular in years.

Whatever, Amethyst. Reed used to write about religion, and while I think God is only real because so many people believe that he is, I am much more invested in art that means something; in art that matters.

Reed wishing he was ten years younger doesn't mean shit if it's not so he can right some wrong, or try to help people, or even tell himself not to sell out for less fans and less fame.

What was he thinking when he left Accentuate the Assent for this Grape Gardens bullshit? And why does he talk to naked women on the internet but ignore people who dedicate days to drawing cute, anime-styles portraits of him?

There has to be a reason. What is the draw of someone so innocent to so much corruption? Is this part of his stunt? Is this…

I sit up and deposit my sketches into the seatback folder in front of me.

When did this start again?

I open my phone and I call my photos. I scroll through All Photos, pass Videos and Moments and Favorites. I even scroll by my Grape Gardens folder, my ATA folder, and my Reed folder. I click on the one titled "Fucking Amethyst" and I scroll through Instagram selfies with irrationally poetic captions, pass true pornography-styled pictures of him, and I slow down when I start to see the whiteness of tweet screenshots.

I hit the home screen and go to Google because I don't remember when the band was formed, and, okay, Grape Gardens existed months before Reed selected Simone as fan-friendship of the year. But these photos of him, my God.

Even in Grape Gardens, he wasn't Amethyst yet. Not fully.

He's got the vibe of a 70's porn star, sure, but he's got on a turtleneck and his sleeves only reveal his forearms, and his pants are high-waisted, and what is the message here, Reed? Because it still doesn't fit with your new sound.

I go to images. I looked into this early stage Grape Gardens from a year ago, but not so in-depth, and really if I want to understand why Reed is slipping into the darkness of selling his music by selling his sex appeal instead of just believing in the merit of his work, well… Well, it's disgusting as an artist, but as a businessperson, it's fucking genius.

How many guys in bands or on TV shows have written books and had them sell out in a week simply because their name is on the cover while Natalie's novels go mostly unnoticed because she doesn't already have a household name?

Success is linear in a way that isn't fair. Natalie wants book sales, so she needs to do interviews, but hosts only want to interview people with book sales. It's a vicious cycle, and even when you jump onto the wheel, it doesn't mean you're a part of it. You're hanging on to the outside by your pinky, and every roll threatens to eject you. Famous actors and musicians and novelists who have had famous actors and musicians play their characters on film, they all strap into first-class seats on the inside of the hamster wheel and sip martinis. They ask you to buy their stuff as if they need to ask. As if they need you to give them more money.

People like Natalie run promotions giving away her

stuff just for the word of mouth, and only a handful of people respond.

So, okay, maybe when I question Reed, I already know some of the answer. But that's only from the side of me that knows money makes the world go 'round in the sense that we need money to eat. We can't exist in this world without money. Without enough money for the necessities in life, we die. Period.

It's fucked up, but it's logical. What can we do?

But the side of me that values art, that interprets meaning, and analyzes language, that side of me is appalled.

Reed is the electric current of creativity so powerful that it blasts through a dank, dingy basement bar and awakens within even the most nihilistic human in existence the spark to understand another person.

I desperately want to understand him, and, yes, we all know I do in a way most people who worship him don't, but I want to know even more.

I want to know what his favorite color is, not what the gimmick says his favorite color is. I want to know where he sits when he writes, or where he stands, or where he goes inside his mind when he's holding a guitar and creating the notes of an unborn song.

When all we had to go on was Amethyst, fine, I'll admit that it wasn't outlandish to think he didn't go anywhere; that the lyrics lack substance because he's all show and no content. Just a husk. But Accentuate the Assent has meat inside their shell. They're poets and musicians, and they're filling and whole, and Reed was so pure. I mean, wasn't he?

I enlarge a photo of Grape Gardens before Amethyst was Amethyst, and I see its origin is Facebook. I click the link.

I inhale something deep and nervous but very determined to figure out the core of who he is— this nugget of truth hiding inside the lie— as my phone closes the image and switches out my screen to Facebook.

There is no caption, just a date. November 28th of last year. They're such a new band. It's so odd. This starting over. This mid-life crisis, maybe. This changing of identities. I don't know.

But there is Reed with his hair parted to the side, not the middle, and it's blond, and his blue eyes are still magnificent, and he's in muted colors like mustard and dirt, and it's so opposite the bright purple and the flashy glittering pink. It's calm and smooth, not rough and sharp and sexual. It's faded tweed and gentle. It's not harsh, silver handcuffs. I don't know what this is, or what it meant paired with the music.

I scroll through a very limited number of photos— limited like his Instagram; these little tastes of who he wants us to think they are— and just thirteen pictures later, three months after the first official Grape Gardens post, there's Amethyst. Not fully developed yet, but his hair is purple, and he's traded the humble brown of 70's clothing for the severity of 80's rock— a black leather jacket, and a thick silver chain. But Reed is still there, still present, and I sit up in my seat, and I set the phone down on top of my sketches on the tiny seat-back tray table, because hanging from the chain isn't a lock or a spike or a collar; it's a cross. Just like the one original Reagan wore. Just like the one I discovered past Reed wore. Just like the one I knew was truly him without ever knowing why.

Nine months ago, Reed was still fighting Amethyst.

Reed was still in there, alive and making choices. But Amethyst dyed his hair and changed his clothing. Amethyst tried taking over, and Reed remained.

Twelve pictures later, seemingly out of nowhere, after photos of him wearing white sweaters and red sunglasses and playing a guitar on stage, Reed is gone.

Amethyst replaces him in June. It took three months to overpower Reed, but he won. It's here in this photo. It's in the way Reed's head is hanging. It's in the chain he holds in his hands. It's in his cut off T-shirt. It's in the way his back leans away from the camera, but his hips hold firm.

This isn't sweet Reed in a sweater, and this isn't delicate Reed checking his phone inside the suit of a rock god.

This is Amethyst, and I wish he'd given me some clue as to where he came from and why he came.

Three days later, after a string of five Grape Gardens merchandise promos, there's Amethyst in the photo I saw on Grape Gardens' Instagram that first night when we connected.

He's lying back in the ostentatious colors of his new character. He appears out of it, out of his head, out of consciousness, out of this world. And the band— he— writes to his fans announcing his birthday, calling himself a frontman, and asking for drinks.

The first and most easy method of downfall. *Buy me a shot.*

There are only eleven comments, and when I click on them, the first one is a photo.

A profile shot of Reed, his brown hair styled into his face, his chest adorned by a shirt with cut-off sleeves,

bracelets made of plastic and prayer beads on the wrist that
bends so he can grip his bass's neck. Reed's right hand is
on the microphone— just black and regular. His eyes are
open, and his neck is straight, and he isn't pretending to be
roofied or wasted. His knee is bent. A hole exposes the
skin there. His jawline threatens to break the skin
wrapping around it, it's so prominent. His nose is still its
original aquiline, Roman perfection. He isn't smiling, not
per se, but he looks happier than he does in anything
recent I've seen of him.

Here's Reed in 2011 the commenter said, and
watermarked the photo with his name. Reed didn't reply to
the commenter; didn't even like his comment. I wonder if
that's because he isn't a woman, and further still, I wonder
if it's because he isn't a woman with a following. I had
higher hopes than proof of 'objectifying asshole', but Reed
is a man and men get passes for being disgusting way too
often than they should.

Closing the comments, I can't help but scroll through
the newfound photos. Photos of Reed drinking from
plastic cups like these basement bars serve. Reed holding
fire in his hands as he stares at the camera through red
sunglasses. Reed lying across his band mates with his
leather jacket open. Reed having alcohol poured into his
mouth. Reed with his eyeliner so smeared that he looks
like a corpse with big, hollow eyes. Reed's spray-painted
banner. Reed in front of it with his chains wrapped around
his neck. Reed's spray-painted banner with a smashed
television in front of it. The smashed TV is spray-painted
too. It says "ANARCHY" and probably because Reed
thinks he's Prince Vicious-Bowie-Rotten. Or at least he did
in June of this year.

I keep scrolling and I keep thinking of how small his steps were on the stage the night I was too drunk to actually meet him, and how that doesn't correlate with the photos I see here of him leaning back into his guitarist as if he's a drunken girl at a frat party; as if he's been roofied and now thinks 80's Big Hair Babyface is his knight in shining armor.

The way his chin was always lowered, even as he sang so boldly the vibrations of his throat sounded guttural and animalistic, it doesn't align with smeared lipstick all over his face in a shot so close-up he's blurred.

There are photos of him leaning against walls, but his hips are pulled away from them. He leans against vans in this way. Against a member of his band I didn't see on stage that night. None of it makes sense with who he *has* to be.

But then another swipe reveals something true. Something pure. Something so Reed he couldn't hide it behind plastic pants and thick, steel chains.

Reed is standing on stage, a brief second in half an hour's worth of sex and violence, looking down at his guitar. His eyelids aren't heavy. His body isn't swaying and his head isn't falling aside. In this second, captured and shared and visible to all who search his name, Reed is simply an artist. Reed is a musician. Reed is a poet.

And there's hope in this photo. Hope that whatever madness appears in these stills is only a mask. Hope that Reed is everything I thought he is.

I swipe again, my thumb shaking in nervous excitement, and I'm rewarded. My patience is rewarded. My unwavering faith in my angel, my Amethyst alien, my muse, my Reed, has not been in vain.

Pixels, mechanics, electricity, battery operated life; it's all come together on my screen in a blending of colors and shapes and patterns to show me an image of Reed remaining inside Amethyst.

He stands with his side toward the camera in his zebra-printed, painted-on pants and his 90's Babs Bunny T-shirt cut off into a crop top. His arms hang by his sides, but they aren't loose and drug-limp. They're tight to his frame. The muscles in his neck are tight, so much so that they're visible behind the chains and the spiked dog collars. Beneath his purple hair, his secret lips are pressed into another's— those of 80's Hair Babyface.

It's something should-be sexual. Like certain men and their lesbian porn fetishes, some women find erotic thrill in watching two men fuck. I think Reed knew this, and I think everything he's done thusly— from his would-be roofied eyes to his naked torso to the chains and collars and leashes— has all been pursuit of some alternate equality; some world where men can be worshiped for their shapes, where they can be admired for their beauty, where women catcall two pretty boys as they fondle each other. I think Reed likes the idea of being sexualized, and I have to wonder if it isn't because he lacks the sensation of being admired.

Admiration is really so much more than it seems. Admiration is a deeply felt appreciation for a person, for what they do, for what and who they are. And if someone did hurt Reed— just like my vicious woman in Reagan's story represents— if someone broke his heart, or made him feel inadequate, then any kind of admiration might feel as good as being loved.

What Reed can't understand right now, what that hole

inside of him doesn't show, is that loving the idea of what someone is isn't anything like loving the reality of who someone is, and surely I can't be one to lecture anyone on appreciation and love when I was too concerned with embarrassing myself in my drunken state to even say hi to him; to tell him how impactful his performance was, to try to make him see how I'm not a fan of what he does and yet I admire him for it.

It isn't cheap and it isn't hollow, not what I feel. And maybe I can't describe it properly, and maybe that's not even my fault. Maybe there isn't a word yet conceived for this type of connection, or maybe there is and maybe I'm too self-centered or too shallow or too stupid to know it.

I don't know. But what I do know is that Reed wants to be sexualized for this act of affection shared between friends because it's clear to anyone truly witnessing the photo that this isn't an act of real affection.

Again, it's very calculated— this image he wants us to see of him— because it's meant to be two men kissing one another, and all it really is manipulative and uncomfortable.

The discomfort isn't found in 80's Baby Hair, no. His brow is loose and unweighted. His lips aren't tightly closed. His hand is on Reed's neck, and his other arm dangles slack.

Reed's expression, though we can only witness it from the side, is entirely different. Like his body, his face is tight and closed off. Sealed away with his secret lips. His eyes are squeezed shut so hard his lashes are buried inside the folds of his flesh. His jaw is clenched. His cheek has a rigid line through it. His lips— oh, those secret lips— they're sealed into a line that lifts up into what can only be described as the smile of someone shy when all eyes in the room turn to him. I think he's embarrassed here— embarrassed in the way a socially anxious person feels when they're forced into answering a phone call from an unknown number.

Reed is here inside the trappings of manufactured sexuality. Reed is timid. He is meek. He's too shy to kiss anyone in front of the two other people in the room, and he's too shy to kiss anyone in front of a camera, but he wants to be objectified in any way that will bring him attention misconstrued as love, and he's so sheltered he thinks smashing TVs and kissing other men is somehow shocking and punk rock. It's evident in his caption on the photo: *All we are is creeps. We're here to give you the creeps.*

Reed, my darling little sweetheart, smashing TVs was only terrifying in the 60's, and kissing other men is perfectly normal if you love them or if you want to fuck them.

When you do these things, oh, dearest one, you just prove how innocent you truly are because they don't mean what you think they do.

Either way, I'm happy for it because it gives me hope that if I'd go back to that photo comment on Reed's birthday post and click the photographer's name, I'd find Reed in the list of his friends.

Of course, Facebook doesn't work the way Twitter does, and profiles are different from pages, and when I go the commenter's page, Facebook informs me that his friend's list is private, and the last thing I want to do is request an online connection to someone whose only link to me is Reed.

But I do have the idea to search for Reed's Facebook

instead of the band's. I was supposed to do this anyway, and he distracted me away with his handsome face I want to draw and kiss and sit on and slap.

When the page result load, two pop up with the same photo— a photo of Reed's face with his mustard clothing from the 70's, so I'm assuming neither have been updated in a while— and I click the first one.

It's an actual profile, one that I can be friends with, but I won't send it a request— I'm merely a god inspired by my god— and I scroll down to see that he hasn't posted here since July.

Amethyst is here inside the posts he shared. Twitter photos of him outside a bar in a birthday girl sash, and images of his purple hair and homemade crop tops.

He posts things about the genius of Michael Jackson, and I super agree, and a part of me is angry that only nine people have liked this because Michael Jackson was the only true mega-star earth will ever know, but the other part is oddly happy.

When I post things to Twitter, even if they aren't meaningful or funny, I average more reactions than nine. Reed isn't the unattainable rock star. Reed is just a humble artist, and somehow that's more pure. I guess I'm a hipster or something because I want what's mine to stay mine, but I'd rather fight off four girls and five guys than thousands of each.

He posts to Facebook about fantasy. He questions reality. Three or four people react to this content, but if it doesn't prove again that he and I are connected— or at least like-minded— nothing will.

His mind isn't here for the masses. He's here for me. I for him. It would be glorious to discuss concepts of time and of thought and of what makes reality real, so long as he's still the person he used to be. I don't know if he's changed, if he's become the person he's pretended to be for these few months. Because alongside beautiful posts about respecting animals there is shit about wanting red glitter pasties and God being a woman.

There is no god, Reed, only people, and maybe you're right because maybe I'm the vision in your head when you type such nonsense.

It's like he's struggling between personalities here. Parts of Amethyst telling us about the wonders of sex and violence versus parts of Reed telling us about his favorite cereal.

He posts that he's in a bondage bar but there's no photo so, no, I don't believe you. He posts about being tipsy but, again, this brag-natured boy doesn't share proof.

I've come to recognize your patterns, Amethyst. I know when you're you and when you're Reed trying to be you. But all of this digging is for naught because it's months old and has no reactions.

Still, I can't help but cringe a bit at the fact that this is his profile, not his public persona page, and that his mom and dad have to read posts about him wanting to be spit on.

I scroll to the top of the page, back out, and click the Reed Barry below it. Same photo. Same name. But a page this time, not a profile.

This has been updated even less frequently. The last post was from last year around this time. It's a photo of the band— one on Grape Gardens's page from the early days of a whole year ago— and he's standing there with his blond hair and his thrifted sweater.

It's not the Reed I prefer, and somehow it seems even less him than whatever this current alien bs is, but seeing it again and again really makes you wonder what his vision for it was.

You can tell there are more fans here than on his profile because his headshots get twelve likes instead of five, or maybe these are the people who fell off when he went all Johnny Rotten sex-crime-victim on them.

Either way, I scroll through only three olden-days Grape Gardens photos before I'm treated to something so miraculous it has to be divine intervention. A video.

Reed, as my beautiful Reed, with blond hair and a regular old T-shirt on, sits in what appears to be a coffee shop with a guitar on his lap.

I'm quick to turn up the volume in my earbuds. Quick to click play. Quick to expand the video until my screen is nothing but Reed and his regular hair and his face free from all obstruction. His regular clothes. His acoustic guitar with a cute cartoon ghost spiraling out of the sound hole.

It's adorable; he is. Everything is innocent, and his blue eyes with his blond hair seem so much more fitting than they do with his purple, or even with my red.

The way he strums is so swift and slow, so precise and yet so free. It's attractive. The way his fingers look as they hold the neck of the guitar and the pick is much more appealing than anyone else's in the same action.

And his voice. I don't know why he makes the music he makes currently, and now I'm wondering why he lent himself to that auto-tuned clean vocals of Accentuate the Assent. This right here... I'm not one for soft music, and I'm not one for slow sappy shit, but this is so perfect it's obscene.

He closes his eyes when he sings, and his voice travels so powerfully I can feel his chords slipping from my ears into my head. My mind absorbs him. He gives me more.

He moves his head and his shoulders shift slightly, everything so in tune with what he's singing, and when the short clip is over and the next shuffles on, the image alone hits me with such force that I'm urged out of my hunched position over the phone until I feel the seat against my back.

A few tendrils of hair fall into his face. His eyes are closed again, and his brows lift and crease and raise and furrow as his voice melts each word into the next so seamlessly you'd swear he'd invented his own language— one comprised of English and melody and musical notes, blended together to create the most immaculate rendition of some stupid boy-band member's solo shit. It'd be unrecognizable to anyone at the label who worked on it, and that's the power of Reed I sensed and crafted into Reagan by design.

He can take something fake and corrupt and pawn-like and make it sound like a ballad built on flesh and blood.

He takes porn and makes it poetry. How else can you explain the beauty that radiates from every photo of his roofied haze and handcuffs?

I needed this. I needed to see that this idea of him I swore I knew for fact wasn't just another fiction I've created in my mind; and I think all this proof does is further my claim that everyone I've ever thought I created actually exists.

Maybe their realms aren't alternative to this one.

Maybe they're just people with whom I've not crossed paths yet.

This art in my hands, this true and incredibly soulful artist, I know he still exists inside Amethyst. I can sense it as strongly as I had the night in the bar. Maybe I've been tripped up, and maybe those are just cries for help. Maybe everything he's doing with his musician friends, with whatever or whoever hurt him in his youth, with his porn-star 70's clothing, and his Sex Pistol's lock-and-chain is reaching toward something else, some greater purpose. Maybe it's all a part of his artistic expression. Maybe he's living his life as one big performance art piece.

I take note of the dates of these videos— all from last year— and, I swear, I am so close to cracking this code. This relationship, this change in him. Why did he lose the plain-Jane boringness of a t-shirt and the guitar and replace them with dog leashes and drugs? Where is the change? And why? And why can he make poetry pornographic and pornography poetic, and is there maybe some sexuality I'm not aware of yet that blends the two together?

Maybe none of this is meant to be anything, and maybe it's just my eyes finding a human being so appealing that my libido makes everything he does into something it isn't. Either way, wanting to save him and protect him is only part of the emotional draw; the other part is wanting to own, entice, and fuck him until none of that other shit even matters anymore.

I keep scrolling until I've consumed every video he's recorded and sung and played with the pure talent of a true artist, with the emotion of someone too acutely aware of the depths of human complexity, and I'm back to Google now, back to the place that gave me these insights and these links; and I can't help but see the irony in how this fucking phone in my hand has caused my utter disconnection from every one of the hundreds of humans on this plane while simultaneously linking me even further with the past, present, and potential of this one man I've never even met in person.

I can feel my heart thudding so rapidly inside my chest that it starts to push what can only be nerves and impatience and an overabundance of concern for a fucking stranger up my throat in the acidic form of bile. I want to gag when I think about this angelic figure with his soothing voice becoming used and being taken advantage of and convinced to drink and smoke until his chords rot away; until he can't even moan in an appealing way, and, Jesus God, if you are real, forgive me for getting wet at that same thought.

Then I see a screenshot of a tweet. This isn't a recent tweet. I can tell by his profile picture.

I call it up, I zoom, and he's smiling in the photo and his hair is brown and boring and beautiful, and all I can imagine in this moment is how delicious that metal wrapping around his lip must have tasted to anyone lucky enough to pull his secret lips into their mouth.

And then I see her picture— hers. The one lucky enough to touch Reed, to taste him, to fuck him. That's not to say I'd believe it if I read somewhere that she ever got to. After all, Reed's aura is pure white like fresh snow. It's calm and tender. It's innocence fallen from the stars, or God, or Mount Olympus because an angel got bored with the heavens and wanted to try wearing human flesh for a while.

Jesus, did your warrior pick the most handsome body.

My fiancé is the most amazing woman on the planet. End of story.

It's simple, and, sure, it's the kind of thing that makes eyes roll. It's that young love that gets written off for youthful lack of experience. It's the malarkey that comes with flesh relationships, and the hopefulness that this person was designed, crafted, and created just for you. It's not something I would ever tweet. But it's wholesome in that naive way that makes everything else I just said seem pure and appealing. It's virtue in a smiling couple who both wear button ups and khakis.

Like Reed in the photo attached, she's got plain brown hair. It's wavy but not in any way that suggests effort. She's got eyeliner on, but it's simple. Her face isn't smooth the way airbrushed models' faces are, and whatever she was trying to do to be attractive to him was in her joy, not her body.

And Reed in this photo, my lord, this is the best I've seen him. Not to say this is the most physically attractive— I think I prefer the blond, fallen tendrils to any of the various styles I've seen— but this is the most physically aware of himself it seems he's ever been.

He's smiling like she is, and the energy of both people is so apparent it's contagious. I, sitting here in this miserable plane cabin with only a two-foot wide aisle separating me from fucking Marty, am smiling.

And the way this movement makes my lips crack— Jesus, I'm begging for something to scowl at.

I reach for my chapstick and apply it as I stare at this photo. This miraculously delivered peek into past Reed. The date, it's the oldest thing I've found since those those links. It's Reed before the bondage. Lucifer before the fall.

Not that I'm saying Reed's the devil, but wasn't he supposed to be the most beautiful of the angels? And isn't that such a cliched comparison? I'm only pointing out how fitting all of that seems.

Really what I'm questioning now isn't just what type of music has Reed always wanted to make versus what kind of music has he been forced to make— artistic expression versus a sellable product. Now I'm wondering if he's able to play so many instruments— the guitar in those Facebook videos, the keyboard in his new one— because the talent was forced upon him.

He seems so whitebread here in this photo, and so does his girlfriend. So cookie cutter they're practically the Santa and Mrs. Claus equivalent of your great-grandparents showing you old photos of how hot they were in their twenties.

He doesn't look like someone who wants to be a rock star. He looks like someone who would've settled down with this girl at twenty-five years old, gotten married, had kids. He looks like he would've been that person from your hometown who pursued family portraits while you were pursuing career. He looks like his wife would work at the Gap part time, just to feel like she was contributing, until she gave birth to the first child. This girl in the photo, she looks like she'd fit that mold well.

It's shocking to me, imagining someone so immersed in their on-stage persona that nothing of his real life has even infiltrated his Instagram once, but in my initial understanding of who Reed is, it makes total sense.

I wonder if, like Reagan in my comic, Reed went to Catholic school, and if his parents wanted him to gain the skills of musical composition and ability to fluff up his application for colleges. I wonder what they had in mind for him; I wonder if they were shocked when he auditioned for local bands, or if they expected him to.

I wonder what his mom thinks now he's trying so hard to shed the skin of a god-fearing, small-town, whitebread, blue-collared family man by cloaking himself in sex and drugs and rock 'n roll.

I wonder if she blames herself.

You see, this is another key difference in parenting styles. People push their children into becoming so much, and being so much, and knowing so much, and being able to do so much, that when they grow up and have the freedom to channel their own passions and desires, what they want becomes so muddled up with what they should want that they have no idea how to be who they really are, not if it negates everything they were supposed to be.

Be good. Be the best. Be number one.

These may seem like lovely desires for your children, and maybe you think you're encouraging them to be great, but really all you're doing is solidifying in their minds that they aren't great, and that they never will be. By telling them to *be* something, to work *toward* something, you're not telling them that they are something. You're not telling them to see what they are, what they are doing, what they are good at, what they are achieving.

You're not teaching them to live in the present. You're not showing them everything that's wonderful right now. You're teaching them that the desired life or talent or job or definition of success is external to them in this very moment, and they grow up believing that happiness is somewhere to be worked toward, and they're adults who can't look at themselves in the mirror and feel any sort of knowledge or acceptance or confidence because they aren't striving to be themselves; they're striving to be better than who they are presently.

That's why people like Reed are so fucked up at thirty, and why they feel a sudden urgency to attempt to dismantle everything you represent; it's because they've achieved everything you wanted them to achieve— a record deal, a fan base, a career based on talent— and they still aren't happy because their girlfriend left them, and their god isn't living up to his end of the bargain, and they haven't been taught to value themselves unless those false idols, those accessories to success, are presently in their lives.

Luckily for me, having been handed everything, I wasn't taught to strive for anything. Don't work for it. It'll come to you. And so when I sit down with my desires, I don't worry about being single or having a small apartment or caring for no one outside of my fish, because when I'm drawing and sketching and inking and writing, everything that is material around me slips away. None of this matters. I wasn't taught that to be successful I have to gain a lot of money from what I'm doing. Money was just always there. And I wasn't taught that everyone else in the world had to agree with my definition of success because my mother always told me how beautiful I was even when I was sick and pubescent and terrible.

When Reed sits down with his desires, he sees them as comparisons to those of others. *Will this song be the most popular in its genre? If not, if I'm not the best, then what's the point?* But that line of thinking comes directly from the unspoken show-don't-tell of parents of overachievers. *Be the best. Be better. Keep reaching. You aren't good enough where you are now.*

And when that's paired with someone committing themselves to only you and then cheating on you, well, you don't create the ego of someone who is so sure of himself he's able to create whatever he wants regardless of who enjoys it.

So maybe I'm lazy, and maybe there are maggots in my sink, and maybe no one except my grandparents (and after that uncomfortable conversation in the airport, maybe Marty) would care if I died today on this flight, but I know who I am. I know what I create, and I am confident in it. I know it's good. I don't care if other people don't see it. And in return, I not only walk through this life with a better sense of self, but I also walk through it hand-in-hand with people all over the country who come to conventions just to see me and tell me they relate to my characters, and we understand each other.

I think I'm the only person on the planet who understands Reed, and I wonder if music wasn't his choice, or if it was totally his choice, or even if it was partially his choice.

I don't imagine he taught himself so many instruments, nor do I really see it likely that he had a personal passion for each of them.

If it were just singing, or just guitar, or just piano, then maybe. But someone so skilled in all endeavors denotes a sense of overachievement that one is instilled with by their upbringing.

Or maybe that's just the interpretation of someone so apathetic she doesn't even buy food for her apartment. I don't know.

The shift here now with Reed just seems more personal. The change in personas isn't a message to

corporations who deem him too virtuous to be Sid Vicious.
The break from holy to sin seems to be a rebellion the
success of his first band never gave him time or
opportunity to experience.

The one loose end seems to be the perfect girlfriend
to this perfect man in this perfect family with perfect
beliefs. But a quick search of her username, *@JoJoRoy*, with
his reveals that image, the idea, the fantasy, almost never
correlates the reality.

If this picture is worth a thousand words, no would
imagine a string of them reading: *How could you cheat on me?
Wasn't I enough? You always said I was. I thought I was. Why
wasn't I?* but sometimes fiction is more beautiful than
reality, and in those times reality is more painful than
anything we visualize ourselves a part of.

I wonder if she loved him, and saw herself marrying
him, and wanted it to be him with whom she shared a
future when the time to settle down arrived, but at the end
of the day— maybe a really stressful one at work— she
just wanted to get off.

This isn't justifiable because your boyfriend is touring
somewhere far away from you, but I wonder if those
simple necklaces and the coffee shop sit-downs and the
biblical messages hidden inside his lyrics weren't more
deeply ingrained into Reed's psyche than they are for most
people.

I think about my friend, Brad, who was raised
Catholic and hates God so much now that he claims he
doesn't believe in Him. Maybe I'm just projecting, but how
could I write a story without filling in the gaps?

"Oh, my good gosh in heaven," I hear, and there's the
tiniest bit of pressure on my forearm. I look over, and I

see Marty.

With one raise of my arm I both remove his hand from me and point to the earbud in my ear, but he rolls his eyes, a small smile on his lips, and says, "I can hear it when you're listening to music, Bexley." He leans his head around to discreetly look behind us, then in front of us, then he looks back to me. "Everyone can," he says, and he shrugs a little.

I exhale loudly enough that he knows I'm annoyed, but he doesn't shut up.

"Be mad all you want," he says. "But you're a ball of emotion right now. It's visible, and it's very rare, so…" his head tilts a bit, like he's trying to shield himself with his shoulder, and he blinks away before asking, "Is everything all right?"

Everything is fine. I'm all right. I worry for Reed, though, because I can see him so clearly and I feel him so vividly that I can only imagine how utterly alone he is. Can anyone see the writing behind the writing on the wall— the SOS in the blurring eyes of a rock star; the screams of pain spray-painted over by swear words and sin? Why isn't everyone he knows looking at these photos the way I'm looking at them now, seeing the messages Reed is clearly embedding into his art? Why can't anyone appreciate him for how in-depth his talent truly is? It's maddening.

"Oh, Bexley," Marty says, and when I look over to him, he's blurred and out of focus, and my sinuses burn, and there's a tremor in my lungs that feels too powerful to be only physical. "Oh, my goodness." He lifts the seat arm and turns toward me. "Bexley, I…" he places his hand on me again, and his brows are all up in his hairline and crinkled. "Are you crying?"

AMETHYST

Chapter 28
To:
From:
Subject: Closer

I'm just trying to write. Literally I've got my markers and my pens and I've inked everything I've already done.

There's a lot of pressure. As soon as we landed, my phone lit up with Bridget's excitement.

Apparently the opening guy canceled, which she expressed remorse over initially, but then her Brits announced who would be replacing him.

Within a matter of twenty minutes, her emotions swung from disappointment to despair to hopeful to excited. Even-more-excited-than-usual Bridget is worse than Marty.

I don't know what it is about eagerness that digs around at the pores in my epidermis until it creeps inside my skin and makes my entire being seem to crawl with the infection of excitement, but I really hate it.

I can't stand the feeling in my stomach, either— that rolling about that's clearly connected to nerves, but nervousness isn't a part of it, and you're standing totally still in your body, and you're not telling it to move, but that pit inside you that you can't see or touch or hold still just does whatever the fuck it wants anyway.

"Bex, you have to eat something," Marty insists and

my earbuds are still in and I'm staring at my phone, typing out the dialogue for the next few blocks. "Seriously," he says and, again, I feel his hand on me, on my shoulder this time. "You've been working really hard and you've been very focused. It's been great!" I just want to get through this stupidly ornate lobby with its hard, echoing floor and get into my room. "You have to eat and sleep, though. Let me buy you dinner!"

"Okay," I say, taking out an earbud as I stop and turn to him. "Where are you thinking?"

His brows jump up, and his smile grows, and I didn't even think it was possible for him to look more thrilled than he usually does. "Really?" He says, then adds. "I mean, the hotel restaurant seems fantastic. They have vegan options and everything!"

"Yeah," I say, letting my eyes roll around the ceilings and the wallpaper and the visual ambiance of the lobby. "That sounds good." I pop my earbud back in place and hand him one of my keys. "Bring me some kind of chicken wrap. I'll text you if there's wine in my mini-fridge."

"Oh," he says, looking at the key like it's a complexity of life when he takes it. "Okay, I mean, sure, but I thought—"

"You're a doll," I say as I head toward the elevator.

When I get in, I regret everything about myself. What is it with elevators being made of mirrored materials? Especially in hotels. No one looks good rolling into these things. No one.

You're either fresh off of seven hour fucking flight, your hair disheveled and your skin dead-looking because you had be awake at 4:30 in the morning, or you're falling in drunk with some hot guy you met at the hotel bar who isn't even half as attractive in the morning as you remembered.

It's not cute. None of what happens in hotels is. So why are architects constantly trying to show us what we're doing inside them?

Maybe it's some reverse-tactic. Maybe they want us to take a look in the mirror and stop our bullshit, but if that's the case, go be a shrink or a start a cult or become a yoga guru. Whatever. Just don't try to make hotel elevators the sanctuary of our souls.

The only thing less real than the soul is salvation, and the closest thing to salvation is saving someone else.

Someone like Reed. Someone so gloriously ideal. Maybe we've come to better understand him, and maybe his intentions are more clearly artistry and rebellious depth, but that doesn't change the fact that someone so innately good, so unbelievably pure, is setting himself up for disaster by simply faking half of the shit he photographs himself doing.

As I spread my folder out across the dresser with one hand, I go to Reed's Instagram with the other. Of course, he's posted nothing new, so I go automatically to the tags. There's something new from The Sandman— a video of backgrounds appearing red and yellow with his oversaturated signature. Flames are added in. The sounds of screams, some of which sound like they were stolen from satisfying sexual encounters while the others sound like horror film actresses fake-dying in static.

All while Reed sings on his knees, his back hunched over, the only part of his head visible is his purple hair. One hand grips his locks as he breathes life into the room by exhaling his words. Sure, he looks the part of dangerous seduction, and he plays it well, but it can't really be him. Can it?

Maybe he's consumed enough alcohol that drinking vodka from the bottle every night is now ordinary. Maybe he's partook in enough debauchery to think the sin he was singing about in Accentuate the Assent was the norm. Maybe it is.

Maybe Reed went from being a committed guy who posts cute photos of his fiance to the type of guy who gets drunk in strange cities and fucks whoever will have him there. Obviously his taste in wardrobe and women have changed. It wouldn't be a stretch to think it started with something small like blacking out at the bar.

I guess he needs to be corrupt to be saved from it so I draw Reagan as Reed displays himself. I sketch him in a fishnet top with spiked collars. I draw hands with long acrylics unzipping his plastic pants. I draw a blonde standing before him in nothing but a g-string and heels, and I draw his bandmate next to him with his arm around his shoulders, licking the skin above his chain.

Don't get me wrong. This isn't a condemnation. Well, not entirely.

While the part of me that reacts favorably to every objectifying position Reed twists his body into is very much alive, it's only the initial response my body has to the physical sight. Sure, Reed's face is perfectly crafted, and the black he's strewn all around his eyes makes him look doll-like and dead in a way that's far more appealing than it should be, but it makes the creamy tone of his skin all the more obvious, and the brightness of his blue eyes shines more visibly against the drastic black surrounding them.

He's mastered the appearance of innocence during sex.

A fucking genius. Because even with his naked torso exposed, with the tight bindings of a belly-chain connected to his handcuffs, he knows how to tilt his head just so, how to bend his back, how to push his rib cage, and shift his hips. Even his legs and feet— together at the knees but sprawled and disjointed everywhere else— tell us he's about to engage in something primal, something sweaty like the strands of hair falling in his eyes, something dirty like the concrete floor he's lying on, all while expressing some sort of sorrow found in his features. Something that says *I'm getting fucked but only because it takes the pain away.*

I think if he's handcuffed, it's out of his control. He won't need to ask forgiveness for the sin of carnal pleasure if he's chained to the bed and can't escape it.

Oh, Reed, what I wouldn't give to help you in these endeavors, to be the one who brings you to release while absolving you from the guilt of the very same sin.

But this reaction to his photos, this piece of me that's turned on by the idea of 80's Big Hair fucking Reed hard and rough while some woman massages his erection, it's not something that's going to fulfill his need for such photos.

What's going to address the emptiness he feels at the core of his being, what's going to remind him that he is valid and that he does matter and that he is desirable and lovable and perfect as he is, is what I'm creating in honor of his influence: My masterpiece, this retrospective commentary on all that Amethyst is.

And that deadline, it's the date Bridget is so excited about. It's why I have to finish this. Finish this, send it off with Marty to my publisher, and have him copy and piece together an actual physical version of it so I can go to this stupid fucking show, and watch Reed's eyes as he receives my devotional.

Something more spiritual. Something we can't perceive unless we're open to it. This connection he and I share, and my understanding of him, and the unwavering support I can provide, it's what he really needs. It's true friendship. It's devout. I worship.

What I can't understand is why he's confusing people like Simone for people who genuinely care about him. All she's done since their first interaction is proven she's interested in him for his platform. Why would he engage with someone who not only seems too worldly for his experience level but also who openly brags about befriending guys with status? I mean, her tweets range from flirty Instagram messages with band guys to fucking people from TV shows she "won't name but let's just say he's evil incarnate". And her age just means she's spent years perfecting the fuck-to-gain scenario. Crafty bitch. I like her.

His logic though... Is there any here? Or is this the type of person whose low self esteem hurled him into a lifelong cycle of accepting the treatment he thinks he deserves? God, just let me save you, Reed. What the fuck are you doing?

At the height of my emotion, a knock on my door, airy and light, brings me out of my head. I hear the sound of the door opening, and truly the downside of getting lost in Reed is losing concept of time. At least this time I was sketching while I was contemplating.

"Hey, Bex," Marty calls, and I try to hide what I'm working on. "Oh, wow," he says, setting two large reusable bags down on the counter. His hand hovers over the drawing as his body circles the dresser, and when he's face to face with Reagan and his imminent threesome, he gasps.

I roll my eyes and try again to shuffle the page into the folder.

"Oh, wait," he says, looking up to me and smiling nervously. "I wasn't babysitting. It was just... May I?" He reaches toward my stack, and I release my grip of it.

He stares at the sketches. His brows lift and lower and rise and furrow. He leans in as he turns certain pages. His fingers dance across inked versions of Reed, of my Reagan, of Reed as Reagan as Amethyst, and he breathes so audibly it has to be on purpose.

"This is..." he purses his lips, turning toward me while his eyes remain on Reed in my penmanship. When he finally looks at me, he says, "It's dark. It's violent, but not in the way your works usually are. It's not blood and gore and heroes and demons. It's something more internal than physical. Some violence of the spirit." I stare at him in silence, arms folded and closed off. He can tell I'm studying him. "It— it's very good," he stammers.

I eye him still. I keep my arms tight. I try to break him, and he wavers a bit in nervousness, but he doesn't crack.

He offers only another smile, but this one is far more timid than usual.

"Hmm," I twist my lips. No dry skin pulls this time because I'm so used to emotions and physical expressions of them now that I remember to apply chapstick more often.

"What's wrong?" He asks, and I'm waiting for a real opinion, but he says nothing.

"It's good?"

"Yes. It's dirty... Ever grittier than your usual stuff. I

can't say——" he spreads the pages out gently with his fingers. "There's physical violence, sexual violence, drugs, murder... So I can't say I support anything here, but considering the direction of the story and who Reagan is at his core, I wouldn't say your message is that these behaviors are acceptable."

His fingers trace the inked lines of my Serpent Woman, and his eyes devour every pen stroke of her and Reagan's intimacy. "Not that some of it is entirely meritless," he adds. "But context..." he looks up. "Context really matters in these scenarios."

"Yes, it does," I say, and I notice how shaken his hand has become, and I consider all the things he noticed about me that I never would've noticed about anyone. Not anyone except maybe Reed, but then I notice everything about Reed. Even the things he doesn't want anyone to see through layers of persona and filters and filth.

It's this expression of Marty, this new confession that's proven just how shy he really must be inside of all that pep, that allows me to see him as something beyond the unwavering positivity and crisp khakis and button-ups. Something more human about him. Something that reaches out for whatever darkness it can find without actively participating in it, and I wonder if he's drawn to my comics the way some people are drawn to porn. I wonder if he ever engages physically in the thrills he allows himself to mentally consume.

Does he, like Reed, find an outlet for the oppression of a strict moral code by nearing himself to someone who holds so little respect for anything or anyone that she partakes in it all without concern?

If Marty and his bland naivety can be broken, then

surely Reed and his innocent perfection can bend for me.

"Marty," I say, and I rest my hand on his. "What would better context be?"

"Better?" He blinks down and then looks up into my eyes. "I think the story's perfect…"

"I wasn't talking about the story," I say, and I step closer to him, close enough to smell his aftershave, close enough to touch him without having to reach.

He swallows. I hear it. And he looks frightened, but he doesn't back away.

He isn't a part of any darkness, but he'd like to be, and when I move my hand from his, when I slip it up his arm and across his shoulder, his body turns instinctively toward mine. His eyes widen. He doesn't know if I'm Aphrodite and he's my watered-down Ares for tonight, or if I'm a hungry lion about to consume this evening's prey.

"Are you—" he exhales through his lips and then he licks them. His brows are creasing over his eyes but they stare at me, at my lips; they glance worriedly to my eyes. They follow my hand when it comes down from his shoulder.

Marty doesn't need a lot of convincing. He doesn't need orders or commands. He's so naturally submissive that his body bends to the motions of my hands. He's responsive to slight touches, tender pulls.

Before he knows it, he's lying in my bed, and when I unbutton his shirt, I stare at his bare flesh and imagine the inked symbols of Reed's chest. I imagine the collars and the chains with loops made for leashes, and when I urge Marty between my thighs, I look at his brown hair and, in my mind, I paint it purple.

Willingly I hallucinate. I try to remind myself of why

I'm doing what I'm doing.

It's difficult to be so subdued in these moments, to have to adjust my approach to such a need-based desire by considering the delicacy of the other person. But if I take Reed home, if he wants to give himself over to me completely, I can't just fuck him like he doesn't matter. He's already so used to being treated like he doesn't matter; what kind of god would I be if I let him continue thinking it? What kind of friend, or soulmate, or follower would I be? A shitty one. And I'm not going to be shitty to him. I'm not going to hurt his already fragile self perception, and I have to remind myself when I'm reaching into Marty's pants and grabbing him that the hero always sacrifices for the one they love.

The things I do for you, Reed.

No one in your life would put your potential needs before their own, and I say "potential" because I really don't know if you'll want to fuck. I don't know if you ever have. I don't know if that's why you were cheated on. I'm convinced it's got something to do with why half of your slogan invites people into such action.

I see your rebellion, and I know it's only to set right the forces that have destroyed you. You want revenge, Reed, and I get, but I don't know how far you take the cause.

I don't know if you're pretending— is the air of sin punishment enough? I don't know if you're genuinely committing all the acts you boast about. I don't know if you're rebelling by performing sinful deeds or if the rebellion is a product of your rage.

Trust me, you have every right to be angry.

Everyone has failed you. Your parents who sheltered

you, your ex who took advantage of that, the record labels who didn't prepare you for the people who bullied you so publicly. People like your guitarist who uses your rebellion for shock value. People like Simone who seek to be envied.

You're a pawn to everyone you've ever met. Until me.

Me, I'm lying in a hotel bed with pictures I've drawn of you strewn about like the idolatry of some great god, and here I straddle Marty as a form of worship.

I'm preparing myself for you, Reed, for the things you might one day need from me, and when I lower myself onto him, when I feel his body connect with mine in a way you brag about but have probably never experienced, I hope you're lying in a hotel bed too, and I hope you're thinking of me— of the woman you wished your ex was, the woman Simone will never be, the woman who will love you and cherish you and won't ask you to change so that she's capable of it. I hope you're thinking of me, this potential perfect partner, and I hope you're sliding your hand down your abdomen, your fingers fluttering over the prominent bone of your hip, and I hope you're hesitant.

I hope the world hasn't corrupted you. I hope you haven't wanted it to. I hope you feel a flicker of shame for what your hand is about to do because that's what the innocent Reed I know would feel, and I hope you do it anyway.

When I imagine you, Reed, I see your eyes closing delicately. I see your secret lips parting. I can hear the soft expulsions of air you try to force through your nose, but the expansion of your lungs is too heavy, too fast, and I hear the way the air rolls from your unwilling lips instead, in the form of a moan.

These things, these images and sounds, they're what

keep me from grabbing Marty's hair and jerking his head back. They're what stop me when I want to sink my teeth into his lower lip, his neck, his skin.

I'm in control of my body. I don't let it run on instinct. I move with careful precision, slowly, slowly, slowly, and I do it because I know you won't want the violent delights you say you do.

Climaxing is easy, ladies, if you forget where you are, and because I'm lost somewhere with Reed, Marty starts clamoring. "Oh, Bex, did you— Oh, wow. Oh, that was... You're beautiful... That sound... I'm trying—"

I want to tell him to shut his fucking mouth, but then this endeavor would've been pointless. I'm learning. I'm changing. I'm adapting to what my muse might want, not because he is important, but because I think he is.

A god appreciates her subjects, and Reed has given so much to me that this is the least I can do, and honestly I didn't realize how difficult it would be.

When I feel Marty's hands on my back, I want to rip them away. I want to throw them off. I want to press him into the bed, using my shins to pin those wandering arms down, and let him use his tongue to pleasure me because, really, he's so fucking lucky I'm letting him enjoy this time too.

But I don't. I wouldn't want to scare Reed when I have him. He's too delicate for any type of domination, no matter how many submissive collars he wears.

He might think it looks appealing, but we'll have to work him up to it.

Mine. I hear it again, and it's all in good time. It's coming. And so is Marty.

Chapter 29
To:
From:
Subject: Bathbombs

Fucking Marty bought me bathbombs. They were in the second bag he brought with the food.

"I know they're not your style," he said, "but they're very relaxing."

Fucking was relaxing, but I suppose he didn't know that was going to happen.

The bathbombs are shaped like snowflakes, and it's so obnoxiously holly-jolly I'd throw them away if it weren't an obvious sign from the universe.

I brought a board to go across the tub so I could sketch in here, but the light is too bright. Invasive. I feel like I'm on display.

So I took the snowflake in my hand, careful not to crack its delicate, compacted powder, and I carved with my nail the lines that would transform it into a Star of David.

It's remarkable how similar in appearance these two holiday shapes are— just as Reed and Amethyst are twin souls inhabiting one body.

What's troublesome about such a similarity, however, is how very misleading it can be.

The Star, a powerful symbol which some interpret as the union of the six male segments of god with the seven female ones, is also called the Shield of David. A shield; a protective symbol, one that meant death in a particularly dark point in human existence. This symbol has represented a peoples' great faith for the three knots of the Holy One, blessed be He; Torah; and Israel. Six basic lines crossed into something so vast and old and profound that it displays the extremes of both the beauty of the soul and the agony of the flesh.

Take this symbol in comparison to similarly shaped snowflake. This seasonal representation of something small and meaningless. What did snow indicate but December weather? It denotes nothing of faith or hope or love. It bears no reminder of suffering, and offers nothing to be respected. It's inconsistent and changeable. It freezes. It melts. It evaporates. It's nothing, and it represents nothing.

Seeing the Star, witnessing its basic lines, proves that splendor and beauty aren't always housed in the more ornate and eye-catching branches of points and circles and waves of something intricate like a snowflake. It reminds us that internal power doesn't need flashy appearances. It proves that something powerful can be as small as a pendant and that something insignificant can be broad enough to cover miles of land.

It shows Amethyst in his pinks and glitters and zebra-striped pants as all surface with no substance, and holds Reed in plain hair and t-shirts as the ultimate vessel of morality and truth.

As I lower the snowflake-turned-Star into my water, witnessing it crumble as the invading liquid surrounds and seeps inside it, a vision overtakes my mind so vividly that what my eyes view here in the physical realm is imperceptible to me.

What overtakes reality is an image of Reed, of the darkness surrounding him drawing nearer and nearer to him. It follows him from all sides when he walks, and when he looks over his shoulder to ensure his escape, the black walls of spiritual decay are brushing against his back.

He grips the opened sides of the jacket he's wearing, pulling them across his chest, holding the jacket closed around him tightly, and his shoulders rise around his neck, and his steps quicken, but instead of running from the darkness, he walks inside it.

He can't go anywhere that it won't follow, and as he sings, it trickles down across his notes to turn them dull and gray, and it creeps inside his open mouth, slithers down his throat, and coats his lungs with its despair.

He chokes. He grasps at his neck, but the darkness, once a mist, is thickening with each expulsion of his newly-crafted words, and it's oozing down the walls around him, spilling onto the ground at his feet until they're covered in its oily manifestation.

It climbs up his legs, wrapping around his thighs like vines, and spreads across his pelvis, his hips, and up his back.

Reed falls to the ground, his palms bracing his fall and getting stuck in the discharge. The disembodied darkness coats his hands, rises up his forearms until it courses across his shoulders and meets the void he's gagging up from his lungs.

His face, his eyes, his secret lips, his throat, all are covered in the phantom liquid. It's overtaken his body. Reed is drowning in the darkness.

After a long moment, maybe an eternity, slowly,

revealing only centimeters of creamy flesh at a time, it dissipates. It looks as if it's falling away, slipping off of his body, but nothing pools on the ground or at his feet.

As more flesh becomes exposed, I witness the sticky ooze, not falling away from Reed, but seeping inside him; his pores absorb it more and more until his appearance is free of it.

Reed, once a victim of the stalking footsteps of the void, is now a house to it.

It lives inside him, festering and gurgling until his hands rush to his hair, and in fists he tugs at the locks until they tremble and shake and curl and twist and become purple.

He screams, and his cries come out differently than his songs— empty and hollow and meaningless— his throat shackled now by chains and collars, and the sound of his own voice causes him to weep.

The tears slip from his eyes in thick, black droplets, and when he wipes at them, they smear their darkness over and under and across his radiant blue eyes.

It dulls them until his countenance is unrecognizable, and his body bends and twists and stands in the discomfort of the invading entity.

Nothing of Reed remains externally. Now, as I look at him, I see only Amethyst.

And for a moment after the vision clears, I'm still not in reality.

My mind sticks to Reed, to Amethyst, to everything that he might never have been if it weren't for whatever shift changed him so profoundly.

I wonder if it was the constant pushing to perfection of his parents. I wonder if it was the rigidness of his upbringing. I wonder if it was his cheating girlfriend, or the endless comments on Accentuate the Assent's photos telling him he looks like a girl and that his religion is bullshit, that their lyrics contradict their faith when they swear, and that these metal musicians look like members of a generic boyband.

I mean, there was so much darkness encompassing him that he surely wasn't even aware of. So much disrespect, so much contempt. Hate. Jealousy. Disloyalty. I really can't be shocked that he broke in the face of it, but I am impressed with the strength it took to withstand it for so long.

I just can't understand why someone with such radiant energy would be receiving so much negativity. Everyone in the world is you pushed out; the universe responding to itself.

How could he receive anything but love and pride and loyalty back?

He praised his fiance publicly. He put his soul into his songs. Everything he did was innately himself, and now he's manufactured that once-intrinsic divinity.

Manufactured.

I bring my sketch pad to the board across the tub, and I look at my drawings of Reagan. I see Reed in him, even when he's absorbed in Amethyst.

Or maybe Amethyst is a part of Reed.

One can repress evil thoughts, can't they?

House them but choose not to act?

I'm not saying Reed hasn't been corrupted, but what kind of person would fake a friendship to gain a bit of validation in his new persona?

I mean, let's think about it. Let's think about when

Reed first started showing up on Facebook in chains and leather. Let's think about this rebranding and let's consider what type of audience he would be newly targeting.

Surely by spraying *FUCK EACH OTHER* across your banner and your album, you'd be targeting an adult audience. You'd be targeting the antithesis of your Christian-metal-electronic fan-base.

Maybe this was all an endeavor to be seen as something more widely accepted as masculine. Through reckless living, through the drugs and the sex, through the friendships of porn stars and punk rock girls, Reed solidified Amethyst to anyone watching him that he was, in fact, a rock star.

Donned in the traditional trappings of an 80's hairband nightmare and a 70's rebellion of punk rock, Reed must have been smart enough to know that appearances only go so far, and on top of the myriad of insults already hurled at his face, hair, accessories, and persona, surely "fake" or "poser" weren't ones he wanted to add to the list.

So he takes pictures at bars with drinks in his hands. He leans over railings like his limbs are liquid from the intoxication, and he holds empty bottles over his head so we associate his lips and his tongue and his mouth to the liquified icon of altered perception and the sweetness of its poison.

He does that, sure, but isn't that all still his projection?

A card of fate dealt to him when, through the various posts and throwbacks and obsessions over his songs, a tweet comes through from someone who catches his eye.

Jealousy might say it was because she's pretty. Judgment might say it was because he's sexist.

Truth reveals itself, however, as I sit here in the fizzing mess of snowflakes and stars and symbols and the synergy of good versus evil, in the form of arbitrary numbers we recognize on this plane of existence as dates.

What better way to promote your new edgy band to a hundred thousand dudes addicted to sex and sex idols all while solidifying yourself as sexual and deviant than to befriend women who, with a single tweet, can do both?

A part of me rejoices. If he's using them, he doesn't want to be them, and if he doesn't want to be them, then he isn't Amethyst, not fully anyway. But the other part of me is disappointed. I'm downright angry. He is *using* them if that's the case, and if he's using them— even for just a hit of their own respective statuses— then he's somehow worse than the guys who only follow them for the photos they jerk off to.

At least they aren't doing anything these women aren't fully aware of.

I draw Reagan as Reed as Amethyst, but this time instead of the serpent woman lingering between his legs to tempt him, he stands alone, faceforward. Snakes slither around his wrist and rest against his leg. Their eyes beat inside of his, and when he speaks, it's with their forked tongues.

My phone lights up and it's a new photo of Reed, and I won't be tempted. I am the master of the universe held in my hands and it's my pen that commands Reed inside of Reagan.

If my God won't bend to the will of his supporting-soul and story, I'll make him.

But something tells me his strength of mind falls prey to anyone with an assertive tone.

Be genuine and good, Reed, his mother might have said and so he was. *Be bad, Reed, and be a rock god,* the masses could've countered, and so he did.

Be you, Reed, I'm saying here in these pages, and he'll finally be allowed to see the world through his own perspective.

I just pray to whatever god, if any, is out there that who he is isn't Amethyst.

Chapter 30
To:
From:
Subject: A Table in a Sea of Tables

"How does it end?" Marty asks, and when I look over to him, I see that he's flipped through every inked block I've completed. "You've got to be close," he says, "I can feel the tension building between the Serpent Woman and Reagan's friend."

"It doesn't matter how it ends," I say, and I look back down to sketches of Reagan dressed as Reed dressed as Amethyst, standing in the middle of an empty city street, snow falling all around him.

Like I dreamt last night, his breath is visible and he stares at the puffs of heat as they absorb into the air. They remind him that he's alive. They confirm it. Everything around him is numb.

Since the void filled him, there's been nothing. No sensations of pain or of pleasure, and every sin provided to him by the Serpent Woman in my text— by the myriad of serpentine people feeding off of Reed's innocence and creativity in our realm— has promised sensitivity, both emotional and physical.

Dismayed by the breaking of these promises, but no longer disillusioned by the falsehood of their hopeful expectations, Reed has accepted his defeat.

He no longer anticipates the sting of tearing flesh when he smashes his guitar and splinters stab into the skin beneath his nails, nor does he await the euphoric release at the climax of his intimacies.

I've witnessed it through visions and in dreams.

I've seen Reed try to live by God's righteous commands, and now I watch him exist separately from them.

But there is only so much love and loyalty one can express without receiving any back before giving and giving without gaining leaves an empty hole in the belly of the believer.

In time, that hole, empty and unprotected— left vulnerable without the shield of belief and hope, weakened by the expectation of turmoil and pain— becomes sore with heartache and infected by fear until these gut wrenching conjectures fester and ooze and seep into the mind.

Once the mind is invaded, once the fairytale expectations turn sour, once the wearer of this wound winces away from anyone or anything that could potentially love them, there is almost no returning. Not without the aid of someone so understanding, so divine, so godly that she could only be his savior.

With Reed standing on the precipice of a changing paradigm, he can either look up to the vast universe above him and see that his fate was written in galaxies with a pen and a paper and a woman ready to clean him with caresses and heal his sores with consideration and attentiveness, or he can choose to stare down into the rocks below him, grip each side of his open rib cage with his blistered hands, and rip it open enough to house the destructive hallucinations and naked, nameless bodies which caused the spreading of his internal sickness.

Nothing matters in this life when a person is placed here at this crossroads, when the universe begs him to reconsider all he's experienced and he's ever known and toss it aside for everything opposite of the future he envisioned.

"I don't know what Reagan will choose," I say to Marty, and I uncap the pen that solidifies everything thin and frail and gray into thick, unrelenting black. "Which path would you choose?" I look up to him, and his eyes are intent on mine. His brows pull together, a hint of motion shifts his lips, and as they open to speak, he's interrupted by a man holding one of my comics.

"Hey," he says. "Can I still get an autograph?"

"Certainly, you can!" Marty's pep returns— and thank God. I wouldn't want to break his little brain with some spiritual debate between desire and destruction— and after he takes the man's money, he slides the comic in front of me.

"Hi, Bexley," he says. "I mean, is that okay that I call you Bexley?"

"It's my name," I say. "What's yours?"

"Jacob," he tells me and I write it across the cover. "Wow," he breathes. "I mean, sorry, but, like, just the way you write the letters. Pretty rad that you're writing my name. Like, that's me you're writing to."

"Yeah," I say and try to smile, but all I can think of is how natural Reed's smiles look— all big and wide and full of perfect teeth— in every three second video I've ever seen of him autographing something for a fan of Grape Gardens.

"Lotta the times," Jacob says, "When I read your stuff, I think you're writing to me too."

"Maybe I am," I say, and I consider what subconscious, higher-self experience pushed Reed's pen in the direction of words like *stillness* and *runaway* and *angels*, and I wonder if everything everyone in the divine circle of humanity creates only exists because someone else, someone they've never even met before, needed to hear it, or read it, or witness it.

"Wh—what?" Jacob looks confused when I look up to him for the first time since he stepped in front of my banner, and then he says, "Holy shit, you're really that pretty in person."

"Thanks," I say, and I wonder if he's ever even looked at my Instagram photos.

"Just figured a lot of that was filter," he says.

"We filter ourselves enough for other people," I say. "Insignificant things like how we really feel about someone, or what we really think of something are naturally filtered through our brains before we say them out loud. I can't imagine filtering something as important as a face."

"Oh, yeah," he chuckles. "Your commentary on how the world works," he taps the comic I hand back to him. "It's what makes your shit so good."

"Thanks," I say, and a thought occurs to me. "So, wait, you're saying your interest in these books isn't the violence, or the sex, or the paranormal creatures?"

"I mean, that stuff's badass, especially the way you draw tits," he pauses, briefly horrified by himself. "Sorry. I mean, that stuff's cool, but I like the way it all means something, too. Makes you feel like less of a loser if your hero-porn-vampire slayer fantasy says something serious about your culture when you close the page, you know?"

"Yeah," I say, and I think about Reed, and his displays of violence and sex and alien status. "Yes, I know. Thank you, Jacob."

"Yeah, cool," he smiles. "Thank you."

The pressure of Marty's gaze is on me so I look over to him. "So it doesn't matter how it ends," he says. "But it has to have an ending."

I honestly don't even want to consider it.

A part of me, the part that reaches out for Reed, is too eager to hold a pencil correctly. I want it finished. I wanted it completed. I want to hold it in my hands, but that's the part that twists my stomach into knots.

The thought of something so spiritual and so cerebral becoming physical. It seems a miracle. But it's just clutter.

Making more shit seems pointless. Creating seems counterproductive to the point where it becomes destroying.

The world is cluttered and where's it all going to go when I die? Who's going to keep it? Whose closet is it going to junk up?

Or will it go in a landfill, and when will those fill up? When will we have to tear down rainforests to make more garbage dumps, when will we have so much trash that we can't keep the purifying trees?

Forests will be a luxury. We'll look back on them as treasures we took for granted. The dystopian future every writer of the 50's foresaw was full of machines and robots and humanity falling victim to their control.

We here in 2019 live that fiction turned reality. We don't fear our technological captors. We've got Stockholm syndrome far more than Belle ever had with the Beast. We fall asleep with our phones next to our faces and we hold them in the morning the way we used to hold the ones we love.

Yeah, the sci-fi writers of the past got it right. Like I said, we're the closest to god a mortal can get. And what we see now is a future without machines, one without plants or animals or many people. We're killing everything that helps us live because we love everything that doesn't matter, and eventually all the shit I create, all my books, all the crafts people sell all over Etsy— there are going to be too many of them for the world to hold.

Down with the trees.

We don't have the luxury of having woods. We need space for our shit because all we really produce is shit. And fuck it if Reed doesn't agree, if he's pure enough to think art is magical in all the right ways. It's evil. Prophets and false idols. Ancient Greece. We predict the fall of civilizations and instead of hearing our divinity, the human-humans burn us at the stake or lock us in straight jackets. We're forced into lobotomies if we're female. We're ridiculed for our sensitivities if we're male. Who gives a fuck anymore? I don't.

It's all for Reed, I tell myself, and a voice replies, *Mine.*

```
Chapter 31
To:
From:
Subject: Home is Where the Heart is
```

Marty thought we'd be having dinner together after the convention. I corrected him.

"Well, our flight doesn't leave for six hours," he'd said.

"That's about three hours of work," I told him.

I should've spent the time napping because by the time we board, it's pitch black outside and I'm ready for a warm body and a bed. Not Marty's. Not again.

I think of Reed, of how close we are to finally forming the final piece of our growing friendship-bond.

I imagine us touching, killing the other's skin cells with a brush of the hand; peeling away small pieces of one another when we embrace, and swallowing the cells of the other when we kiss. I imagine us sharing DNA, sharing atoms, becoming one body.

We're one spirit, aren't we?

How incredible it might feel to meld our physicalities together until the space we occupy is filled with one mind, one soul, one being.

I fell asleep.

And now that I'm awake and looking at my phone, I really wish I hadn't.

A notification tells me Vinny thinks my apartment is indicative of something diagnosable, and that's not even the worst.

An alert tells me that Reed tweeted in the middle of the night. At three a.m., and I wonder if he was awake on a bender after his set, or if he was locked away in his room, looking out at the foreign city before him, wondering why he's alone both in this moment and in life without a partner.

AMETHYSTALIEN @reedbarry
Honestly don't know why I try. Deep down, I wanna find someone. It'd probably be nice to be in love. Just keep pushing people away, Reed. Your defenses are so high.

I swear to God, we *are* one person.

I want to reply to it. I want to message him. I want to tell him that I know why he pushes people away, and that he's right to. I want to tell him how no one in his life is worthy of him, and how no one appreciated him how they should've.

I understand why he's defensive. I know where these mechanisms come from.

I'm here, Reed, you don't have to scold yourself ever again. I won't let you. I'm here to lift you up, to remind you of your beauty, and make you see that other peoples' mistreating you was a product of their idiocy, and not a commentary on your worth.

You're worth everything, Reed. You're the world to me.

But I swipe the notification, and I click "view", and I

try to see the tweet, to see his name and his handle and his photo above it, to see the timestamp, to view it all in its original form, but it's gone.

Tweet unavailable.

He deleted it.

It must have been one of those moments where your logic can't reign over your emotions. That second of truth slipping by inside a lie. Those moments when the world is crashing around you and the barista at a coffee shop asks how you are and you almost cry.

But he caught himself. And he deleted it.

And it's fine.

No one needs to see that side of him. The world isn't worthy.

But I saw it, and no matter how badly we both choke on the desire to experience care and concern and connection, when our eyes meet for the first time, he'll never again question why no one else was right for him.

I'm here. And he's mine.

Mine.

I go through his replies. Nothing new. I look at his likes. Nothing new. I go to Instagram. No new posts. No new story. No one's screenshot the tweet and tagged him in it.

No evidence.

Maybe it didn't even happen. Maybe this was a private conversation— the universe talking to me. A confirmation. The time has come.

I hurry through the airport. I tell Marty I'm heading home and that after he gets my bags, he needs to head there too.

For a moment he thinks I'm wanting to spend time

with him, but no, I don't. "The story," I say. "I didn't bring it all."

Marty keeps what I took with me. He needs to get it to the publisher. He needs to stop at Staples before that, though, and make me a copy. He needs to bind it nicely so it doesn't look like a copy of a manuscript. I need to give it to Reed.

Better yet, a digital copy would be more secure. A failsafe. Bridget might spill a drink. It might rain.

"Scratch that," I yell as I run away from him, "Make me an ebook!"

When we arrive, I'm quick to rush in.

After I check on my fish, I gather up the missing pages, and I attempt to exchange them for my bags at the door.

"I've got it, Miss," he winks, and I think he's trying to be flirty. He maneuvers around me, "Where shall I drop them off? They are on their own little trip still, aren't they?"

"They've reached their destination," I try not to groan. "Just drop them there."

"Well, not on the ground," he smiles and waltzes over to the bar that separates the entrance room from the kitchen. He's about to place the designer duffle bag down but then he recoils all at once. "Oh, Bexley," he gasps. "Oh, my goodness gracious graces."

"It's fine," I say without trying to prevent myself from groaning, though I don't know what he's seeing.

"It's not! When is the last time you cleaned in here?"

"I Swiffer once a month," I say and shove the pages against his chest. "Have you forgotten the part where I need this immediately?"

"Oh, sorry," he says, "Of course not."

It's an awkward goodbye because Marty leans in, like he thinks he's going to kiss me, and I tell him we aren't a couple. "Just get the copies bound up nicely," I say. "And send me an ebook."

Then I text Natalie.

You know what time it is.

She must be editing because she replies before I can even unzip one of my bags entirely:

Done already? That's gotta be a record. Are you back from ny yet?

I reply: *Just got back.*

The usual then? She texts.

Thirty mins?

Perfect.

We have this agreement, Natalie and I. We read one another's books before publishing. Just to get some feedback. This one is more important than the masses though. This one is for Reed. This is going to save him. It has to be perfect.

I throw my laptop bag on my shoulder, and I send Vinny a quick thank you text for feeding my fish, promising him dinner as a thank you, but we haven't actually hung out just the two of us in months.

I text Marty, telling him to pull over, take photos of every single page of my book and text them to me in order. When he asks why, I tell him to just fucking do it. I tell him he has thirty minutes.

No sooner than I sit down in my car and turn it on, I hear my text alert. Then another.

Since I haven't left the garage yet, I check them to

make sure he's getting everything in the photo, that they're legible, not blurry.

They're fine, but I don't text any approval, and as I back out of the garage, the alerts keep pinging.

When I walk into the only twenty-four-hour diner in town, Natalie is already there.

I sit down across from her, and slide her my phone.

"What's this?" She asks.

"The manuscript is with Marty."

"Well, why am I reading it if it's already at the publisher?"

"Because," I groan as I pull my laptop from the bag. Haven't we discussed this? "Marty has to get me a copy together before Tuesday."

"Because?"

"Because of Reed," I say, opening the laptop and then my email. Doesn't anyone pay attention to me?

"Reed?" She huffs. "The guy you think is your destiny?"

"He's not my destiny," I roll my eyes. "He's God."

"And the role of the book is... You're saving him, right?"

"Just read it," I say, and I take a sip of coffee, and I watch her roll her eyes.

I can tell she wants to fight it. She doesn't want to get lost in this story. She wants to be able to say it's terrible so she can prove me wrong about Reed. She wants me to be serious.

Before she knows it, though, she's leaning closer to the phone. She's zooming in on certain pictures. Her brows jump and crease and wriggle.

I type. I write. I document this— our story— and then I go to Instagram.

I study the new photos people from last night's show have tagged him in, and I'm so frustrated about falling asleep on these overnight flights.

I should've been there for him. I should've been watching.

People have saved images and reposted them. Reed was busy last night. While I slept. He was at a party. It was dark but what was visible looked unimpressive.

Someone screenrecorded a video posted to The Sandman's Instagram story.

He sat at a round, particleboard-looking table. The necessities for rolling joints were spread across it. He took a hit, handed it up to Reed who stood beside him.

Reed, decked out in black and pink and chains and spikes; Reed who, by image alone, embodied all that was rebellion and sin. Reed smiled shyly. He looked downward.

The Sandman, still gripping it between his fingers, pushed it toward Reed's secret lips.

Whoever was holding the phone hollers encouraging peer pressure.

Allowing the joint to touch his lips, Reed looks as he did when Baby Face Big Hair's lips pressed into his own. He allows the sin. He doesn't fight the contact. But he isn't comfortable in it. He isn't causal. And when The Sandman cheers with the phone-holder, when Reed looks away shyly, a puff of smoke slips from Reed's open lips, but not in the smooth linear exhale of someone who'd inhaled the substance. A cloud. It comes from the mouth, not the lungs.

Reed tries. He really does. But he won't have to fake anything. Not anymore. Not with me.

It's beautiful, really.

Sad in a way.

I mourn Reed's loss of himself while I rejoice in seeing he remains.

Maybe purity can overtake the void after all.

Amethyst won't win.

Mine, the voice growls to me, and I realize the only person standing in my way is him. The Alien.

But the timer is counting down, and it won't be long until I'm standing face to face with him, ready to exhume his corpse from the defeat and disappointment the world has hurled at him, untie him, free him, allow him to rise from the dirt which has stained his soul and resurrect the beauty of his past.

Whether or not he's given up on the idea, salvation is an option, and I am more than qualified to be the deliverer of purity from the void.

"Well," Natalie says, and I look at the time in the corner of the laptop.

Somewhere between seven a.m. and now, she'd plugged in my phone. I'd say time is irrelevant, but that's not true. To be relevant, something must exist, and this email draft diary proves that time doesn't.

How else would two hours of pleasure or of fantasy feel like ten minutes? How else would ten minutes of torture feel like an eternity?

I wonder how long those seconds felt to Reed when eyes were on him, insisting he confirm his deviance; all the while he knew his foot would never slip even the slightest step out of the strict moral line.

"Well?" I say, but it isn't a curiousness that causes the word to come. It's a dare. I dare her to question me now. I dare her to insult our connection. Call me crazy. I'm ready to hear it.

"I can't believe you did this in under a month," she leans back. Her brows are raising as she stares down to the phone, then her eyes blink up at mine. "You wrote it, you drew it, you inked it. It's complete."

"It's a biography," I say, "They take less time than fictions because their events have already happened."

"Sure," she says, coming back to the table. Looking up to me, raising only one brow now, she says, "But you don't know that these things happened, and if they did, there's a lot more to reality than human beings have ever considered."

"Yes," I say, "That's the point."

"Okay," she exhales. "Okay, you share something with this random guy you've never met. Let's say I believe that. What happens if he doesn't?"

My face twists so badly I think I've pulled some muscles in it. She stares at me.

"What?" I tsk. I scoff. The nerve. "Have you read it?"

"Yeah, and it's a good story, but it's not his life."

"It's a representation of it."

"Bex, there are demons who turn good guys bad—"

"For a writer, you're taking this very literally."

"Because I'm afraid you're taking it literally."

"Oh, please," I say, taking my phone back. "Don't be afraid for me."

"Bexley," she says, following suit when I stand up.

I close my laptop. I don't need to see Reed, not like this, and I don't show her because she doesn't deserve him.

And I don't know why I thought this conversation would go any better than our last. "You're being extremely idealistic, and trust me, I never thought I'd say that to you. That's why I'm so worried."

"Everyone's worried when I don't care. Everyone's worried when I do," I say.

"Maybe there's something to that," she says.

"There isn't," I say, but there is cause for concern.

Reed is a spiritual being. Everything he does is art. Even now, even dressed as some paradoxical 80's dream, an amalgamation of opposites, it all comes together on his body in a way that's not only aesthetically pleasing, but also indicative of each little segment of his personality.

He's Vicious because he wishes he were more aggressive. He's Bowie because he's beautiful.

Throw a blanket around his shoulders and he'd be the reincarnated Christ, or at the very least a hyper-sexualized Gandhi.

"Maybe just appreciate the story he gave you."

"He didn't give me a story," I say. "He gave me his life."

Chapter 32
To:
From:
Subject: Vinny

"Hey," I say as I enter the clinic from the side door.

"Oh, hey, Bexley," Angel says. "Vinny watch your fish again?"

"He did."

"Where'd you go?"

"New York."

"Oh, so fun!"

"It was fine," I say, because it wasn't fun. It was tedious and tiring, and I had to put a lot of work into that novel to get it done on time, and it was difficult being so near to Marty.

All for Reed, I think, and a voice replies, *Mine.*

"Did you bring him more thank-you muffins?"

"Not quite," I say, and she really should be focusing on her work. I'd like Vinny to get finished on time today.

"You're later than usual," she says.

"Uh-huh," I reply, and I take out my phone.

I open Instagram. I type an R in the search and click the first name listed in my suggestions.

"You're usually a thank-you breakfast person," she continues, and, no, I'm not a breakfast person; I'm not even a morning person. Coming here early is appealing, however, because they've got the entire day ahead of them and I can be in and out quickly.

Today, after talking with Natalie, requires a bit more time.

The things I fucking do for Reed.

"Oh, Miss Martin," Vinny says as he emerges from a room.

"Hey, Doc," I say.

"How are Marlowe and Chaucer?" He grins as he hands Angel some paperwork. "Am I in trouble?"

"Quite the contrary," I say, and the paper bag crunches something beautiful when I lift my arm a bit. "I brought thank-you presents."

"No cookies or coffee or muffins first thing in the morning?" He smiles and his face looks like a Ken doll's.

"That's what I said," Angel chimes in.

"No, I was actually thinking we'd do a thank-you dinner this time. Spice it up."

"Well, we're done as soon as Angel gets this last client checked out. What'd yah have in mind?"

"Pizza. Delivery."

He grins.

"And I have cream soda," I say as I open the bag and show him its contents.

"Like old times," he says.

"Like old times."

"All right. Cool," he giggles a little and takes his keys from his pocket. Holding one up, he says, "How about you head up and get the pizza ordered, and give me, say, fifteen minutes?"

"Perfect," I say, and the keys are in my hand.

Mission half-say accomplished, and I go outside. The

keys aren't labeled so I climb the wooden stairs to his apartment.

For whatever reason, I imagined his keyring would only hold three keys— his clinic, his pharmacy inside it, and his home above it.

I imagined that they were all labeled as well.

While I call the pizza place down the street, I sit on the futon. Still such a frat guy. Total bachelor. I respect that. But this place is all marble floors and old wood-carving railings. He should've let Bridget have this place. Her room's decor is ostentatious but in the right way.

"Schavell's," a voice says. "Todd speaking."

"I need to place an order," I respond, picking up one of the keys and scanning for any marks that might suggest what it unlocks. "Delivery."

"Sure," the phone says, and I recite the same order Vinny and Bridget and I used to get as I lift up two more keys and try to find a mark, a line, a dot. Anything.

The phone repeats my order, and I interrupt, "Wait, no, no wings. Those were for Bridget."

"Okay, no wings," the phone grumbles, and why would one person have so many keys? "Give us fifteen," the phone says after I tell it Vinny's address.

"Sure," I say, "And, Todd," I drop the keys and look to the phone, "If you were a pharmacy key, what would you look like?"

```
Chapter 33
To:
From:
Subject: Men who aren't Reed
Section Two
```

I'm not entirely sure how we've gotten here. To say my logic is becoming flawed would be an understatement, and I have to wonder if this qualifies as a crime of passion.

If you're still here with me, if you're still reading, close the binder. Delete the email. If this is the printed page in a manila case file, put it back inside and burn it. Erase your hard drive. Erase mine.

What follows now acts more as a confession than a diary entry, I realize that. But I suppose I continue on because I believe so strongly in the intended outcome of the universe, of God, of whatever puppet master is pulling all of our strings.

You see, the alcohol was a must, especially when I discovered the pharmacy key wasn't going to be so easily stolen, and I never wanted to hurt Vinny. He'd just get a little tipsy. He'd get drunk. Maybe he'd black out and wouldn't remember taking me to the pharmacy or giving me its key. Either way, he'd wake up and just remember having a fun evening with me, and I'd be home with Marlowe and Chaucer preparing for the impossible idea— fucking thanks, Natalie— that Reed may not come willingly.

Instead, I awoke on Vinny's couch to the sound of his wailing.

"What the—" he's exhaling, panting. He groans.

"You're fine," I yell in response.

"Bex?" He shouts. "Bex, what the fuck?"

"It's fine, Vinny." I am so tired of this shit.

I guess I remembered his tolerance being a lot different than it is now. I mean, when his eyes fell shut during our third movie, I thought he passed out.

I slipped away, still careful of disturbing him, with his keys.

After trying two of them in the back door of the clinic— which is attached to the apartment in the same sense a basement might be, though there is an actual basement, and a garage on its other side— I gained entrance to it.

I went beyond the reception area, walked by the ten or twelve exam room doors until I found the door, discreetly hidden between the employee restroom and the x-ray room, that would open into the pharmacy.

For future reference, Bexley, none of the brass keys unlock the pharmacy, even though the knob is brass. Smart, Vinny. Very smart. And, Bexley, it's none of those little silver ones with the round tops that look like mailbox keys or something. So congratulations, Vinny, you threw the potential drug thief off twice. It's not logical, then it is. Not brass, normal size.

And maybe it was the heat of the moment, maybe it was some weird guilt for thinking about stealing from Vinny, I'm not sure— I know it wasn't concern for Reed because I knew, and I still know, that he's going to see me and follow me anywhere— but the name of the drug I'd need to sedate someone, to make them pliable, was completely absent from my mind.

A vision as clearly in mind as reality was before me. Instead of seeing my hands there in that room, scavenging drawers for drugs, I saw them in a memory scanning old notes for previous novels— notes given to me by Vinny for a comic called Darkened Deals. *Special K*, my mind said, and then it whispered, *Mine*.

I scanned for drugs beginning with "K", still uncertain if Special K was even something I'd find here. Perhaps that had been from a different comic. My mind was frantic, screaming at me about how I should retain some of the real-world shit I write about when I'm accessing these other realms.

I wished, at that moment, that this were all part of some great fiction I'd been writing, that this were a line in Reed's story of freedom, so that a person from somewhere far away might whisper the words I needed to me.

Instead, the door flew open and Vinny stood menacingly in its frame.

"Bex?" He said in his deep voice. Confusion painted across the bits of his face not cast in the shadows of the dark room.

I'd remembered that one from the shady types in my writing— don't turn on the lights if you're doing something sneaky and/or illegal.

"What are you doing?" He asked, the same stern tone in his voice.

I know I pursed my lips— quickly as I'd developed my new habit for chapstick, I'd forgotten it— then I offered, "Research."

"Research?" He said, and I'd begun to worry Vinny might actually be upset. Then he swayed, caught himself on the frame, and laughed. "Why does research bring you to my pharmacy?" He was still smiling and stepping into the room.

"Well, it…" I blame the alcohol for my slow response. I'd been planning on not getting shit-faced drunk at Reed's show Monday night, but now I'm thinking it should be a water only kind of night. "Like," I played up that drunk-girl voice I've heard a million times over at those small-bar shows, "It was this lightbulb moment. Sitting by you, it made me think about your work, and medicine, and you know how my stories go." I chuckled and mimicked his earlier sway.

"What's this story about?" He asked.

"A rock star," I said.

"Rock star," he said, leaning against the counter I was rummaging through. "What's the rock star doing?" He hiccuped.

"Being corrupted," I said.

"Wow," he whispered at first. "You're really attached to this one."

"Nah," I said, "Not really," and I tried to imagine Marty, or Bridget, or anyone else I don't give a shit about, but an explosion burst inside my head releasing, instead of fire and shrapnel, images of Reed, of his secret lips, of the smile he tries so hard to hide because he wants to be taken more seriously than he was in Accentuate the Assent. It was fucking beautiful, but existed in the wrong moment with the wrong set of mind. "It's just… I need that drug we used for Ryan. Was it called Special K?"

"Yeah," he chuckled, eyes widening as he moved

across the room. "Ketamine." He removed a vial and tossed it to me.

"Okay," I exhaled. Easy enough. I looked over my shoulder, tried to remember what I'd already searched through. Where are the needles? "So," I held the bottle in my fingers. Flipped it. Stared at it curiously, and moved nearer to him. "How do you open this thing?" I didn't look up to him. If I saw his suspicion, I'd surely crack. I mean, who would ever buy that I was that stupid? Who am I— Bridget?

Luckily, he chuckled. "You don't open it, Bex." He swayed. One hand fell on my shoulder and the other reached above me to a cabinet. "You use a needle."

"Oh," I said, and thank God he's such a lightweight for a man of his stature. "Let me see," I said, taking the needle. "How do you do this? I need to get inside Reed—" I looked up, inhaled the heat of my anger, then let it out. "Reed's mind." Like I cared if Vinny heard me say Reed's name. He wasn't going to remember it anyway.

"He's your character?"

"He's the rock star."

"Weird name," he said, and I felt my fever developing. My jaw clenched. "It's better than 'Vinny'."

"Everything's better than Bexley," he said, and in any other circumstance, I'd have enjoyed his joke.

"So how much of this do I need to knock Reed out?"

"Well, large dogs…" his lips closed and he brought his hand to his head. "Reed's how tall?"

"I don't know," I said, getting frustrated and needing answers. "Five foot ten."

"Kay," he said, stumbling around, knocking the shit on the counter around as he reached for a calculator.

"He'd need about— Six would knock him out. You wanna make him agreeable and not OD him, right? So you'd need— Yeah, three CCs will do it."

He took a needle from me, filled it to the proper mark. "Like that," he offered it and I took it.

"Perfect," I said.

"Yeah, for your story."

"Yeah," I said, "For my story." I pushed the plunger forward so any remaining air was out of the barrel. "And you think this is the correct amount?"

"Should be," he closed one eye and his lips lifted on one side.

"Should be?" I said and he hummed confirmation. "Well," I said, "Vinny, this is serious," I looked at him sternly, but he didn't offer more assurance.

"It's just a book, right?" He asked, and I became offended by the suggestion that books weren't that important, but also the fact stirred inside my head that if Reed doesn't comply I can't shoot him up with ketamine if I don't have enough to knock out a large dog. This was a very serious dosage. There was no room for error, and with that in mind, with the rage surging through me like wildfire ready to burn down every hospital, every clinic, every engineering firm, every college that teaches its science students that their practice is more important than that of those studying English or history or art, I looked Vinny in his drunken eye and said, "We must test the theory," and I shoved the needle directly into his neck.

He wailed and pulled away from me, and I withdrew the needle. I followed him where his drunken shock toppled him over onto the floor. "It's not that serious," I said, gripping some piece of machinery used for testing blood, or shit, or piss, and slapping him upside the head with it.

Whatever it was originally used for, it worked wonders on silencing Vinny. It calmed him. And when he stopped squirming and grabbing at his neck, I took his forearm in my hand. "Now, Vinny," I said very gently, very calm and collected, "The contents of this needle must enter a vein, right?"

His eyes were frightened but his mouth refused movement.

"Fine," I said, looking back to the blue streaks in the inner elbow crook and scooching my feet nearer to him. "If I'm wrong, it's your funeral," and I pierced his flesh with the needle and emptied the Special K into his bloodstream.

Now I'm not accusing Vinny of miscalculating the dosage. He is, after all, much larger than Reed in both of the visibly gaugable physical manners. He's got, bare minimum, five inches on the guy, and more muscle mass than I've ever seen on someone so nerdy. It just didn't achieve the desired effect.

I expected this shit to knock Vinny on his ass. I wanted him out cold when I shot him up.

The effect was actually better than anticipated. See, it made Vinny very, very agreeable. I mean, there wasn't anything I couldn't talk him into.

I asked him to give me seven of the nine vials of ketamine in the pharmacy, and he said, "sure," while slurring and swaying around. I offered to get them myself since he was obviously pretty toasted, and the man thanked me for it.

My God, this shit's amazing.

He gave me different needles so I wouldn't be reusing with so many vials. Cleanliness is next to godliness and all of that, but it's also illegal so everyone who goes to Vinny's practice and is reading this can sleep soundly at night knowing he isn't shooting Lassie up with dirty sharps.

"The ketamine," I told him, "Is in case Reed doesn't come willingly." The ketamine is a failsafe so long as Reed is only the picture of innocence. It's only if he not only refuses to talk to strangers, but also doesn't want to fuck them in the back alleyway. "What do you have that would be appealing to a drug addicted rock star with plenty of options?"

"Oh," Vinny sounded enthused for someone so close to death, "You need the little gold key with the oval top."

I filed through the keys on the keychain and when I found it, I held it up. "Okay. Go."

"Third drawer on your left side. Second from the top."

I arched a brow at him, testing him. Was there something legitimate in that drawer, or were the drugs messing with him causing him to mess with me?

I went for it. Wouldn't you have? And when I opened the drawer, I was pleasantly surprised. "Ah," I said, removing a bottle and tucking it securely into my pocket. "Tramadol."

"Just don't give that to anyone," he started to nod off, "I could lose my license."

"Oh, Vinny," I said, slapping his cheeks to wake him up. *Imagine Angel coming in here tomorrow morning and finding him dead,* I thought. *With my fingerprints everywhere.* When he opened his eyes and they focused on mine, I smiled. "I wouldn't dream of it."

"Good," he said.

"You know, we probably should get you to bed."

Before I can't get you out of the crime scene.

"Yeah, cool," he said, and when he walked by me, he smashed into the counter.

Shit. I was going to have to help him back upstairs.

"Bex, seriously!" Vinny calls again, interrupting my writing. What is it with everyone around me not respecting my time with my job?

"I'll be right there," I call back, and he grumbles around.

I guess I should tell you how he ended up in the basement.

You see, I realized after Marty saw my distressed apartment, and after Vinny said he could give me the number of a great psychiatrist he went to college with, that my place is kind of dirty.

I started to try to clean it, I truly did, but there was weeks worth of empty French fries bags and old paper plates and moldy Starbucks cups. It was just too much for one person to do with such time constraints. I mean, Reed's show is *tonight*.

I considered a hotel. I considered his van. We're something more than soulmates. Our spirits are bonded without us ever having had a conversation. Would it matter where we were so long as we were together? No.

But last night I considered, now that I had a very pliable, very wealthy man's apartment to my disposal, that pretending this were my home for a night or two wouldn't be so bad, would it?

I've seen people in rom-coms do worse in the name

of love.

So with Vinny's arm slung over my neck, we rounded the stairs that led up to his apartment and opted to use the ones behind the building— the ones that descended into the basement.

It was a fucking nightmare. Even in my heeled boots, Vinny's six inches taller than I am. He's beefy, and that big-assed body looming over me while his feet skidded from one step to another felt like the presence of a flesh-and-blood grim reaper.

I could just see myself coming this far— writing and inking an entire graphic novel in a few weeks' time, drugging my best friend's brother, stealing his medication, and now plotting to steal his home— just to fall down some concrete steps and die under the immense pressure of Doctor Action Hero's beefed up body with less than twenty-four hours until Reed's show.

Somehow we made it, though, and if that isn't proof that the universe is on my side in this, I'll never convince you.

Once I slung his arm away from me, Vinny fell pretty quickly. I wasn't about to check for a pulse— I'd had enough of my foray into the practice of medicine by that point— and if I saw blood gushing from his head, I just didn't need the stress of that considering my current predicament.

I ran up the stairs quickly, and I heard him groaning around and asking why we were in the basement and where was I going and explaining that this wasn't his bedroom.

I kept trying to lock the door in some way that he wouldn't be able to open it from inside, but I had no such luck.

I was forced to go back in and delay my plans further.

I searched for chains, for locks, for anything that I could use to secure the door, but I only found plywood and empty boxes and some old, moldy tubes that looked like a dog had chewed part-way through.

"Hey, what's that?" Vinny asked. He was still on the ground, but he'd gotten his head up. He was attempting to balance on his forearm enough to sit upright, but I stopped that with a little kick of his shoulder. "Why's that? Why'd you do that?" He asked, but when I leaned down, he became distracted. "Why do you have that? There's a clean one upstairs in dental."

"It's okay, Vinny," I said, taking his very agreeable arms and moving them behind his back.

The idea was illogical. Using tubing to tie someone's hands up, I mean. But so many ideas are entirely backed up by logic just to fail in practice. This was the opposite.

Perhaps it was because of how old the tubing was— it was harder than it should be— or maybe it was because its integrity had been compromised by the years or the dogbites, but it was thin, almost rope-like and I could tear it open so that it was no longer a cylinder. It held him pretty well. I can't lie.

I went back upstairs and started hiding all traces of him, except for a photo he had of Bridget and I at some dumbassed football game they dragged me to two years ago.

Authenticity, it added. Nice.

See, Reed, this is my home. This is my best friend. We went to the show together— your show— and we watched you. Now you and I are here and we're looking at her. Isn't it strange how perfectly timelines cross and mirror one another? Isn't it all so divinely crafted?

I went into the kitchen next to familiarize myself with everything's placement.

Oh, yes, Reed, forks are in the drawer directly beneath the sink. Bowls? Two cabinets to the left of the sink. Cereal? Yes, on your left; third cabinet. Milk's in the fridge. I've got two percent and almond. Take your pick.

When I rid the refrigerator of family photos and a "number one vet" magnet, I moved to the hallway, expecting to have to correct only two bedrooms maximum. Instead, I was met with a fork in the road— two sloping walls that enticed me equally to their respective directions.

I can't believe how many times I forgot that this isn't an apartment above a clinic. It's a gigantic house gutted into a clinic and a home combined.

Thankfully, Vinny added some modernity to this otherwise antique home because the lack of sharp wall intersections and hard corners will be helpful if I do need to give Reed a quick three cubic centimeters.

I read a study once that said most people, when presented with two equal options of right or left, will choose right. I went left because of it.

I was treated to a spare bedroom that must be Bridget's when she crashes, but because she and I are "best friends" I felt justified in leaving it as such. Next to her room was a spare bathroom with evidence of only her.

At the end of the hallway was a large linen closet, and I dug through it until I found sheets appropriate for Reed— black satin with elegant ruching that crossed horizontal pleats of fabric into vertical ones.

I wasn't sure what was on Vinny's in the master bedroom— or where it was in the "apartment" for that matter— but I knew Reed deserved fresh linens, and this beautiful, dark comforter and pillowcases, like those only the wealthiest of the undead would slumber within, were too correct not to use.

I kept them bundled in my arms as I went back down the hallway— the while imagining Reed's skin against the satin, against mine, mine against the satin and him— as found that two accordion doors across from Bridget's bed-and-bath revealed the washing machine and the dryer.

Oh, of course we can get your pants cleaned up, Reed. Just down the left hall and on your right.

Another piece of necessary knowledge committed to memory.

The other hallway has a game room on the left— in case Reed wants to play pool or cards or even some classic PlayStation 1– and a home theatre on the right. Curling up with some horror films and popcorn doesn't sound too bad, does it? And at the hall's end is the master bedroom.

I went inside slowly, careful to eye each and every inch of each and every wall.

Luckily, Vinny kept his decorating for the rest of the home. It made making this mine a lot simpler.

All I had to do was hide an old textbook from vet school and his notes about a dog named Belles and her pyometra.

It's strange, but when I opened the closet to deposit these items, I became very concerned about Belles because these notes say this condition has to be addressed immediately. She needed surgery. Get your pets spayed, folks.

I sat down in the middle of the large closet and read until I saw his updates. Apparently she keeps coming in for fluids since the emergency surgery, and as I leaned back, enthralled in Belles and her story, a dress shoe came toppling down from somewhere. I looked up at the shelving behind me, realizing that this closet— this closet in a room meant to be mine— is filled with men's clothes.

Not to worry. I formed a plan.

I shoved the books back into the corner where the hanging slacks on my left met hanging t-shirts in front of me, and I left the closet.

I took the sheets Vinny had been using— plain, white cotton and totally unacceptable for someone as inhuman as Reed— and after I threw them on the floor, I redressed the California king in black satin.

As I rounded it, I imagined Reed's head lying against one of the pillows; the darkness of space surrounding him, contrasting the tones of his hair so that the amethyst strands appeared a galaxy inside an endless void, and if I'm being crass and blunt and totally honest, I can't wait to fuck him.

I wondered briefly if I had time to rub one out, but the thought of objectifying Reed in such a way made my stomach turn.

Instead, I ensured that both bedside tables were free of dust and dirt and evidence of Vinny.

When I opened the drawer to one nearest the window, I removed the gold wristwatch.

The last thing I need is Reed thinking I've got any man in my life but him.

After tossing it into the closet, I exited the room, then the apartment. I got into my car. Phase two required a trip home, and I wished I'd planned this better. I forgot to ask Vinny how long the effects of good old Special K would last.

Chapter 34
To:
From:
Subject: The Mirage

I wiped the sweat from my brow when I got back into my car and left my apartment.

I'd loaded it up with the contents of my closet and bookshelves. I packed my shoes into the trunk. I brought framed photographs fans had given me at conventions, photos of my family, photos of Natalie and I, photos Bridget took at shows. I brought my own graphic novels, my notebooks, my laptop.

In my front seat, I strapped Marlowe and Chaucer in. I drove under the speed limit for their safety, which came with the benefit of not getting pulled over, not looking suspicious, not getting a DUI, not being caught for kidnapping— though I'm still not certain whether or not you can kidnap someone by locking them in their own home. Either way, it's surely illegal to drug them, so I was thankful my fish kept my car at forty-five.

I stopped at a gas station to obtain deadbolts and those sliding locks with the chains. I got a hammer and nails. I got screws and a screwdriver. Spray paint. Handcuffs. Zip ties. Rope. Chains. Serial killer 101 or BDSM goddess. One can never tell. Soon enough I'd be both.

I purchased electrical tape and duct tape in zebra stripe and regular silver. I grabbed a dog leash when I walked by it. I didn't know exactly what I was doing, but I wasn't going to find myself in need of another trip.

This was all to use on Vinny, but it was for Reed, however indirect. For his benefit. So he wouldn't be exposed to cruelty or violence. So he wouldn't be tainted or frightened. So we could be together without stress. For our time together. For our life together, our future, our reunion of spirit.

But I got more direct items, too. Pancake mix because Grape Gardens' tour manager uploaded a photo of the band eating breakfast one morning a month ago. Hershey bars because Reed tweeted about his addiction to chocolate six years ago.

I care so much, Reed. I want to nourish you, but not just with food. I want to nourish your spirit with the giddiness only sweets and someone's consideration can provide.

I'm here, Reed. We're so close to being so close.

Once I got to Vinny's, I was going to make it my home, and with him in mind, I got a charger for an Android in case I couldn't find his and needed one.

As soon as I returned, I went down the basement stairs. A quick Google search suggested alcohol would intensify the effects of the drug I'd administered, so I wasn't entirely sure what I'd be walking into.

Luckily, he'd passed out by then.

I began tying his hands with rope behind his back, but if the drugs didn't kill him, how would he eat?

I scrapped the idea and tossed aside the rope.

I placed a chain loop against one of the wooden

beams and used the hammer and a stake to secure it there. I zip-tied the chain around one of Vinny's wrists, but I immediately worried that he'd use his other to release it somehow. I decided to chain his legs together the way I'd seen countless movies depict prison inmates. I don't know if holds in actual jails, or if they even use it, but it worked here, and he was still close enough to the stairs that giving him food wouldn't mean traveling into the darkness of the room.

I took the phone from his back pocket and used his fingerprint to unlock it, then I changed the passcode.

Wanting no more surprises, I surveyed the rest of the basement area and found that, when he'd remodeled, he split the gigantic basement into sections— a garage for the clinic, a garage for his apartment, a basement section dedicated to holiday decorations and old boxes labeled "photo albums 1934-1976" and "gram's stuff from attic", and finally a general basement area, which became his prison.

I sealed each door with padlocks and replaced the knobs and locked them with keys. This endeavor seems simple enough, but I ended up needing the internet for step-by-step photos.

I found just one window in Vinny's area, and I spray painted it black before drilling screws into it so that it couldn't be opened.

When I left, I deadbolted the basement door closed, then I padlocked it.

As I made my way up the stairs to the apartment, I texted Angel, and everyone else in the clinic group chat— Vinny, you're so helpful— not to come to work tomorrow. A water main broke. Everything's flooded.

I'm not sure if that's something that can affect this building, but a broken water main got Donnie Darko out of school for a day, and luckily no one in today's society questions anything that keeps them out of the office.

I placed Marlowe and Chaucer on the mantel below the living room television, and I covered the futon in gray sheets from the linen closet before I filled it with so many pillows and stuffed animals that it appeared cozy and inviting.

No more dorm room life, Vinny. Sorry.

After I hid the shelves of DVDs behind my books, I went into the bedroom and placed a specific book in the drawer of the nightstand on what I imagined would be Reed's side of the bed.

When I exited the room, I took the groceries into the kitchen. I put the pancake mix where it made most sense. I placed the chocolate in a basket by coffee pot, and in so doing, I realized how little I knew about this particular model.

It sounds insane, but my comics have taken me across the country, and I've met a lot of men. When my mood is stable, when I'm not thinking about how pointless everything is, when I'm all right accepting that life is meaningless and all I'm meant to do is breathe until my lungs stop moving, I bring these strangers into my hotel room.

Other nights, I'm not as stable. Some nights when I'm in foreign cities I know I'd go out for a drive. I know I'd be writing with both hands off of the wheel and both eyes off of the road. I find comfort in fictional people on those nights, and if that comfort causes a collision that kills me, what do I care?

I can't get into my car and write when I'm not home, however, and on those nights, when I meet someone attractive, I go home with them. I follow them out the doors of the convention centers, and I get into their cars, and if I die by their hands after I take pleasure in their bodies, who cares?

If life only means living, if there's nothing more to existence than existing, if there is no greater purpose or meaning, then what does any of it matter to anyone?

The point is that I've not been murdered by any of those strangers, so I've awoken to a lot of new beds in new places, and new staircases or new hallways that lead to new kitchens. Every kitchen has had a different coffee pot, or machine, or instant maker. Every power button is different, and every brew takes a little more time than the last, and you add water in various places— the back, left, front— and some of them steam, and some cook, and some just heat water so grounds can absorb into it.

The point is that knowing how to work your own coffee pot doesn't mean that you know how to work anyone else's. And the point is that everything does mean something because all of those nights— at home or afar— when I should've been dead, I survived. Why, if not for Reed? If not to prepare me for him now.

I flipped on the light in Vinny's kitchen— the small overhead just above this little breakfast nook— and I studied the machine before me. I pressed every button in case Reed doesn't know how to make my morning coffee, and when I grew confident in it, I reached to turn the light off.

My focus wasn't as intent on the machine as it had been the first time I reached for this light though, and the room around me was brighter with it on, and something off to my left was visible when it hadn't been earlier.

I could feel my face twisting in confusion before I became aware of the emotion itself, and I stood back from the counter in the little breakfast alcove, and stared at the wall behind it.

Either I was seeing things in the darkness, hallucinating, or there was a gate there. Maybe I'd accidentally injected myself with the ketamine meant for Vinny's vein, and I'd forgotten it— I wasn't sure. I pulled his phone from my pocket, though, and searched for the effects of the drug. My suspicions only half-confirmed, I read that small doses can make you forgetful but that they won't make you hallucinate.

That didn't really confirm or counter that I'd slipped some into my own body, but at least I knew the gate was real.

I approached it cautiously for I couldn't fathom its purpose. When I got closer, I noticed a little serving table across from it, and a phone next to the table.

I touched its intricately woven black metal, and its shaking tin echoed like thunder down what seemed to be a long corridor. Where did it lead?

I slid it open, and felt for a light switch. I couldn't find one, so I used the flashlight on Vinny's phone to illuminate the hallway. It was a staircase.

In trepidation, I trod the path before me. Each step felt like a foot closer to the gates of Hell, but alas no brimstone or fire was found at its end.

Instead, it led to a glamorous door— a door that fit the architecture of the house in its original state. How odd.

I opened it slowly, peeking through the small crevasse

I'd created as if I were the narrator of Poe's Tell Tale Heart, and indeed such a comparison was confirmed when the thin light of my phone fell onto an eye. It wasn't vulture-esque in nature, but it was closed and draped in recognizable skin. Vinny.

This secret kitchen door led to the basement.

Chapter 35
To:
From:
Subject: Up to Speed

A quick Google search explained that this was a separation of servants from their employers, and I was disgusted. I hate how people have treated one another. I hate how they do.

"Bex!" Vinny yells again and I probably should feed him.

I'm just so tired. I spent so much time fixing this place up, setting my stage, that I probably got an hour's sleep. I need to nap before I see Reed. I need to be rested when we meet. I can hide how dead I feel with makeup. I can paint away the sleep deprivation. I am an artist after all. But what I can't hide is the amount of time it takes me to type a word, to speak one, to think of one.

I need to be on my game when we're together, and I'm genuinely not even concerned that the outlook is bleak at the moment. I know what will happen when we're together. I know how we'll feel. I know that everything leading me to that point, to the first second of our eyes meeting, is purposely planned by the universe, designed by God himself, to make that initial spark ignite so intensely that the smoke detectors set off in the bar.

Mark me, it will happen. He will adore me. Maybe he

won't know why initially, but he will. He'll follow me. And if I have to make him pliable at first, the effect will wear away and he'll stay. He'll thank me for luring him in, for drawing him to me. He'll wrap himself around me, and he'll tell me that he wants me to see how willing he is now.

I can't wait for it, and I get lost in the idea of it, and I feel it as if I'm already there with him, as if he's already here with me, and fucking Vinny screams at me again.

"Bex!"

"It's Bexley!" I scream back and I throw my laptop onto the coffee table. Plastic to glass crashes around it. The remote under its left side has it slanting, and so help me God if it's broken before Reed can read himself in my words because of Vinny...

"Bex?" He asks, surely hearing my feet stomp across the floor. "Bexley, I mean…"

"What do you want, Vinny?" I ask.

"Shouldn't I correct you?" He huffs. "Shouldn't I say 'it's Vincent'?"

"Say whatever you want," I tell him. "I don't care."

"Why am I down here, Bex?" His eyes close tightly and he turns his head. "Bexley."

"If you're trying not to piss me off, or earn my trust or whatever, stop. Entry-level psych classes from ten years ago aren't going to teach you how to talk to me."

"I'm just trying to figure out how we got here."

"Your brain is science and math. Mine is art and fiction and abstraction. You won't be able to x + y = z this."

"Bexley, stop talking like you're a character in one of your crazy stories—"

"We're all characters in this crazy story, whether it's

mine, or God's, or the Fates'."

"What—"

"I can't help what I do. I can't change what's happened. It's like someone's hand has been sketching me through life, telling me what to do and what to say, and I've never cared about any of it because it didn't make sense. The truth is we're all characters, and we all have writers who inject us with thoughts and feelings, and inkers who give us eyes, but none of it is ours. We do as they tell us, as they draw us, and when we question it we find the plot holes and the parts that make no sense, and we can't understand people because our authors are always changing our lines. But when you near the end, when you see the happily ever after on the horizon, you realize everything in your life was foreshadowing, and the universe is rounding out your character arc, and you know you're going to feel something you've never felt before because it's time for the conclusion. This is it. This is the end. But don't be afraid. The apocalypse is just the page before the sequel."

"Bexley, you're scaring me."

"It's okay to be scared," I say. "It's all right. You don't get it. You're not in touch with what God wants; you're not a God, not like I am."

"You?"

"Me. Me, Natalie, Reed."

"Who— Your characters?"

"Not mine," I say. "But creators understand each other. You may never see it."

"Bex, please." He reaches toward me from the bottom of the stairs. "It's cold here, and I'm in pain. I slept on the concrete, and I've got shit in my system that I shouldn't have. I'm hungry, and I just... We can talk about whatever you want. Let's just— Bex, where are you going?"

I'm going to the kitchen, Vinny. You're hungry. And I crush up some of the Tramadol, and I sprinkle it on his toast and his coffee, and I'm thankful for the practice.

"Here," I say, slipping it through the gate. "Don't make me close this door."

"Bexley, I need out of here."

"Just wait for now," I say. "It'll all make sense eventually."

I try to give him some decency. I try not to lock him in like a prisoner, but he just refuses to shut the fuck up.

I shake the gate and ensure that the padlock is secured, then I close the glamour door.

I go upstairs. I close the gate and lock it with a newly installed padlock too, and I'm getting good at being a handyman.

Then I go to the bedroom— my bedroom; mine and Reed's— and I curl into the black hole of satin sheets, and I imagine my Amethyst Alien here next to me.

Soon, I think, and the voice whispers back, *Mine.*

```
Chapter 36
To:
From:
Subject: A Show
```

Bridget is making her way toward the barrier again.

I stand here at the bar, sipping my drink. Nursing it, I'm careful not to overindulge.

Tonight, I consume only Reed. Only his soul, and his spirit, and his heart, and his flesh. Tonight I don't need an excuse to fade away from existence, and tonight I have no desire to be anywhere else but here.

Tonight this dingy basement bar looks like heaven, and the soundcheck of drums and out of tune guitars seems the opening melody to a choir of angels.

Tonight, wrong is right, and all that has been broken will be restored.

I hold the comic in my hands— the graphics of Reed's face, his body, his soul. It's called up on my phone so that every time I unlock it, every time Bridget texts me, every time someone from my world-before-Reed contacts me, I'll open the screen to him. To my destiny.

I hold the story of his fall against my chest, and I pull it more tightly into my ribs, hoping it'll cleanse me of the burning gin trickling down my throat like liquefied fire.

I'm ready for Reed tonight.

I'll bear witness without the blurred vision and

spinning rooms. Tonight I won't care what Bridget texts. I won't care who she wants to fuck. I don't care how many videos she takes.

Tonight is meaningless out of Reed and his resurrection.

When he steps onto the stage, I am awakened. Blood pumps through my veins so intensely that I can feel its flow inside my wrists. My neck. I tingle.

When he presses his secret lips to the microphone, his hand moving down the glittering pink, I tremble in anticipation. The foreplay, the need.

My skin shrinks and rises when he finally releases his voice into the atmosphere of our world. Here we are together, a hundred people, sectioned off by the walls of this room like my characters are sectioned off by the lines of the panels I draw for them, like Natalie's characters can only see what she writes; and if God has simply written a script for us, if he inks and blocks and sketches each moment of our existence, I can't thank him enough for writing Reed into my story.

But the thought remains that Reed is God with his voice, and his fingertips make music, and I am God with my writing, and my fingertips make worlds.

Together we could create or destroy, or create and destroy, and if he wants me to smear his makeup with my lips while we make love or with my fists while we fuck, then I'll wreck whatever purity remains inside him, and in that destruction we'll craft a new beginning.

Life is waiting for us, Reed, waiting for us to write it, to draw it, to score it.

My drink never goes empty, but I ask for two more. As Reed sings, as he pours his soul out to the crowd, the bartender pours vodka into one glass with Coke while the other stays virgin.

It's Reed's choice. I wait until no eyes are on me and I slip a bit of social lubricant into both glasses. It's the illusion of Reed's decision. Pick one. Tainted or no, but aren't they both?

"Don't forget, Grape Gardens family," he exhales breathily into the microphone while his forearm, covered in a furry black sleeve, wipes his glistening sweat from his forehead, taking with it his amethyst locks. "We'll be over at Grinning Donkey tomorrow night too. Small and intimate, but our friends from Party Stream asked us to support."

Bridget texts:

Still down for that one, right?? You know I have tix! Yummy is the best way to describe Aaron.

And before can I answer, she texts again:

Aaron is Party Stream's vocals/guitar/lyricist/HUNK

I reply: *Sure.*

Sure, I'll be there, Bridget, but as Reed's soulmate, his partner, his new world.

I'll be at every show, reminding him of his worth as he works off his contract, and when the time is up on whatever type of deal musicians enter into, he'll be able to create whatever he wants.

He'll be free with me, free of doubt, free of falsehoods, and free of corporate bullshit stunting his release.

Oh, the release I'll give him.

His secret lips stop moving. The music slows. Stops. Everything is silent and he breathes, "Thank you."

He leaves the stage.

I wait. I anticipate.

The perfect moment is necessary. I can't be standing next to fans, to shallow adoration. I can't be aligned with everything I'll never be to him.

I'm reality, a god amongst parishioners, and because he was on that stage tonight and I was among them, I shall not be misidentified as one of them.

I am here— flesh and blood divinity— just as he is, and I expect to approach his table when the headlining band begins and his devotees have dissipated.

Ok, Bridget texts, *I'm liking your weird little Canadian band more and more.*

Mine.

I don't reply. I need to focus. I call up the graphic novel, Reed's fall, his life, his story, and I stare at Reagan in a scene on page thirty-four that bears an eerie resemblance to the scene before me in my world.

Reed lights up when people approach his table. When he smiles, his eyes crinkle in the corners. He's genuine, and when he shakes people's hands and hugs them, he looks like he's as excited to meet them as they are to meet him. It's beautiful.

By the time the next band begins to play, the last of Grape Gardens' fans is finishing up a transaction. I see plastic slip across a small white square in the drummer's phone, and in exchange Reed hands the girl a CD.

The girl next to her says something and he looks down to the table. His fingers wiggle as his hand wanders over the various items, and when it stops, he reaches down. He picks up a sticker. Hands it to her.

She shakes her head and lifts a hand. It seems a rejection of the offer, but she's smiling, and I think he's giving it to her at no cost.

It's endearing. Reed is giving. That girl will go home and put that sticker on her notebook and tell everyone in pre-algebra about how her favorite singer is so humble and kind, and she'll start to appreciate people for more than just their faces.

Maybe Reed doesn't see it that way, but I do. I see truth.

80's Baby Big Hair puts his hand into a skin-tight pants pocket and a pack of cigarettes accompanies it when it emerges.

He packs the cigarettes as he talks to Reed, and as the box bounces off of his palm, I wonder if he's even old enough to smoke.

Not that I'm complaining because it gets him away from Reed. The drummer remaining seems like an issue, but I remember that I have two drinks, and either one Reed picks will make him agreeable and whichever is left will make the drummer so.

I take the drinks over, and Reed must sense me coming because he looks up. Our eyes meet. It's glorious. Heaven and good, hell and fiery, and we're trapped here in this club on this earth between the two ethereal states.

He smiles and his head follows his eyes when they fall, and I'm getting closer. He looks up when I find my way to his table, and I say, "I was waiting for one of you to leave because I can only carry two drinks at one time."

He chuckles, and in a slow blink of his eyelids stained gray, my sight is consumed by the stillness of the night glistening inside his crystalline eyes.

No wonder he identifies colors with gemstones. His eyes are strength and stillness and certain the way a rock is, but they are the deep blue of sapphires and the pastel of aquamarine, and even the dimmest light reflects upon their surface like moonlight in the ocean. I'm sure my lips have parted, and I have to consciously tell myself not to gasp or say, "wow," or fuck this up with my amazement for him.

"I'd say that's a very sweet gesture," he replies and his voice is delicate when it isn't singing his soul, and it's as soft as his skin looks, and his lips aren't hidden and secretive but he still bites the lower one into his teeth. His brow lifts playfully, and when he's gained the confidence to continue, he finishes, "But how do I know I'm not the one you planned to leave out."

"Because this glass," I lift my left hand, "Has alcohol in it," I lean forward, feigning a whisper as I wink to the drummer, "And your band mates look fresh out of seventh grade."

"Nah," the drummer laughs, taking the glass from my left, "I graduated two years ago."

"I'll buy it," I say, "But not the big-haired kid."

"Good call," he winks, taking the glass from my right hand as he rounds the table, "He's just started grade twelve."

Reed chuckles, but he's looking down again, and I scold myself because how dare I ignore him like this?

He feels my gaze on him. He looks up with his eyes and tilts his head a bit. His cheek almost finds his shoulder and he lifts a hand to the metal loop hanging from his chain. He tugs at it. "Guess that leaves me out," he smiles but only with the corners of his lips.

"It does," I say, "So you get to pick your poison."

He looks up again, and I smile and raise my brows questioningly.

"Oh, you don't have to—"

"But I want to," I say and I can't help feeling like the   serpent woman in my comic. Encouraging, encouraging, but to what end? "You've got to at least want some water after that set…"

It's dark but I swear his cheeks flush. The floor steals his eyes from me again, and his teeth press into his secret lips the way I want to bite them, and he giggles— he *giggles*. "Okay. A water."

"Okay," I say, and when I turn toward the bar, he speaks again.

"Wait," his boldness is gone when I look back because those sapphires are on the ground and the amethyst locks of his 90's boyband-bangs are falling into them. Nervously, an exhaled laugh leaves those incredible lips, and he begins to round the table. "I mean… I can go too. You don't—" he shakes his head and he cuts his words off in frustration. "I just mean you don't have to go get it… For me."

I exhale and smile as I turn back to him. "Relax," I say, and I reach out and I place my hand on his, and he's even softer than the satin sheets on Vinny's bed, "I've got you."

His eyes gaze up to me beneath his lashes, and he is the picture of perfection, all shyness and good, and it takes every bit of strength in every one of my muscles to lift my hand away from him, but I do it.

I keep my eyes on his, and I want him to know that when I say I've got him, I don't just mean tonight. I don't just mean the drink. I mean for every night from this moment on, and I mean for anything the world might throw at him.

I'm a shield, Reed, but not the way makeup and masks are shields. I'm the protective nature of an animal, a pride

lion, the alpha wolf, and you aren't just my beta male;
you're my mate and you're my cub and you're the runt of
the litter and that's what makes you so special. So perfect.

I lift my chin and lead with it when I turn. He needs
me. He has to sense it already.

I can feel his eyes on me, and I wore this tight dress
on purpose. Its black matches the ink on my left arm and I
hope Reed asks me about the Roman numerals above my
elbow because we are the same, and we always have been,
and at some point in our respective lives, we each chose to
tattoo the year of our birth on our arms.

The difference is that mine reads "eighty-eight" and
his reads "eight eight" because Roman numerals don't
work the way our numbers work, and if Reed had me
sooner, I could've helped him.

I try not to let my pissy mood affect my face, and
thankfully I can test-smile at the bartender before I need to
look at Reed again.

"Two more?" The bartender asks.

"Water this time," I say.

"You gonna drop your own shit in that one too?" He
eyes me.

"I'm not roofieing anyone if that's what you're
thinking."

"Then what are you giving them?"

"Nothing they don't ask for regularly," I say, and
maybe that's true of 80's Baby Big Hair, and honestly I
thought the drummer was too dull for drugs, but maybe
not.

"Whatever," he says, and I believe he genuinely
doesn't care.

He sets the glass of water down and looks at me, but

only for a second. When he turns, I check my surroundings quickly and slip my not-a-roofie into the drink.

Reed isn't looking at me when I turn back, but his eyes dart around from the contents of his table to the floor to his feet. Resting his chin in his hand, Reed leans over his table, and I can count his ribs beneath the creamy skin of his back.

He straightens up when I near him, and the large metal links thud against his collarbone, and instinctively, as he reaches for the offered water in my left hand, I lift my right to the injury.

"Didn't that hurt?" I ask, and I brush my fingers over his clavicle. His shoulders curl in on him. He looks down to my caresses, and I pull away. "I'm sorry," I say.

"No, I..." he looks up at me. He pauses. His brows shift like maybe he doesn't know what's okay, or why it is, or if it is, and his own hand reaches for his collarbone, and he exhales something sad and small. He smiles. "I guess I'm not used to something so... Tender." He flushes.

Jesus, I can't believe this is real.

"You seem tender," I say gently, and his eyes find mine. "Underneath all of this viciousness, I mean."

He chuckles, looking away, and his fingers trace leather and chains and metal spikes. "Maybe I am," he looks up, "Maybe I'm not."

"Maybe you don't need to mask it with me," I say, and he brings the water to his lips the way he brings the microphone to them. "Don't hide," I say playfully, but only because I know he's too shy not to, and he drinks the water.

"Thank you for this," he says.

I encourage, "I want to see that all gone, young man. You had quite the workout tonight."

He chuckles, but I know he feels cared about. I'm taking care of you, Reed. I want you to stay hydrated, and I want you to be slippery when I suggest we leave together.

It's not as nefarious as it sounds, and, dear reader, you know that to be true— unless you're an FBI agent just punching in and picking up where the last guy left off— because you know all I want to do for Reed is free him.

"I get sweaty," he grimaces.

"You get into your art."

"Thank you."

"For what?"

"Calling it art," he says, and he brings the water to his lips and hides them behind the plastic.

"Doesn't everyone?" I ask.

He says, "No."

"I can't imagine why," I say, and his brows crease and he lifts a hand to his eye.

"Before, I wasn't edgy enough," he rubs his eye and his palm smears the makeup everywhere, but it honestly doesn't look that different from the other eye's adornment. "So I changed." He exhales and takes another sip, and I'm ecstatic. "Now they're pissed that I'm faking it."

"Are you faking it?" I whisper, and my eyes narrow in on him, and I want to see his eyes and his lips and watch for any nervousness associated with lying.

"Bro," a voice calls from behind me, and the pressure of an arm is suddenly present on my shoulders. "Thanks for the Coke," the voice says, and I stand up straight which moves me further from Reed and I hate it. I look to my left, and it's 80's Baby. "Added a little something to it though. Hope you don't mind."

"Knock yourself out," I say, and I mean it.

I can't wait for this set to finish so they can sign more CDs then sneak away into the bathroom or their van to fuck.

I cross my arms over my chest, and I look back at Reed. He's studying me, watching me from the corner of his eye.

"Their set's almost done," Reed says. "I'm not sure anyone else will wanna see us, but we hang out here in case." His hands wring the glass of water— almost empty— and he says, "Do you think I'm faking it?"

I loosen my arms, my expression. I move against the table and I wish it weren't between us because all I can think about is fucking him on top of it. "I don't think you fake the core qualities that make you a musician, an artist."

"But..." he says so softly I practically have to read his lips.

"But I don't think you're Amethyst anymore than I am."

He swallows, and his lips part, and before he can say anything, the silence is interrupted by another fucking person.

"Can I, like, take a pic with you guys?"

I look to my right, and I step aside. Reed watches me as his drummer says, "Of course!" and 80's Big Hair moves around the table, and the three other people invading my space with Reed all stare to him.

I turn, and Reed comes around the table too, but he touches my arm. My attention goes immediately to the small spot his fingertips merely grazed, and I hope the electrical current passed between us was powerful enough to leave a bruise. I look up to him.

"Don't leave," he attempts an order but his tone is pleading.

"Yes, sir," I say, and I'm so good at giving him what he wants. I start to walk away. His eyes are heavy on my back, so I look over my shoulder and wink to him before pointing to the bar. He smiles and dips his head, and he's slippery when he gets over to the girl with her phone ready for a photo.

You're mine, Reed, and the voice laughs loudly. *Mine.*

Chapter 37
To:
From:
Subject: K-Holes

Only four people total visit Grape Gardens' table after the headliners finish, and Bridget texts that she's going around back to try to see them getting into their bus.

I've learned to rideshare when she gets this urge, as the band still has to pack up, and some smaller ones hang out for a bit backstage, and she dedicates way more time to false idols than I've ever wanted to.

I text her back: *I'll Uber.* She won't come back in looking for me.

The lights have come up, but it's still dark in here, and I watch Reed's drummer start to pull T-shirts from the rack behind them— the same rack used to chain and cuff Reed in place— and it calls up the imaginations of porn directors in my head, and all I can see is Reed's secret lips parting in pleasure, his brows tightening over closed eyes as he moans, his bare skin glistening with sweat.

80's Baby Big Hair licks his lips as he talks with Reed, and then he disappears into the night with a girl who looks too young to be here, but so is he.

Reed looks up to me for only brief seconds at a time, and when I catch him, he flushes. He plays with the loop on his chain. He bites his secret lip.

The illusion of the bar around us is merely that. The music playing behind us is drowned out by the lyrics of "Echo", and by Reed's voice, and by all of the words that were just his calling to me.

Everything around him is blurred. He is the focal point of a painting unfinished. He is everything.

As Reed folds the t-shirts, the drummer takes the boxes of CDs and posters around the table and through some secret little door no one but those with "backstage" access can enter.

In a bar this small, it's almost funny, but looking at Reed's fingers wrap nervously around the laminated pass labeled "ALL ACCESS" makes it seem legitimate and fully rock star.

Of course, that's just the nature of someone like Reed; someone so extraordinarily beautiful in every movement of his body, every blink of his lashes, every whisper of sound from his lips. They make everything they touch seem abnormal in the most artistic way.

He's alone now though— that's what really matters here— and I go to him.

"Need some help?" I offer, and, fuck, I do sound like Reagan's serpent woman.

He smiles, lifts the pass in his hand to eye level, and says, "Can you believe this is plastic?"

I lift my hand and gaze into his oceans as I brush my fingertips along the pass. "Yes," I say. "It feels like plastic."

"Now feel me," he says, offering his palm as the pass falls from it and bounces from the string attached to his belt loop.

"Okay," I say, and I lower my chin and my voice is all

seduction, and I want to feel you in so many ways, Reed. When I run my fingertips across his palm, he shivers. "I feel it too," I say.

"Like we're one," he says.

I exhale, "Yes. We're one."

"Like we're the same person."

"Yes," I say.

"And we're the same as the plastic that makes backstage passes, and the trees that make paper, and we all breathe the same air."

"Well," I lean back because I forgot about K-holes and if he's this fucked up already, I need to move quickly before I can't get him out of this room. "Technically we breathe the by-product of trees, but I guess so."

"You know," he says, and his eyes glass over, "A few months back, Clint hooked up with this girl I've known since I was sixteen. She was way younger than I was but we were really close. I was really upset when he hooked up with her. It was like he defiled my little sister, but he didn't see why I was mad. He kept saying how he wouldn't have done it if I was interested in her. It's not like that but, I mean, I see where he's coming from. He doesn't have a sister, and he's way younger than I am, too. He's younger than she is! I think I forgive him."

"That's great, Reed," I say.

"I don't know your name," he says, "We're the same person but I don't know your name."

"Of course you do," I say, and I touch his hand. I encourage the ketamine high, the togetherness it creates in whatever mind it's affecting. I supply false memories. I make claims he can't argue. Come with me, Reed. Come away with me. "I'm Bexley. You know me."

"I do?"

"Yeah. We're the same person, remember?"

"Oh, yeah," he smiles. "Bexley is such a beautiful name."

"You flatter me," I say quickly, "Listen, Reed—"

"I wanna cuddle," he says, but maybe it's the drug.

"Perfect," I say, "But it's too dirty in here—"

His lips pout and, my God, do I want to taste them, and he crosses his arms over his bare chest and he looks away. So vulnerable. "But I wanna cuddle," he whispers.

"Yes, dear, we're going to."

"Dear?" His brows lift over his widening eyes, and he smiles something beyond beautiful in genuineness.

"My dearest one," I grin, "Better?" His smile pushes his cheeks into his eyelashes, and he nods. "Let me take you home," I say, offering my hand. "We'll cuddle."

"Okay," he smiles, taking my hand. "Okay, Bexley," and, Jesus, I could climax just watching those secret lips form the syllables of my name.

The ketamine is coursing through his system, and his voice is small and perfect. "We really are the same person, aren't we?"

"We are," I say, and we walk through the bar, and no one even looks at us because Reed is God but he isn't the headliner. "We really are."

Chapter 38
To:
From:
Subject: Kinks

The Uber driver doesn't question me when I load a slippery man covered in chains and dog collars into the car.

He looks in the rear view mirror at times. He lifts a brow here and there.

Ultimately, with the way Reed's dressed and my arm covered in tattoos, he probably thinks this is an everyday occurrence for us.

Soon it will be. Soon we'll be traveling the world together, and soon I'll be able to protect him and keep him safe, and I won't need to dose him to do it.

"Do you know any of my music?" He asks.

"I know one song," I say, and I know others but "Echoes" is the only one I really like.

"'The night is calm'," he quotes himself and he looks out of the window and he rubs his fingers on the glass.

"'I want to connect to something else'," I say and he looks over to me, "'About you.'"

His face falls, and he leans into me, and his hand moves to my face, and my eyes close so I can surround myself in his touch, in our connection, without the distraction of his beauty.

"I don't wanna chase you," he says, and it's too poetic

and too pure and too transcendental to be the drugs.

I open my eyes, and his are wide open and focusing, and his pupils dilate when we drive by streetlights, and the air really is still. "No sound to my footsteps," I say, "Because I'm not running anywhere."

When we get to Vinny's, Reed tries to find his wallet to pay the driver and I have to remind him that he doesn't have any pockets.

"Let's get you to bed," I say, and we walk up the stairs while he looks at the stars, and he's convinced by Special K that the universe is righteous and interwoven with everything inside it.

It's only further confirmation of everything I've been saying. I mean, Reed could've become extremely melancholy on this drug, or he could've fallen asleep in the cab, but he didn't.

He became convinced of the unity of cells and spirits, and we might be the same as plastic and trees, but we are still the same as each other.

I open the door, and when his little saddle shoes slip him inside, he pauses. He stands there. "I don't know this place," he says, and his eyes look around.

"I know, darling," I say, guiding him through the hall and into the living room. "I know it, and I'm going to take care of you, okay?"

"Okay," he says lowly, and his head is dipping and swinging, and his feet are dragging. "Oh, wow," he says, and lifts his head as much as possible. "Look at this," he reaches for a stuffed pig on the couch, "It's so pink. Wow." He breathes his astonishment, and I tilt his body away from the couch.

"It's very pink," I say, and with my body I encourage

his beyond the kitchen and toward the Y-shaped hall.

"I can't believe this color," he gasps, and he pets the pig. "It's so soft. What is this?"

"It's yours," I say, and we've made it to the hall. "Keep it, love."

"Love," he says, and he sways into the wall, and my hands go to his shoulder and his head, and he giggles. That fucking giggle. "I'm okay," he smiles. Lifts his hand to mine. It fits perfectly. We are one. "I can really have this?"

"Of course, sweetheart."

"Wow," he says. Smiling as he looks to it, Reed pets its pink fur with his hand full of metal and rings. So punk rock. So delicate. I adore him.

"I've got you," I say and I help him away from the wall, and when he looks into my eyes, I swear he's seeing into me.

"You really do, huh?"

I nod, and we're walking without looking, and I'm fucking brilliant for doing so much research on the place before I brought him here. "I really do."

We enter the bedroom, and I guide him to the bed. He sits on its edge and his hands run over the folds in the satin, and he's gasping already and I haven't even gotten his shoes off yet. "I love this," he says. "It's cold... Soothing..."

"Lie back," I offer, and he obeys, and I pull his saddle shoes from his feet to reveal mismatched socks— one with Luigi from Mario Bros., and I love him for not favoring the main character, and the other a faded purple that probably matched his hair once.

He giggles when I lift his leg to remove this sock. "A fan gave me those socks," his eyes close and his body

277

releases any tension holding him up or tightening him. He's entering another world, and this memory becomes as clear as our supposed reality. "We were somewhere in Toronto. Didn't even play five shows together yet." His eyes open, "The color was so intense, and I remembered purple being a fabric color only royalty could afford, and I thought if rock stars were modern royalty, and I wanted to dye my hair to match my socks because I thought if everyone else saw me as something I'd see me that way too."

I don't say anything as I let his foot fall back to the bed, and I lift his other leg and pull Luigi from his foot.

"What do you think?" He asks.

"I don't think it matters what everyone else thinks," I say, and I guide his foot to the bed.

"But what do you think?"

"Why does it matter what I think?" I tease, and I round the bed and sit on its edge.

"Because we're the same person." The serenity in his delicate features fades suddenly, and his brows pull tightly over moistening eyes. He pushes himself onto his elbows. His voice is smaller than usual, and his secret lips tremble, "Aren't we?"

I try to hide how viciously he breaks my heart with a smile, and I stare into his eyes, and I brush his amethyst hair from them. "Yes, Reed. Yes, of course we are."

I feel his rings when he lifts his hand to mine, and the cold metal is shocking inside his warmth. "That's why it matters what you think. No one else's opinion ever made me happy. I think you know me better than they do."

My lips part. He's brilliant, and he's so astute, and he sees invisible things like the bonds of spiritual togetherness, and the ketamine is right— we are one. Staring into his eyes, feeling his skin, sitting here in bed with him, the world is right. Every wrong has been corrected. Every complaint has been resolved.

I feel my eyes burn, and I wish it were brighter in here so I could see him more clearly, but I feel how bonded we are, and he's confirmed it.

Whatever insanity I've done in the name of us, of who we could be together, has been validated. I walked the right path; it led me here. We're united, and he knows it without having any reason to. It's a spiritual certainty that can't be seen or heard or smelt, but he feels it.

"I think the color suits you," I whisper, and I run my fingers through the locks of precious gemstone, and he closes his eyes, and he purrs.

"Lay with me?" He asks, and his eyes open slowly, and he's angelic but seductive. He's everything— alpha and omega. He's beginning, middle, and end. He's wrong and righteous. He's perfection.

"Of course," I oblige him because he's mine, and the voice whispers, *mine*, and when we fall into the satin and memory foam, we fall into each other.

His hands are all over— my hair, my cheek, my neck, my shoulder. Everywhere there is exposed flesh, we connect. Just at the fingertips. Just for now.

I spread my palm, hovering over his chest, and press my handprint into him. I imagine my fingerprints spreading over his body. I lift my hand before I stroke his flesh. I want those claims there. Mine. Mine.

"Bexley," he breathes, and our lips are close, and his voice is delicate and soft, but he's rasping in the night's earlier efforts, and I want to soothe him the way the coolness of satin soothes him.

"Yes, Reed?" Closer and closer; his secret lips are seeking mine.

"How do you know me?" He exhales the words, hums them, tiny moans inside his throat.

"Bridget wanted to see the headliners a few weeks back. I came with her. I saw you. You inspired me." When he exhales, I breathe it in. We are one.

"Inspired?" The ketamine makes him pliable, but no less shy. He bites his lower lip, and it's near enough to my teeth inside my lips that I could bite it for him if he'd let me. "I did?"

"You did," I say, and the worlds between us have become countries, then cities. "Everything you are," I say, and my fingers press against the spikes on his neck, the chains on his collarbone, the harness across his chest, the hem of the plastic pants on his hip, "Inside of everything you're not." The cities became mere miles that shrank into feet, and now we're only inches apart. "An artist is bound by nature to create," I say and I unlock the chains behind his back, "But without concern, we're manufacturing our divinity." The harness lifts from his chest, and I slip my fingers between it and his skin, and I pull it away from his body. "You've given me passion," I whisper, running my fingertips through the red indentations left in his torso. "I want to give it back to you."

His lower lip is quivering. His eyes dart from my left to my right as if the answer will come from my eyes instead of my lips. His whispering voice cracks, "How?"

"By releasing you," I say, and I unclasp the dog collar around his neck, "From everything you think you have to be."

His hand catches mine and he pulls it against his expanding chest. "I feel lighter," he says, and I hope it's not the ketamine talking.

"I do too," I tell him because the weight of the metal isn't pressing down on his lungs and suffocating him, and the weight of the darkness I saw in the world has been eradicated by his beauty.

"I want to cuddle," he breathes, and his arm moves around me, pulling me into him.

His chest is bare and soft. His arms are smooth where they're not obstructed by chains.

My leg rises to his. Our feet intertwine. We reach for one another. We hold each other. The inches have become a space immeasurable, and he says, "But if I want to kiss you?"

"You can," I answer quickly because it's the truth. You can do anything, Reed, be anything, so long as it's with me.

He smiles but it's hesitant; shaken and nervous. His brows crease, and he looks at my lips more seriously than he should, and I can tell his mind is telling him not to fuck this up.

I hate what people have done to him. I hate that this is the worry he has when his biggest concern should be which of us will do the laundry and which will get the dishes because he's too flawless to be inadequate at anything.

His lashes fall over his oceans, and my lids want to follow suit. I can't allow them. I need to see him this close; to confirm it's him. And it is.

The running cliche is that time stops when you find the one, but really it feels more like a screenwriter's description of dying. A flashing sequence of movie frames surrounds him. I see him in bars, singing his soul into pink glitter, and trapped behind silver and amethyst. It's beauty that binds him. And all at once, not like a firework or an explosion, the gentle pressure of his secret lips brushes over mine like a careful breeze that stirs the stillness of the night with a slowly rising sun.

He doesn't move away when our lips part. His hand runs up the back of my neck. He rests his forehead against mine. "Is this a sin?" He whispers, and I want to tell him that kissing your soulmate is never wrong, but it probably isn't right when you've drugged him.

"No," I whisper and wonder if that's taken away it's appeal.

"Good," he exhales, "Because I wouldn't mind doing it again."

"Feel free," I offer, and he accepts.

Slow and concise, his secret lips seek pleasure, but the way his hand moves across my shoulder and the way his fingers caress my skin, the way he leans away when he exhales, it all culminates to one conclusion: that pleasure he seeks is mine.

I want to return the favor. I want to smother him in affection, wrap him up in kisses, clean him with the radiance only spiritual bonds can ignite.

I lean in with a touch of force. I weave my fingers into the galaxy of his hair and pull our separate worlds together. Our gently touching lips collide in the pressure. Inside his throat, a moan breaks the silence of our souls.

I let my leg run further up his leg. I grip the flesh of his back with my nails.

He's mine, and that means I own him. That means I'll

do whatever I want with his body when it's in my bed, and I don't do this out of my own psychopathy, no; I do this because I know him well enough to know it's what he wants.

"Bexley," he whimpers against my lips, and I devour his.

Those secret, hidden lips that press against microphones and metal, wine bottles and glass, they belong to me now, and the only touches they'll experience are soft, wet, delicate kisses adorned with the sharp reminder of teeth telling him that he no longer controls them.

"You want to sin," I whisper between increasingly passionate pulls of skin and lip and teeth.

"I— I—" he stammers, exhales, tries to answer, but it wasn't a question.

"But you don't want to be responsible for it."

The tautness of his muscles releases, and his arms urge me against as he moves closer. His hands squeeze at my shoulders. He's needy, desperate. I've offered everything he's ever wanted.

"I'll take care of you, Reed," I whisper, stroking his hair, his cheek, his chest, his hipbone. "You'll never have to worry again. I'll adore you. Keep you safe."

He hums against my lips as he tries to blend our bodies— already as close as we can be when clothed— even tighter together.

"You have to do one thing in return," I say, and I drag my nails along his skin, "You have to give yourself over to me. Let me have you. Own you. You're mine."

His secret lips won't speak, but they continue their pursuit of mine.

"I'll bind you, Reed," I say and tug at his chains. "I'll tie you up," and I grip his wrist. "I'll do everything you've always been too afraid to ask for. Your art, your performance, you can be that guy here in these four walls with me, and when you go on stage with your innocence intact because I took from you when you weren't able to run, you won't care if they call you a Backstreet Boy or say you're too vanilla. You'll know who you really are when you're with me, and by keeping you chained," I pull at the cuff on the bedpost, "I'll set you free."

He moans, and his hips press into me. His hand finds my hair, and the other my hand and the metal cuff. His secret lips part in passion and forget the pressure to be perfect.

"Cuff me," he exhales, and his unskilled lips ravage mine.

A fraction of freedom and we've come a long way.

"What do good boys say?" I ask as I pull back, and I feel like something out of a fanfiction, but he's innocent and wants to be owned.

"Please," he moans, and his body tremors against mine.

I move to my knees and take the cuffs. Above him, I run my fingers down the chainlink, and I look down to him, and he offers his wrist with his hand palm up. His eyes blink slowly as he looks up to me. His shoulder begins to lean back, but his body is caught between staying near to me and lying back in submission.

He wants both. I want both. So I lock the cuff around his wrist, and move against him.

I slip a leg over his hips, and you could call out position "straddling" but we're not that vulgar, and what we're doing is a spiritual endeavor. I'm providing him the escape he's always wanted beneath his catholic boy upbringing: be sexual, be deviant, but stay obedient to the will of some other force.

I bend my knees so we're touching; my core to his. Our centers together, but separated by the barriers of pants and panties.

His free hand reaches for me. Shaking in hesitation, it continues until we connect, and holds my waist so tightly the seams of my clothing stretch and snap and tear a bit internally.

He's so needy. So wanton. So pure.

I lean down, running my hand through the amethyst locks in his eyes. "Mine," I say, and my hand wanders over his secret lips, and the voice moans, Mine, and then I'm tracing the tattoo on his chest and my fingers are caressing his nipple, and he closes his eyes, and he sighs, "Yours."

```
Chapter 39
To:
From:
Subject: Baby Steps
```

We didn't fuck last night, even though I wanted to, even though he begged me to.

His breathy words, his moaning beneath my fingertips, he truly was mine in those moments, and his acceptance of this, his invitation for my invasion, with that whispered word, *yours*, nearly threw my logic into the wind with all my caution.

"Mine," I confirmed, and I caressed his secret lips with mine, and I let my hands wander while he was limited to just his one.

He whimpered. He whined like a child who wanted something they could not have.

In some ways, by the very nature of innocence, Reed is childlike.

His body is over thirty, but his experiences and his beliefs and his ability to immerse himself entirely inside his creativity, it's all beautiful and it's all what makes him the absolute perfect man, but it renders him naive in many ways people of his age haven't been in years.

"Please," he said over and over, but the profanity, the violence, the sinful nature of his request proved too mature for his secret lips to utter in words.

His body accommodated. His hips would push upward instinctively, and when he'd become conscious of it, he'd lower his chin and blush.

"It's okay," I whispered on more than occasion. "Don't repress it." I wanted him to be authentically him, but it was hard to determine what actually was him and what was the ketamine.

Still, I needed him to be comfortable with our sexuality. It wasn't for my sake— I could fuck Marty again any time I wanted or I could shoot up Vinny and reenact this very scene. I don't want to fuck. I didn't want to last night; not the in the ways I'm used to wanting it.

This wasn't some means to my happy ending. This wasn't a circumstance of biology and desire and need for release.

This was a spiritual awakening for Reed. Everything I've done was for Reed. And I wanted him to be comfortable with the things he expressed publicly as art because he was too modest and too meek to ask for them in private.

He was opening up. Blooming beneath my hips. But I couldn't deflower him, physically or spiritually, when he wasn't sober.

In all honesty, I'm sure I didn't need to dose him. Fucking Natalie with her pessimism and fucking Bridget with her fanaticism and fucking Vinny with his easy-access drugstore.

I mean, this is really why writers don't let their friends read their work. This is why artists are more comfortable with strangers seeing their insides than their family or colleagues.

They all got into my head when all I should've paid

attention to was the universe, and instead of taking Reed's clothes off and releasing him from Amethyst, I cuffed him to a bed and told him he was mine, and I kissed him and touched him and told him we'd commit every sinful act we'll both say he never wanted.

I'll take advantage of you, Reed, if it means you can fuck without feeling guilty.

I'll be the bad guy. I'll play the villain. Maybe you're God, Reed, and maybe I'm the devil, and maybe Lucifer wasn't a bratty child, but his lover's excuse for all the evil he denounced but secretly enjoyed.

Like those secret lips.

"No, sweetheart," I told him, and when I moved away from him, he protested softly.

I laid down next to him. His brows raised and pulled together when he moved onto his side. "You don't want me?" He whispered.

"You're the only thing I've ever wanted," I told him, and it wasn't a line. Fuck, it was the most honest I think I've ever been about my separation from everything most people assume everyone wants.

He looked down his body. His free hand drifted over his stomach and his exposed ribs. When his eyes found mine again, he smiled sadly, "When you touch my skin, I feel it in other ways."

I smiled, reaching for his collarbone. "What ways?"

His eyes close, and his features loosen. "Ways that aren't physical."

"That's because we are more than that," I said, and his eyes remained closed but his hand found mine. "We're more than anyone else could ever be to one another."

"Bexley," his tired voice hummed, "If I fall asleep…

Do you promise to be here… In the morning?"

I promised, and his secret lips curled into a sleepy smile, and I kissed them gently.

It was beautiful.

I barely slept, though. Having him next to me was like experiencing a dream. I had to keep touching him in case I blinked it all away. In case I found myself in my empty apartment the night after his show. In case none of it was real.

Even as I type this, I wonder if it really happened. What's a memory except a story? It isn't happening now, so how can we know that it ever did?

Maybe I'm just sitting in Vinny's living room with my phone, typing out the words to a novel I'll never publish, and maybe I've been writing too long to separate fact from fiction.

As if on cue inside my existential crisis, I hear grumbling from the room.

I toss my phone onto the couch, go into the kitchen, and gather the tray of hot tea and coffee and cinnamon rolls.

I enter. Slowly at first. Just enough to see him.

He's sitting up, his back hunched over. One hand scrubs at his eye, and he lifts the other. A bit of confusion as he looks to the chain and the handcuff, but I can't tell yet if he's Reed or Amethyst.

I push the door open with my foot, and he looks up.

"Good morning," I say.

"Oh," he exhales, looks down. "Oh, hi. Um, I…" his wrist becomes his focus again.

"You," I emphasize playfully as I sit down on the edge of the bed, "Are into some kinky stuff."

His brows raise and then understanding washes over his features. His free hand rises and he rubs at the back of his neck. "Oh, yeah, I guess." A nervous chuckle leaves his secret lips, and then he bites the lower one. He doesn't remember if he came here last night as himself or as Amethyst.

Neither of us can tell the difference at first. We are one.

As it does so many of my favorite photos, his head moves downward. He blinks slowly, looking up. It's Reed in there this morning.

"Don't worry," I say, sitting down beside him with a tray of tea and toast. "I won't tell anyone." I wink.

"You made breakfast?" His eyes scan the contents of the tray, almost as if he's expecting to discover a large pellet of rat poison jammed inside a piece of the toast, then he smiles nervously and those bluer than blue blues meet my gaze.

"Not quite," I say, sliding the tray onto his lap. "I made a hangover cure."

"Hangover cure?" His brow wants to furrow, but it's too shy to move so boldly. Instead, it merely twitches, and he glances up to me from the tray and says, "I don't usually do this."

"Stay the night with someone?" I ask, and I should've been an actress because I know he's never done any of this before.

"No, well, yes," he chuckles, and his shoulders curl up around his lowering head as hesitant fingers reach tentatively for a piece of toast. "I mean, I don't stay the night because I don't really go home with anyone."

His eyes blink up in search of a reaction but he

doesn't hold them there long enough to gage one. "You said that," I say, and I lift one of the cups of tea. His jaw moves visibly after he takes a bite, but slowly, quietly. "You also said you don't normally drink as much."

Adorned with a vulnerable gaze, his eyes meet mine. His jaw stops. Accusingly, his eyes implore mine for an answer. Tell him something, anything. Don't tell him he was violated. Don't say you took advantage of him. Not in a state like that.

"We didn't—" I shake my head. I try to reassure him with the truth, but he looks even more innocent in person. Glistening as he sits there, radiant as the sun sneaks through the blinds just to feel his flesh, he appears more a manifestation of divine light than a man. "Sorry," I say, trying to control my own jaw, slack in amazement, as well as he's controlling his. "You're just—" I curb my words. Close my mouth. I regain control. I'm in charge here, and a voice reminds me that Reed is *mine*. "We didn't do anything that your impaired judgment may have allowed without sober consent. I'm not usually one to stammer, but I was inebriated last night as well, and seeing you now with the clarity sun and sobriety sharpen… Your beauty is nothing short of inhuman."

As expected, he continues to communicate with his brows. They raise in the center. They pull together. They riddle his face with confusion, disbelief, but then a glimmer of joy.

I feel my teeth press into my lip, and though I want to keep my eyes on him, to consume this perfect image of his purple hair messy and falling to frame his face in ways his usual and purposeful part never allow, I try not to be so intimidating. A success, for I'm rewarded with his response.

"That's the…" he chuckles and looks back to the toast in his hand, "Wow, that's the nicest thing anyone's ever said to me."

"I can't imagine that," I say, stroking an ego that needs to be rebuilt. "So many of your admirers must compliment you."

"But they only like me for my music," he says quickly, then he pauses. Looks up to me. "Wait, do you… Is that why you—"

"No, no," I assure him, "I'm not really one for shows or musicians. My friend, Bridget, she drags me places."

"Lucky me," he says softly, and his hand rises so his secret lips can hide away and be safe.

"Lucky me," I grin, watching him take another bite.

Chapter 40
To:
From:
Subject: The Pet

"I have to shower," I tell Reed, and I wink, "Don't go anywhere."

He chuckles, lifting his hand, and the chain clangs against itself, and the cuff locked to the bedpost slides up its ornately crafted wood, "Where would I go?"

"Funny," I say, and unclasp my necklace and toss it to him.

I exit smoothly. I am confidence personified, and Reed can feel how right this all is, how right we are, how much sense we make together.

I roll my eyes when couples call one another their "other half", as if some other person can complete you, but I realize now that my distaste for the phrase had nothing to do with its validity. It's the misuse of the term that irks me so badly. I see that now.

Reed genuinely is another part of me— spiritually, I mean.

Am I a completed person without him? Yes, of course. But is my soul aching with the hunger only he can alleviate? Yes. I know that now. Last night had confirmed it.

But as soon as I close the door behind me, I quicken my pace. I have to check on Vinny. Make sure he hasn't died. But at this point, I'm not sure if having him alive is better or worse than finding him ODed on the basement floor.

"Bex," he grumbles around when I unlock that bullshit Titanic-looking gate. Fucking rich people. I mean, having servants is one thing but ensuring they can't get rise to your level as literally as figuratively by installing such monstrosities… I'm at a loss for fucking words. But at least it's coming in handy for me right now.

I bet if old Mr. and Mrs. Marquart could see their 1890's class divider being used to lock a rich white dude downstairs while a woman fucks some starving artist in his bed, they'd dig themselves out of their graves so we could all witness them rolling over.

Fuck the system.

"Oh, Vinny," I gasp when he makes his way to the gate, "Why, you're alive!"

"Bex, what happened?" He asks. "Weren't we… We had pizza."

"And wine," I say, bending down to shove some of the toast under the gate.

When I stand up, he glares at me, "What? What's this?"

"Breakfast."

"But why am I down here? Let me out."

"Sorry," I say. "Have the toast."

His brow raises. "Bex— Wait… Is this drugged?"

"Yeah, Vinny," I roll my eyes, "I drugged your toast." Even Reed wasn't as suspect and we just met.

"I'm not eating that."

"Then starve."

"Bex, come on. What the fuck is happening?"

"Lower your voice."

"Bexley, why are you doing this?"

"I plead insanity. You already wanted to hook me up with a shrink, right?"

"You can't be mad about that. Seriously? I was trying to help!"

I grit my teeth, "Lower your voice."

"I heard you the first time!"

"Well, you're not listening," I say, "So do as you're told to do, or else your only options *will* be poisoned food or starvation." I move closer to the gate now. I can't have Reed hearing any commotion. "In case you haven't realized here, Vin, you're locked inside a room with no windows and no phone. I've got all of your keys, access to any of your drugs, your phone, your food, everything. Don't make me close that beauty door at the top of the stairs and forget you're in here."

"This just doesn't make sense to me, Bex. I don't understand it."

"You don't have to." I turn. I walk up the stairs. I am the picture of perfect confidence.

When I get to the top, I feel as manic as Vinny thinks I am.

Vinny is in my way. This would've worked out so much better had he just been in Vegas for that yearly vet conference he goes to, but I suppose it's still the universe working for me. How would I have gotten his keys if he'd been elsewhere?

I need rid of him now, though. Without him in that basement, able to yell or scream or alert Reed to him, things would be perfect.

I'd be here in this remodeled grand mansion with the

soul that's known mine for years, the soul that's found itself materializing in the most flawless body two mammals could produce.

I lean against the door and close my eyes.

Please, universe— God or whatever— we've been talking so much since I saw Reed that first night. You've been guiding me. Guide me now. What do I do?

I go silent. Meditation is the opposite of prayer. In prayer, we ask. We talk. In mediation, we listen. If we listen well enough, we receive.

Maybe it's me. Maybe it's mind, but I don't hear anything. I see images of Vinny from ten years ago. I see us with Bridget. I lift my hand to the sting in my eye but I keep my eyes closed. I think, but I'm no certain, that there was some time in my past when I might have experienced happiness.

I see memories of myself laughing, sitting on Bridget's stupid red couch, and I see Vinny smuggling us beer at the same time he lectures us for drinking it.

I see pizza and air hockey games. I see smoky bars that felt luminous by the jukebox colors and breezy from the cracks in the windows.

I don't know if it's this world that's fucked up somewhere along the line, or if it's me who has.

Either way, those bars seemed dreadful after so many trips, after so many jobs and unemployment checks, after friends who are no longer friends, after relationships that failed, after I left college and entered the workforce, after everything that made life seem fun was replaced with responsibilities.

When you turn twenty-five, people stop looking at you like you're a kid. You can't get a pass on a bad decision for youth. When you turn thirty, you wonder why that happens because the person you were ten years ago is so separated from you now that you only see a child when you look a her.

Maybe life isn't supposed to be easy. Maybe everything gets harder as we age. Maybe…

My eyes open, and the sun is shining through the window so brightly it's speckled the ceiling with reflections of its glow. It's different in here now because someone different is here now, and that bar last night felt even freer than the ones I used to go to with Vinny and beat him at pool.

Someone different was there. Someone who caused the puffs of cigarette smoke to gleam the soft pinks and blues of heaven, which is surely why he chose those colors for his lights, for his microphone, for his new banner with the band's new font.

He's here now, and he's making everything new and brighter and better. He's making everything matter. And either that means that Vinny's and my friendship matters, or means getting rid of everything that never mattered.

But my memories are still so foggy, and I don't remember feeling happy, though I do remember thinking I was, and whether or not I've always been miserable can't be the determining factor in where I go from here as far as Vinny is concerned, and I asked for answers. I tried. I've been following the unseen forces this far. I don't see why they've abandoned me now, not when I've gone through all the trouble of getting Reed here, of having him trust me. I could listen better if it weren't for the heat of that or the glare of all its reflections, and maybe if I move some shit out of its path I could think more clearly.

I look to the counter. I go to it. I scan it for the source of those gleaming beams on the ceiling, and when I start to squint, my hand reaches for whatever is blinding me.

Feeling the relief on my heated lids, I open my eyes. I look down to my hand— oh, yes, the universe is still directing me— and I close my fist around the handle of a large butcher knife.

```
Chapter 41
To:
From:
Subject: The Eye of the Storm
```

I don't think I can kill Vinny, but closing the door and forgetting about him feels like leaving those maggots starve to death in my sink.

Either way, death is inescapable. Either way, it's my fault.

Is it true that what you don't do matters as much as what you do? If so, drugging and kidnapping Vinny but not stabbing him to death would be a wash. Leaving him to die... I'm not sure what I can counteract that with. Anyway, starving to death is slow and painful. I've seen enough movies and written enough books to slash someone's throat correctly. Quick and painless.

It feels like action is the choice here.

Either way, I need some time for that Special K to kick in, and even more time for me to get a buzz going.

I'm not going to murder my best friend's big brother who I used to sleep with when I'm sober.

I take a bottle of champagne from the fridge and I mix it with orange juice. I fill a glass for me and a glass for Reed, and I'm not sure how alcohol mixes with the drugs he's taken, so I chug his drink and refill the glass with just orange juice.

When I re-enter the room, Reed is reclining into the plush pillows. One hand rests on the PlayStation controller lying on his gloriously frail chest, and the other is at his secret lips, feeding them a piece of crust as he giggles. When he reaches for another piece, the metal flames against the bedpost, against his bracelets. Still a willing captive.

This time, the voice says, *He's mine.*

His eyes flick over to me, and his face lights up.

"Oh," he smiles, "I love orange juice," and when he tries to move toward me, his bracelets clang and chime against themselves and the cuff. He looks down to it, reminded that he's trapped, and chuckles. "Guess I lost the key," he blinks up slowly, and I've never seen eyes look simultaneously so seductive and so vulnerable.

I move into the room, offering him his glass while keeping it just out of his reach.

When he fails at taking it, his cheeks flush, but he bites his lips as they curl upward.

You are pure, Reed. You're innocent. But you want this.

"Only good boys get juice," I say, and he looks up to me with naive curiosity that begs me to do what we both know he wants without making him vocalize his desire for it. I arch a brow, "Don't you want to know how to be a good boy?"

He bites that lip again, keeping it hidden away inside his mouth, but he manages a shaky, "Yes, please."

"Tricks," I say, and I point to the ground. "Sit."

His hands leave his lap and rest on the edge of the bed. Slowly he starts to lower himself, but the cuff stops him again. He raises that arm and that melodic collisions of metal on metal accompanies his shy laugh.

It's beautiful.

When his knees touch the carpet, when he sits back on his heels, I say, "Beg."

His rushing blood colors his cheeks the perfect shade of pink, it complements his sky-blue eyes and that amethyst hair in a way I *have* to draw, and he licks his lips nervously, and whispers, "Please."

I step closer to him. Breaking character, I lean down. I whisper my reply, "Is this what you want?"

His cheek hollows and his lips pull it closer to his teeth. "I might be… bad at it."

I stand back up and put the orange juice on the nightstand— coasters, Vinny. This shit's expensive— and I move to the bed to retrieve the forgotten key.

I release Reed from the binds he seems to love.

His shoulders fall when his arm does. His head and eyes follow his wrist as it seeks out the comfort of his other hand.

As he rubs the marks left by hours of imprisonment, I can't help but feel conflicted at this solemnity of freedom.

I expected something more joyous. I expected hopefulness and praise and thankfulness. I expected him to rise from his feet, strip off the trappings of Amethyst, and want to start writing real music again.

It's disappointing in that way.

Somehow it's satisfying, though, because the image of this beautiful man cloaked in insecurity and fear is proof of his perfect soul.

How could anyone snap out of something that affected them so deeply as quickly as I first imagined? If it really affected them, they couldn't.

I get our drinks, and I hand him one.

He looks to it from the side of his eye, and his arm stays tight against his side when his hand moves just enough to take it. "Thank you," he says softly, and his shoulders surround his perfect face and he brings the glass to his secret lips but he doesn't drink.

"You're welcome."

We sit in silence for some time. I watch him without staring. It's not that his very presence doesn't invite your eyes to him, and it's not that his body doesn't insist they stay. I simply don't want him to experience the pressure of my gaze. I don't want that weight on his already-insecure shoulders.

I want him to breathe. He didn't fuck anything up, and I know he's feeling that way. His slouching back tells me. His averting eyes. His lowered head.

A part of me rejoices for how accurate my interpretation of him has been so far, especially when Natalie and Vinny seemed convinced of my insanity.

I know you, Reed. I know without ever having met you. I kept your body safe last night. I'm keeping your heart safe now. After I allow you a few moments of silence to still your anxieties, I'll calm your mind.

I take a drink from my glass, and I feel his eyes flick toward the movement.

When I look back to him, his eyes go forward again. They fall. He draws his knees closer to his chest, and he wraps an arm around them. His mouth is still kissing the rim of the glass, but he hasn't yet found the courage to drink from it.

He's embarrassed himself. I've embarrassed him. But how could I look down on him, stare with an arrogance so manufactured I'd win an award for the performance, and bark orders to his shaken soul?

I'm not here to ensure his persona is maintained. Not like everyone else in his life. I'm here because I'm the only person aware of who he really is— or maybe I'm the only person who cares about how his character affects who he really is— and I'm certain this will cause some embarrassment. I'm sure it'll cause hardships, fights, upset.

It's hard when you don't know who you are. It's harder when you know who you are and hate it.

"I'm sorry," he says.

I blink, brought back to reality by his melodic voice. "For what?" But I know.

He smiles and exhales but it combines into something nervous and fearful, "Ruined the mood."

"No, you didn't," I say, and I turn my body toward his.

"I should've just said 'yes', right?"

"No," I say. "No, what you said was exactly right."

His head shifts a bit to one side, and when he comes back, his brows crease slightly. "You didn't... Do what you wanted after I said that." Another nervous exhale that he tries to cover with a smile.

"I have exactly what I want right here," I say, and I pet his hand. "There's a magnetism within you, Reed, something that can draw concern from someone who didn't even care if she existed from one day to the next," his brows lift in the center, and my fingers feel their way around his hand.

I marvel at each solitary touch. Every little connection of his flesh to my fingertips shares an energy between us that is so swift and so small, one might miss it if they were less observant than my body insists I am with him.

"I knew nothing about you, not even your name, but seeing you on stage, hearing you, feeling your presence there in the shared air of that tiny bar, it knocked something loose inside of me. Maybe it knocked something into place. I felt it. I felt it shifting, and I've never felt much of anything before that. For anyone. Not even myself."

His eyes begin to glaze, and the shimmer of the sun reflecting inside his tears illuminates the blue of his irises until they're all I can see.

"I found an old outline I'd started months ago, this story that had a main character I couldn't understand fully," I pause because I'm lost at sea, and all there is is blue above me and below me, and the waves crash in one of his irises, and the clouds shift in the other, "You brought him to life," I whisper. "You brought me to life," and I'm amazed by him. "I wrote the story," I say, setting the glass down and lifting my hand to the drawer. "Inked it and everything," I remove the laptop and bring it down to us, "In less than a month."

He whimpers when I release his hand but I need both to open the laptop and type in my password. I look over to him and reassure him of our connection with my eyes— what we have will always be more spiritual than physical— and he breathes a sigh of relief when his oceans and skies and sapphires and seas are in my sights again. He feels it too.

"That's pretty much unheard of," I say and I grin, "I'm not bragging. It was all you."

He bites his lip when he smiles and looks away. His eyes look upward to mine, and he asks, "Me? How?"

"I don't know," I say, "I mean, I do but it might sound crazy."

He edges closer and says, "Tell me."

"I can do you one better," I say, and I offer him the laptop, "I can show you."

Chapter 42
To:
From:
Subject: Spiritual Awakening

I leave Reed with his story, and I go into the bathroom.

I don't want to influence him and his experience. I don't want to see him break down when his spirit is crushed or his soul is compromised. I don't want to see the memories mirroring pain in his eyes when he thinks of his heartbreak or his first experience with losing trust.

And I don't want to see him stonefaced if none of it affects him.

I flip on the light, and, fuck, I keep forgetting Vinny bought a damn palace and turned a piece of it into his practice.

I tread carefully on the pristine marble that leads me through a small hallway-like opening between the actual hallway and the room. When I round the curved corner, I find myself lifting my hands to the ornate carvings that run through the middle of the walls. Wooden but delicate, and surely crafted by hand.

A large mirror stops the flow of my fingers, and I don't want to see myself as Reed had just witnessed me. Surely my hair is knots and old hairspray, and my eyeliner is worn and running.

Yes, we both need him to read and see and remember alone, but I also don't want him to feel any disappointment or concern if he sees me, the one person who truly gets him, in all of the trappings of the life he's been forced into.

Really this brief separation is as much for him as it is for me. Besides this, I did say I needed to shower, and I don't want there to be any lies in the first twenty-four hours— Well, not any unnecessary ones, at least.

I turn to the bathtub. Like the Parthenon, marble steps lead me to this place of holiness. Cleanliness. Godliness.

In prayer, I bend my knees at the top step, and when the water flows from the faucet centered on the side, my eyes move along its rim until I notice the built-in neck rests on each end, the molded armrests, and the recessed back jets. All this and the girth suggest this was made with lovers in mind.

How appropriate, and how well the universe rewards those who listen.

I immerse myself into the water with Reed in mind, using the plush wash rags hanging on a small bar built into the wall above the faucet to wash away the layers of grime and dirt and Vinny and Bridget from the previous night.

Cleansing, freeing, calming, this water provides release from each stress of the evening and each worry of the morning.

In here, I'm not someone painted for a show. I'm not someone feeding their friend drugged-up toast. I'm not someone who doesn't feel. As they hum against my back, the jets prove that flesh is alive. The blood reacts to them and I itch everywhere it circulates more vigorously.

The steam opens my sinuses. The heat opens my pores. Everything is awakened and alive. Everything physical is as present as everything spiritual, and I'm only waiting now to absorb Reed's body into mine as easily as his soul was given to my soul.

We can become one here, where it's clean. Here, where he can relax in the comforts of the gods. Where he can be himself. Where he can be clean physically and express the purity of his soul.

Unsure of how much time has passed, or of how much of his story he's read, I'm taken out of my fantasies of Reed by his reality.

The door doesn't creak when it opens, but I know he's entered the little alcove.

As I sit up in the bathtub, I see his feet slide across the marble.

"Bexley?" He asks timidly. "I'm not looking," he offers before the rest of his body slips around it. "I just… I need to talk to you."

"Okay," I say, and I press my body against the side of the acrylic so that only my collarbones and above are exposed. "You can look without affecting your chastity," I say, and when he looks, I grin and wink.

He chuckles, stepping forward. His hand scrubs at the back of his neck. His eyes watch his feet as they move tentatively toward the steps. "How do you know I have any chastity?" He asks. His words are soft and shy. He stammers when he looks up and our eyes meet. "How do you know any of the stuff you know about me?"

"I know you," I say, "Because I know Reagan."

"But how?" He asks. "I mean, I didn't read it all. I'm afraid of what else you might know. Afraid of being embarrassed that you know it. Afraid of not being able to lie to you— Well, it's not that I want to lie, I just…" he looks away, clipping his words and shaking his head.

"You don't like the vulnerability that comes with being you," I say, and his head jerks in my direction and then it shakes again.

"Like that," he says. "We just met last night, and you could've known what I looked like before that, and you could've googled me and found old pictures, and maybe even old twitter posts popped up, but I'm not sure what type of google search could've told you how I feel, or how I got this way, or how I want to hide myself behind my microphone when I sing because I feel more naked in my music than I've ever felt without my clothes on."

We share a long moment of silence; my blues dull in comparison to his as they lock. My focus remains on those depths, those windows to his soul, but beneath them I can see his lips part. He feels this.

"You don't have to be afraid of me," I say, "Of me knowing who you really are."

I reach for his hand, and without looking, he turns his upward and takes mine into his. As my fingers unfurl, I feel the heat of his skin, so soft and fragile; so easily broken is the shell of man, and as I brush my fingers against his, I feel a sensation slip between us that is surely a connection not of this world.

His perfect lips grimace slightly. It's something sad and tragic, yet profoundly beautiful for how natural it is, how identical it aligns internal with external. He swallows, and his Adam's apple jumps. Trembling, his secret lips whisper, "How can I trust you?"

In line with his struggle, the course my fingers follow

breaks. My brows crease when I'm stunted. A sliver of cold separates my skin from his, and I wrap my fingers around the ring on his middle finger.

Slowly, I urge it upward, and when it passes his knuckle, he looks down. His head sways a delicate no but his lips remain silent when they part.

"It's okay," I say gently.

The ring slips from his body and I let it fall. His should hunch upward when it pings against the marble and bounces down the steps. His tongue soothes his lips, and when they close, he swallows.

My fingers target the metal that keeps his ring finger from my touch. When I slip it along his finger, he places his hand over mine, holding it in place. He looks up to me, "I— I feel safer with these on." His eyes glisten, and he says, "I know that's stupid."

"It's not stupid," I say, "Armor is meant to protect you."

He exhales, "Armor…" his head shakes in a small sort of denial, but his twisting lips provide his accordance.

"You don't have to wear your armor with me," I say, and softly, slowly, I begin to move my fingers again. I look into his eyes, allowing him the choice, and I continue, "I know you already, remember?"

His lips tighten and tremble, and his brows lift in the center where they pull together.

"I know the sound of your voice when it was still yours— before it belonged Grape Gardens— and I know the hymns hidden your poetry. I know you aren't Amethyst. I know he's someone who comes on stage and saves you from the sadness inside you. I know you dress him up in chains and leave him to the mercy of others

because you don't want to be what they expect you to be."
His hand isn't steady when it releases mine, but it lifts and
allows me to move my own. This is what he wants. I knew
it all along. I'll give it to you, Reed. You can have anything
you require of me. I'll do what no one has ever done for
you. I'll make you matter. I smile gently, "I think you're
perfect in your purity, Reed. I don't think your beliefs
make you any less a rock star, and I don't think changing
your clothes has changed you. This metal," I lift the ring as
I release him from it, "It's the same as any shield. It's
meant to hide the wearer from his enemy, to guard his
tender spots from the injury of a weapon. I think a lot of
people have mistreated you, and I think it's easy for you to
look at everyone as a new version of the aggressor, but
here I sit in my most vulnerable state— No barriers, no
weapons, no shields, and no armor." I open my palm,
offering the ring to him. "You can choose to keep yours
on," I say. "You can keep fighting," and our eyes meet,
"Or you can surrender yourself to whatever that book
you're reading proves we share."

He bites his lip in consideration, and in this moment I
forget who is God and who is a muse, and I see the
overhead light reflecting in his endless oceans, and the
steam rises from the scalding water to create a frame of
heavenly sky around him, and I'm here, Reed, flesh and
blood and soul and body to give myself over to you.

"The surrender is scary," I say, "Because it means we
have to change the way we've looked at everyone and
everything around us for as long as we can remember. For
you, that means letting go of the fear of feeling too much.
For me, it means letting go of years of never feeling
enough. I never cared for anyone. I never loved anyone. I

thought I was stronger that way, happier even, and I fought to maintain my individuality through countless offers of companionship. I never wanted it, Reed. But you changed that. Happily I surrender to you. No games. No lies. No fear."

His fingers reach into my palm and curl around the ring. He holds it, grasps it in his fist.

After a long moment of silence, of his eyes and mine, he opens his hand and the sound of metal on marble vibrates the room as all barriers are dropped between us.

He smiles, tentative and beautifully Reed, and he whispers, "I surrender."

Chapter 43
To:
From:
Subject: Bliss

With bare hands, Reed pushes at the bracelets on his wrists, "If I'm home and I wanna post something to Instagram— even just a story," he says, and chainlinks clink against one another as the unclasped bracelet slips off of his arm, "I put these on before I record."

"It's your image," I allow him his insecurity. I write it off. Excuse it.

"You said it's not me." He reaches behind his neck. "You know you're right."

"But do you?"

"Of course," he sighs, and the movement is visible in his neck because he's removed the spiked collar, and now he's reaching for the ringed one. "The only reason for the image was because it's not me."

"Well, it has to be some part of you," I offer. Like I discussed with him and Ketamine. "Otherwise, where did it come from?"

"It came from the Sex Pistols," I knew that, "And it came from David Bowie," and I called that one too. "I watched videos of Queen, stared at stage photos of Prince, even practiced moving like Michael Jackson. Don't you get it, Bexley?" He asks, and his eyes plead with me, and his lungs are rising quickly, and metal clangs against the floor. "You have to get it. I know you do. Please don't make me say it."

I swallow the lump forming in my throat. I won't pity him. He deserves more than that. He's the only beauty still left in the world, and the fact that this innocence is so flawed makes it even more wonderful. "I won't," I whisper, and his fingers slip over the loop at the center of his chain. "Do you want me to?" I ask, and this offer is just like the bedroom. I'll be the sinner, the fire shining light on the deep recesses of his mind.

"You said it in your book," he releases the final chain from his neck. "'He tries to be his heroes… Because he doesn't know who he is.'"

Water crashes as I rush to him. "When you see yourself the way I do," I speak in cliches with him, but I don't care. I lift my hands to his cheeks, his jaw, his bare neck and chest because he's the virginal Mary Sue, and I'm here to save him. "You'll see the greats as one-hit-wonders."

"How do you know…" he bites his lip. His brows crease. "People always say stuff like that, and then we get to know each other better, and everything they thought would be wonderful ends up being…" he scoffs, "Try-hard, immature, lazy."

"Reed," I say, and he responds to his name the way dogs respond to theirs, all perky and attentive. I grin. "Do you think anyone's ever know you as well as I do?"

He chews the inside of his cheek. Those secret lips hide more than his soul.

He stands abruptly. Shit. Is he leaving? I fucked up. Fucking cliches. Fucking romance novels. Fucking—

"You can't half-way surrender," he giggles and bites his lip as his fingers seek the waistline of his pants. He doesn't have to touch himself to get there, but his fingers are moving slowly down his tempting flesh.

His hands tug at the chain around his waist, and I scold myself for letting him sleep in all of that bullshit, but my eyes are too gluttonous for concern right now.

Right now, I see Reed standing before me. He's bare and beautiful, surrounded by the steam and styling of an ancient Roman bathhouse, and I'm in the water on my knees, ready to serve the emperor.

Metal clangs against the marble, and his giggle calls my attention upward.

"My eyes are up here," he grins, and he isn't insecure or sad with me. With me, he's playful. He's willing. He's free. You're welcome, Reed. I've got you.

"But I'm looking down here," I tease, and I raise my brows when I lower my gaze again.

I watch him as he slips his fingers inside his pants, as they move left and right and pull the fabric from his body.

He's a tease, and it's fitting. His face is seduction, his voice is an orgasm, but inside it he's too pure to just be fucked.

Finally he releases himself from the plastic binding, and he chews his lip as he considers his underwear.

He looks up. A grin forms across his secret lips, and he steps into the water with me.

I chuckle, but I'm disappointed. I wanted him free.

He sits back, and the jets bubble water around him, and he sinks into the seat opposite mine, immersing everything below his clavicle in the hot bath.

I tilt my head. Purse my lips. Is he trying to get me

aggressive because I will command.

He sits up, and his hands rises from the water, holding the only remaining fabric between us, and he tosses it.

"You're beautiful," I say.

He looks away shyly as he accepts the compliment, but he connects our stares when he offers one. "You're beautiful. And you're a poet, and an artist, and you feel safe in a way I've never experienced before."

My hand is wet but he lets me pet him. I caress him. We touch each other.

He's sober now, and when his hands urge me closer, I move against him. I move into him, into his arms, into his lap.

Our lips connect softly at first— a good morning gesture of concern and love— but it takes no time, with my bare body against his bare body, and his core reacting to mine, for our embraces to become passionate, needy, dirty.

His fingers dig into my skin. I bite his secret lips. He moans, and my hips shift over his, and he grows, and I need us together now.

"Please," he whispers, and there's no ketamine in his system. There's no tramadol or Gabapentin or alcohol.

All that's inside his perfect form is Reed, and then his perfect form is inside of mine with me.

Chapter 44
To:
From:
Subject: Knives for Lives

We lost track of time. We were connected.

All around us was the cleansing steam, once hindering fog, and heat bubbles of jacuzzi tubs replaced those of lakes of fire.

Everything was Reed. Everything is Reed. Without the drugs to coerce him, he still believes I'm the same to him.

I am his savior. The father, son, and Holy Ghost he can fuck. He's free, and he knows it's because I see him, and I accept him the way no one ever truly has.

Be innocent, Reed. Be shy and meek and Christian.

I don't buy into the bullshit you believe, but it's heartwarming to watch you— with your amethyst locks dripping wet around your face— as you sit naked in satin and read the Bible.

The best of both worlds. Heaven, hell. Naive and vulnerable. Fiery and passionate. You like to be chained up and bossed around, but it's because you're too delicate to ask for anything, and you know just from reading my work that you don't need to ask. Not with me. I know you. I knew you before we even met.

This is transcendental. No one will ever believe it, but sometimes fact is everything you believe fiction to be.

Sometimes you expect the cynic to fall victim of her own nihilism. Always you expect the psychopath to find her motives in insanity. But here we are.

You're in the black satin sheets, free and fucked and frantic to finish reading the story of your life.

You want me to write a follow up. You want me to tell you what happens now that you're free. You want the fairy tale off our lives, and I offer you these empty emails— my draft diaries of you.

You read them, smiling as you see that this destination was always at the end of your path, even when you felt lonely and misunderstood.

I was there before you even knew I existed.

I was always there.

I am God. I am everywhere. Everyone who sees us will know that.

I go back into the kitchen and leave Reed to our world before it was ours, back when it was only mine.

I'm happy to share everything with him. Come into my world. Live here with me.

I make us some coffee because we haven't gotten that far yet, and as I lean against the counter, I grab the sweeteners and cream for Reed because he's sweetness and light, and I'm the darkness he's been calling out for in his violent art.

I'm here. I'll tie his ankles together and chain him to my bed. I'm red-hair and an inked arm and black clothes, and Reed can go back to his blond and his orange t-shirts and his couple of tattoos.

He can stop writing on himself. Stop dragging makeup down his cheeks. He can stop with the metal binds and switch them for acoustic guitars and spiritual lyrics.

He's free.

And I look across the counter to the knife, the sign from God, and Vinny isn't free, not here in his earthly form, and maybe I should free him too.

My problem is sound control. I imagine a knife in the chest would be scream-inducing. Maybe a knife to the throat would be a helpful silencer. I haven't done this before, so I can't know until I try, but I've got Reed here in this bed a wall away from me, and he trusts me to make him toast and tea with the correct amount of sugar because his tongue is too pure to taste anything bitter, and I know that without him telling me.

I take the knife. Reed's lost to our world when it was mine; he won't hear us in the realm. In this universe, I'm alone in this home, and Vinny is a pest, an infestation of rats, and I have to rid us of the intrusion before it contaminates Reed.

With the knife in one hand, I take a full syringe of ketamine in the other.

Vinny will be flaccid. He'll be silence. He'll be stuck in a K-hole and I'll slit his throat. Nice and easy. Silent.

I open the kitchen's Titanic door, and I close it behind me. I'm slow as I descend. I don't want to alert either man to my actions.

I open the vanity door slowly, then I crack the lower Titanic gate. I slip inside. It's dark with the windows boarded up, which is good because Vinny can't see me, but bad because I can't see him.

His eyes are probably well-adjusted to the darkness now, and I just hope that Tramadol toast isn't wearing off.

I step off of the final step. My flesh slaps against the concrete, even though I'm careful, slow. I keep a hand on the wall so I don't lose my path.

I hear Vinny breathe.

I step closer.

"Bex?" He whispers. His heart must be racing because his voice is shaking.

I say nothing. Maybe it's me. But maybe I'm a demon. Maybe I'm Jack the Ripper. Maybe in some parallel universe, I'm both.

"Bexley, is that... Is that you?"

I hope he keeps talking because I couldn't find him otherwise.

"Bex?"

I've got to be near, but if I reach out, I'll alert him. He can certainly overpower me. The darkness, my asset, is truly my enemy.

Searching for a light switch, I run my hand along the wall. I move my feet in pursuit of it, hoping not to kick into Vinny in the process.

My pinky finger senses something small, something plastic. It has to be a switch. I press my back against the wall so I know he's somewhere before me, and I flip it on.

Vinny groans, and he's collapsed more than he's sitting. His hands rush to his eyes, burning from the brightness of single, old, yellow, dim lightbulb.

"Sorry, Vinny," I whisper, and I lunge at him.

We topple over onto the ground just before the staircase, and I'm amazed at how far away everything felt, how long it seemed to take to get to him in the dark, but I took three steps at most.

He groans again, and his head hits the concrete, but I take no chances.

I jam the needle into his neck and push the plunger

until it empties inside him.

"Bex…" he groans, and I lift the knife, but a sound above us halts me in my tracks.

"Bexley," my name is uttered, but not by Vinny; by secret lips.

"Shit," I say, and I rise quickly, rushing to the stairs.

"These emails," I hear Reed say, and Vinny groans. "Our lives," and he's closer. I try to listen for his footsteps, but Vinny is dragging himself around, and he won't shut up. "Am I really the only thing you care about?" He's nearing the door, the gate, these stairs, and I have to go back down and kick at Vinny, knock him over.

"Yes," I call, and Vinny's swinging at my legs, and he won't fucking die, and I'd stab him if Reed wouldn't hear it. "Only you," I grit my teeth, and try to rip my foot away from Vinny.

"You mean it? It's… It's not an act? Your story, how you searched me, what you wrote, how you are with everyone else… I'm not another… You wouldn't…"

"I wouldn't hurt you, Reed," I'm grunting, and he's at the top of the stairs, and I'm finally climbing them. "Everything to me, Reed. You're my everything."

"What are you—"

"No, nothing," I say, and I'm panting and probably sweating, but I think I've dodged this bullet.

"You're… Doing nothing?" His brows crease, and I think he's confused by the dingy basement, and the gates, but when I start to speak again, I feel a tightness on my leg.

I turn, and Vinny is pulling himself up the stairs. His head is falling, and he's groaning. His body seats and swats up, and he's regaining his footing like a fucking zombie.

"Bexley…" Reed gasps, but before I can say anything,

Vinny uses the last bit of his strength to swing at me.

I move, and he connects with Reed, pulling him down as he collapses again.

I push my hands against Reed's chest, his shoulders. I try to steady him. He can't fall down these stairs. I don't want him breaking a leg or busting open his head, and I didn't want him to find Vinny, but he did. And now we're all three entangled in each other, toppling down the stairs in a confusion of limbs and flesh and bone.

For a second or a minute, I'm not sure how long, there is nothing. Life is an empty void of darkness. I feel nothing.

It was like revisiting my life before Reed, but I remember him, and how I have him now, and how we're meant to be together— bound by flesh and spirit— so surely he'll understand that this was all for him.

I open my eyes. I hope he hasn't run away while I was out, and I feel the weight of an arm around me, and when my eyes adjust, I see glistening locks of amethyst.

My alien. He's here. He's holding me. Comforting me.

Mine, the voice encourages me to get up, snap out of it, and I whisper, "Mine," and I start to move, but he holds still.

"Reed?" I say, and I groan, and it's a struggle to sit up because his weight is on top of me. "Reed?" I say the word more urgently as I roll him over. I try to keep his head from hitting the ground. My heart races but it feels empty, like it's pushing half-frozen slush through my arteries. My chest is hollow. Air is escaping everywhere inside me and I can't catch any of it in my lungs.

"Fuck, no, no," I'm wet and heavy. My clothes are stuck to my skin. I touch my chest, and pull my hand away red. I look at Reed's chest, and his bare skin is splattered the same. And there, just below the tattoo of our birth year, is the blade of the knife I intended for Vinny. "Oh, God," I breathe, "Oh, no. Reed? Reed? No, no, no!"

I can't see his chest move. I hear nothing. See no movement anywhere. I put my fingers to his neck, my ears to his chest, but the knife is where his heart should be, and this isn't a book! This isn't fiction. This is not Romeo and Juliet, and he can be alive in a million other universes with a million other mes, but I cannot be here without him.

We were supposed to build our life together. He's freed. I freed him. I'm here. He's mine. He's everything I hoped he'd be, and he can't be gone now.

"Vinny!" I wail, and he's crumbled up on his side, and there's foam stringing from his lips to the concrete, and this is not the time for him to finally be dead! "Vinny! No, no, get up!" I scream as I grip his shoulders. I'm trying to sit him up, and I tug him toward Reed, and I cry, "Vinny, no! You have to save him! Do CPR. Stitch him up! Vinny! Don't let him die! Don't... God, why? Why?"

I don't even know what I'm saying. I collapse on top of Vinny, on top of Reed.

I cry.

After some time, I shove Vinny's body aside. I lie back in the darkness against the concrete floor. I stare at the ceiling. I reach for Reed.

I roll over. Curl myself around him. I brush his hair from his eyes. I kiss his secret lips. I take the blade from his chest, and I hold it over my wrist. I let his blood drip onto my veins, and then I drag the knife across them.

Made in the USA
Middletown, DE
17 March 2023

26962381R00196